Penguin Books
The Comic



Author of fifteen novels and four collections of short stories, Brian Glanville was born in London in 1931, lived for several years in Italy, where much of his fiction is set, and has been *Sunday Times* football correspondent since 1958. *The Comic* was warmly received by such comedians as Frankie Howerd, Arthur Askey, Eric Morecambe and Ted Ray.

Brian Glanville

# *The Comic*

Penguin Books

Penguin Books Ltd, Harmondsworth,
Middlesex, England
Penguin Books, 625 Madison Avenue,
New York, New York 10022, U.S.A.
Penguin Books Australia Ltd, Ringwood,
Victoria, Australia
Penguin Books Canada Ltd, 2801 John Street,
Markham, Ontario, Canada L3R 1B4
Penguin Books (N.Z.) Ltd, 182-190 Wairau Road,
Auckland 10, New Zealand

First published by Martin Secker & Warburg 1974
Published in Penguin Books 1979



Made and printed in Great Britain by
Richard Clay (The Chaucer Press) Ltd, Bungay, Suffolk
Set in Linotype Times

# *Chapter 1*

There was this lunatic, see, he was working in the garden of the asylum. Great big garden with lush lawns, bushes cut in funny shapes, rockeries, greenhouses, flower-beds full of geraniums, roses, lupins. And this woman, she was the Lady Mayoress, came walking round the garden; she'd been visiting the place. She met this gardener and she said, 'What lovely flowers. What a beautiful garden. Did *you* do all this, my man?'

'Yes, mum,' he said, 'it's me, I done it all.'

'Amazing,' she said, 'I do congratulate you.'

'I done the lot,' he said. 'For fifteen years, I been doing everything. The flowers, the greenhouses, the shrubbery. It's all down to me.'

'And you mean they're *keeping* you here?' she says. 'A man with your abilities?'

'You wouldn't believe it, mum,' he said, 'but that's what they're doing. Fifteen years they've kept me. Put in a word for me when you leave, mum; you'll do that for me, won't you, mum?'

'I *shall*,' she says.

'You won't forget?' he says.

'Of course I won't,' she says. 'As soon as I get out of here. A man as talented as you. It's quite ridiculous.'

So she's walking off, she's reached the garden gate, when a brick hits her in the back of the neck and a voice shouts, 'You won't forget, will you?'

I walk round the asylum garden – I'm sorry, what do I mean, asylum? Sanatorium, rest home – past the geranium beds, between the shrubs and round the rockeries, and this is what comes into my head. That's the terrible thing about being a comic; every picture tells a story, every situation triggers off a gag. All the years being quick on your feet, never being lost for a laugh; warm-up gags, exit lines, get-you-out-of-the-shit lines. That story – it must be older than me, but it's the one I think of, going round the garden; only where do *I* come in? Am I telling it or am I in it? Am I the comedian, or am I the gardener? After all, the gardener looked sane enough, didn't he? Sane enough to con the Mayoress. And most of us here, a lot of the time, *we* seem rational enough.

Not that poor old dear sitting under the hedge over there with her knitting, the one they call Penelope, busy on that scarf or shroud, or whatever the hell it is, that she's never going to finish, anyway, because she'll suddenly unpick it all and start again. But most of us. And most of us don't know what we're going to do next. How do I know that I won't throw a brick?

'Good morning, Colonel!'

'Morning, morning!'

Military bearing. Crisp corduroys. Sane as you or me; which isn't saying anything.

There were these two colonels in the club, see. One of them said, 'Heard the latest about Carruthers?'

The other one said, 'No.'

The first one said, 'Gone native. Living in the jungle with a chimpanzee.'

'What, male or female?'

'Oh, female of course. Nothing queer about Carruthers.'

Jesus, won't they ever stop coming? Sometimes I feel I'm going over the edge again, I'm going back to what I was when they brought me in here, and then I start to shake, the fear gets into my guts, the sweat starts out on my face and I begin to pray, please God, no, please, God – don't ask me what God – don't, don't let me be a computer again.

Which was what I was for Christ knows how long. Weeks, years. I don't know. You don't measure hell in time, it's got a time of its own, and that time lasts forever; while it's lasting.

I tried to explain that once to Dr Weiss. What a hope I had, as much hope as I had of making him laugh. The original wet Saturday night in Wigan or Württemberg or wherever he's from.

'It is, of course, a regression to a state of total dependence. Like a baby. There are no episodes, only eternity.'

'Doctor,' I said, 'you're clever, Doctor, you really are, but you don't *know*.'

What I was, was a computer. I was programmed. You pressed a button, touched off a circuit, and out came a joke. There were a million buttons. Psychologists: that was one of them. I could go on forever about psychologists. So this psychologist jumped on top of the girl, right there on the couch, and then he said, 'Well, that's settled *my* problem; now, what about yours?'

Landladies. Milkmen. Scotsmen. Irishmen. Jews. Holidays. Honeymoons. Vicars. Button after button. Story after story. And no way of resisting, holding back. They pressed the button, and you gave. I wasn't living, I was being lived. Being used. The whole, sodding world was using me, and I couldn't bear it any longer. The hatred started building. Stronger and stronger. Over a long, long time. Growing. Just hating all my fucking audiences, where at other times, other bad times, it had been them hating me. Waves of hatred coming across the footlights, rising out of the auditorium like a poisonous mist, shrivelling me, scaring me.

But now it was the other way, and I hated them because I was powerless, because they could do what they liked with me, and knew it; press any button, get any gag, any story, any song, any response, even any expression. Laugh, clown, fucking laugh! A smile a song and a tear. Press a button and I came on. Press another and I walked off. Press another, and I probably dropped dead. So that suddenly one night at the Sunderland Empire ...

That sounds good, that. Like one of those schmaltzy show-biz autobiographies; ghosted, naturally. Suddenly one night at the Sunderland Empire, a star went cold, and it was me.

Staring out into the blackness and over the blob-white faces.

'Fuck you, fuck you, leave me alone!'

Curtain. Good-bye Sunderland, hallo, nut-house. A nut was born, and it was me.

I'm sorry; rest home was what I should have said. A funny

thing happened to me on my way to the rest home. And when I got to the rest home. Like they crucified me.

Crucified. Always we come back to this crucified.

That's because I'm always being crucified.

But no one can be crucified more than once.

*Literal-minded Kraut.*

In your dreams, I know you are crucified. You have had the dream again?

I'm always having the dream. Christ as comic, nobody ever thought of that one, nobody's ever done what *I* mean to do when I get out of this fucking place; if I ever get out of this fucking place. The London Palladium; like a Lenny Bruce bit, but for real.

'And now, ladies and gentlemen, we have pride and pleasure in bringing you – Jesus Christ, Comedian!'

Organ music; the kind you hear when you come into a church. Curtains part. One spotlight, picking out the cross, and on the cross, like I'm nailed there: me.

'Hullo, there, nice of you to come and see me. Nice of you to come and see where you've put me. No, but seriously. I'm sorry about the thieves, the two thieves, sorry they aren't here. One of them's my agent, the other's the producer. *You're* getting paid, they said, you can do it on your own; got down from their crosses and walked off. I'll tell you something else: you think they didn't make me pay for the nails?'

In the dream, though, I don't talk, I can't talk, and the audience is the whole world, row after row after row of them in an open-air auditorium that stretches back and up for ever; dead silent, except that I know what they're saying, they're saying, 'Make me laugh!' and I can't speak, I can't even think. I open my mouth, hoping that something will come out, something that'll start me thinking, but my throat's gone dry. Then I try to think of something, something that'll start me speaking, but my mind's gone numb. There's a hole in my side, there's nails through my hands and through my feet, but these I don't feel. I'm in terrible pain, but it isn't physical, it's *pure* pain, that you'll never touch with sleep or booze or drugs or operations. The pain is me and I am the pain; up there on the cross, I realized that I used to keep the pain away with jokes, but now the jokes won't come.

Let us talk again about your dream, and why you should believe we wish to crucify you.

Because you tried when I got here, with your shock treatment. Making me sign that sodding paper. When you knew I'd have signed anything, I was that far gone; if you'd given me a paper saying, this entitles you to castrate me, I'd have signed that, too.

'Here you are, take this, you won't feel anything.'

Strapped to that table like Frankenstein's monster, terrified out of my mind, an electrode on each temple, then *whang!* the current coming through, my body stretching, stretching like it's going to break. You say that isn't crucifixion?

Not crucifixion. Therapy.

Therapy! You're joking!

But it worked. You no longer have the paranoiac delusions. The ego has asserted its authority.

What does that mean? That I'm sane again?

Such words are inexact.

Okay, I know the jargon by now. I was manic, now I'm depressive.

In very broad terms, yes.

You think I'm any better off?

Do *you* think you are better off?

I'm still here, aren't I? I tell you what I sometimes think, Doc. In the old days, people used to go and watch the lunatics for a giggle. They didn't need comics then, did they? Now, maybe it's coming round to the same old thing. You ought to charge your visitors, Doc.

You use jokes as a defence. It is one of the difficulties of your analysis.

A defence against what, Doc?

A defence against facing your reality.

Not that again, Doc, do me a favour. *What* reality?

Each individual has his own reality. The joke is your escape.

Escape from what, Doc? I'm still here. I'm still bloody trapped.

From reality. From responsibility. From suffering.

*I couldn't see him, lying on the couch, but I could picture him, all right, fat pink cheeks and straight silver hair, sleek as a sea-lion, wearing his* interested *look, like he was watching you in a cage. Very interested in me, Dr Weiss is. Never met anybody like me.*

I admit it is a fascinating opportunity to investigate the nature of humour.

Doctor, you wouldn't see a joke if it jumped up and bit you.

I am interested in the meaning and significance of jokes.

Look, Doc, you can pull 'em apart until there's nothing left, you'll still never know what it's like to face a thousand drunk animals in Glasgow on a Friday night.

I am interested in what it feels like to *you.*

*You couldn't win.*

Now he said, 'I would like to talk more about your Messiah complex. If we can resolve this, then I still believe that we will have resolved your difficulties.'

'Maybe you'll have resolved away my jokes and all, Doc.'

'As I have said before, it is quite possible your jokes are only symptoms.'

Very deep about jokes, the Doc.

'We know well that the function of jokes in their listeners is an economy of psychic tension.'

'Come again, Doc?'

'By which we mean that, temporarily, an inhibition is lifted, the result of which is laughter.'

'Like when your mother-in-law falls downstairs and breaks her leg?'

'The significance of the mother-in-law's function has been very thoroughly understood. But what we are not so sure of is the nature of the gain in the psychic economy of those who *tell* jokes.'

'I've always told jokes, Doc.'

Which is true. Go back as far as I can remember, and I'm telling jokes. In fact I think he's right, it *was* a defence; or it began as a defence. At home, at school. My father, big bastard, keeping that pub in the Mile End Road, always handy with his belt. 'All right, John; upstairs and wait for me.' My mother had a pretty good right hand, too.

At school, with all the tough kids. Half of them went to Borstal, and three-quarters of those must have gone inside. I can still open a paper and see this one's been done for robbing a bank, or that one's been knocked off for running a protection racket. Lovely lot. Me all long and skinny, far outgrown my strength, no good at fighting, football, anything like that, pushed around by all of them in the playground.

Always the most terrifying part of any day at school, that, when the bell went, the lesson ended, and out we all came in a great stampede, on to the asphalt with the high wire netting round it, to keep the beasts in the zoo. And they *were* beasts, too; predatory, like dinosaurs. 'Give us a penny, then! Give us a chip, then! Give us that sandwich, Lofty!' Arse hanging out of their trousers, most of them. They were bad days, those, down the East End. *We* didn't have much more than they did. Everything going on the slate. Brewers coming down hard on the old man for bigger profits. Happy old East End. 'Knees Up Mother Brown', and all brave in the Blitz. Packed like cattle down the bloody tubes, night after night, lucky to get a place even on those terrible bunks, sleeping on the platforms if you didn't, bombs whistling down, anti-aircraft guns banging, sirens howling like monsters, half suffocating. It makes me puke to hear how some of them go on, film stars, comedians, who've got out of the East End and tell you how wonderful it was, when they're living in Park Lane or out at Sunningdale in a house with a swimming-pool.

One thing I knew before I was even ten years old: getting out was the important thing, leaving it all behind you; the horrible little cobbled streets and three in a bed. People mucked in because they had to, because they'd never got two sixpences to rub together, making a virtue out of necessity.

Yes, I know how they billed me when I started out: Johnny Lucas. 'Maybe It's Because I'm a Londoner'. I'll tell you something: that song stuck in my throat every time I sang it, but in those days, every comedian had to have a song. Bob Hope sang, 'Thanks For The Memory', though at least he used to play around with the lyrics; or his writers did. Max Miller sang, 'It's My Mother's Birthday Today', Arthur English sang, 'Powder Your Face With Sunshine'. It was one way of getting off the stage, though if you ask me, some of them didn't deserve to get off alive.

Anyway, I made them laugh at me. Like Dr Weiss would say, who probably never laughed in his life, that was my defence. 'You're yellow, Lofty!' they'd tell me in the playground. 'That's right,' I'd say, pulling my eyes into slits, 'I'm yellow; my mother was frightened by a Chinese laundryman.'

'Screwed by him, more like,' they'd say, the bastards, but they'd laugh, and it'd get me off the hook.

*It's no coincidence that this lanky Cockney's signature tune is 'Maybe It's Because I'm A Londoner'.*

*'To me,' he said, with a proud glint in the spaniel-brown eyes which can fill so easily with pathos, 'being a Cockney is something to be proud of. If you're brought up in the East End, it's a wonderful feeling; it's something that sticks with you for the rest of your life.'*

Like the stink, the dirt, the lice. That time when they evacuated us, in 1940. To a tiny village in Northamptonshire, a million miles from anywhere, with these cards round our necks; like refugees. Billeted on a tiny house, my older brother Ted and me, the one who's a copper; above the local sweet shop. The first night we were there, they had us down the village hall and examined our hair for lice; the lot of us. I'd never felt so humiliated. Only ten, but it's stuck with me ever since; the worst thing that ever happened to me, till I knew what it was like to stand up there in front of people, and not get laughs. Treating us like inferior objects; animals. 'Slum children.' The first time we'd ever heard those words, because to us, the slums were our world, all we'd ever seen except for odd day-trips to the sea. Fields, trees, cows; what did we know about them?

The first couple of weeks we were there, I was terrified of cows. I'd scuttle across fields, sidle along the hedges, looking at the strange monsters that looked back at me with their great, stupid, brown eyes, and mooed. Like an audience.

This ambivalence towards the audience is also most interesting.

It's simple enough, Doc. If they laugh at you, you like them. If they don't, you hate the bastards.

Also in group therapy, Dr Tomkins tells me you have shown the same tendencies.

God forbid I ever had an audience like that. Or like you, Doc. No offence.

*As if you could offend him.*

Let us consider the significance of this remark, and to whom it was really addressed.

*To you, you cunt, to you.*

Dr Tomkins. Welsh Twit.

Know the one about Dai Baker, Doc? Got home and found his wife in bed with Dai Plumber.

We aren't here to tell funny stories, Mr Lucas.

We're not here to be entertained by you, Lucas.

Mr Stubbs, the bank manager. Tight-arsed in a stiff white collar. Washes his hands a hundred times a day. Heard they took him away when he insisted on counting all the money in the bank every evening, personally.

I've never played funerals, Mr Stubbs.

Five of them, besides the doctor, sitting there like God in a white coat. Stubbs, Mrs Casey, a stocky sort of Irishwoman, very smug on the surface, full of all kinds of pretentions; you could tell she had net curtains across her windows. Colonel Graves, poor bastard, served in India, so stiff-backed and proper it must have been hell for him to join in, mahogany hand twitching on his knee like a puppet's; Mary Smith, fat Australian blonde with freckles who was always bursting into tears; Ivan Roberts, a kid of about nineteen, with hair falling over his face, so embarrassed it was hard to get a word out of him. Some audience. And yet they *were* an audience; in miniature. Or like an audience. After all, what was an audience; unless it was a Royal Command Performance or a Variety Club lunch, or maybe one of the West End night clubs? Just hundreds of people like this; dull people, square people, screwed-up people, only with this difference. You were up here, and they were down there. Literally up on a stage. Whereas in group therapy, we were *all* down there. I was one of them. No worse, no better; there was no protection, even if there wasn't any obligation; they hadn't paid money to hear me, I didn't have to make them laugh.

To begin with, I couldn't stand it; it was like having the lice picked out, all over again.

'This is exactly why we want you also to have group therapy,' old Dr Weiss said. 'To alleviate what we have been calling this Messiah complex.'

'I wouldn't come down from Heaven to save *that* lot,' I told him. To me, all they were was scab-picking sessions; you pick my scabs, I'll pick yours. You prod me on my father fixation, and I'll hit you over the head with your penis envy. It didn't take long to learn the spiel, and it didn't do much for you when you'd learned it. Hair down, gloves off, and come out punching, that was our group therapy sessions. Just made for that lot, I was; suddenly they'd got a star they could pull down to their own miserable level. Except for young Ivan, who was too shy, and the Colonel, who was too much of a gentleman and hardly spoke at all; in fact I think he was more pleased to see me than anybody, because before me, I reckon it was him they were ganging up on.

'What makes you think you're better than us?' she asked me, the old cow, Mrs Casey. 'Is it because you earn more money?'

'Scandalously overpaid, you people,' said old Tight-Arse.

'It's because he's famous,' Mary said, with a nasty little lop-sided smile she had, when she was putting the boot in.

'Famous?' said Tight-Arse. 'I hardly call *that* fame?'

'Fame is the spur,' said the Colonel. It didn't mean much, but I knew he meant well. He liked to keep things cool.

'Well, shall we try to analyse all these mutual hostilities?' said the Welsh Twit. 'John, in the first place, why do you resent the group so much?'

'Because they're cunts,' I said. I'd been longing to say that. It really shook them.

'Well!' said Mrs Casey.

'Disgraceful!' said Tight-Arse, and the old Colonel, the only one I was sorry about, shot bolt upright in his chair, like someone had spat at the Queen. I got a lot of satisfaction out of saying that, and I know *why* I got the satisfaction, though I wasn't going to tell the Welsh Twit, and he'd never find it out for himself. It was just *because* they were an audience in miniature, because for once I'd been able to tell an audience what I thought of them and really see it get across, see it hit home.

'Cunts,' said the Welsh Twit. 'That's a little generic, isn't it? Not even relevant, in several cases.'

To me, like I've said, these sessions stank. Whoever thought them up must have been the world's biggest bloody sadist. Sometimes I went to them, often I didn't. The only reason I went at all was because Dr Weiss was on at me about it, telling me how much good it would do me, and the one thing I wanted was to get out of this place: well enough to work again. Though the thing that worried me, that never left me, was how I could ever get out without leaving everything that mattered behind. Because what they wanted and what I wanted, what they meant by a cure and what I meant by a cure, were two totally different things; there was a whole damn Pacific Ocean between them. They wanted to cure me, and I wanted to make people laugh, and what I knew and what they'd never admit was if they did cure me, I wouldn't want to make people laugh. I'd be a zombie, a vegetable.

A funny thing happened to me on my way to the graveyard. They cured me, but they killed me. I had this picture: that they discharged me. Guard of honour on the last day. Come out through the gates between two lines of nut-cases, dressed in straitjackets; or maybe under an arch of insulin needles (I'd escaped that, thank God), shake hands with Dr Tomkins, shake hands with Dr Weiss, receive the diploma, we discharge you sound in mind and body; and next thing, I'm back at the Palladium.

Play the music, 'Maybe It's Because I'm A Londoner', stroll on to the stage, take one look at the audience; and don't give a fuck. They laugh, they don't laugh; I'm indifferent. I don't hate them, I don't like them, it's not a matter of life and death any more. I haven't got to prove anything, go through the patter, make the gestures, camp up the expressions. I don't feel better than them or worse than them. I'm like a eunuch, looking at a beautiful woman. That's all I want to do: look.

'Evening, everybody.'

The expectancy, coming across the footlights so you can touch it. Please make us laugh. Because it's a Palladium audience, this. That's what they've come for, to laugh; you're halfway there before you start. And I don't care if they laugh or cry. Because I'm cured. I'm dead. I've solved all my problems; I'm integrated – that's what Dr Weiss calls it; are you integrated, Dr Weiss? Are *you* really alive, Dr bloody Weiss? I'm so mature you can smell the decay from the back of the stalls. A funny thing happened to me on my way from the mental home. I stopped living.

Then living for you is only to make people laugh. *Rident ergo sum.* They laugh, therefore I exist.

The highest form of existence, Doc.

And so not making people laugh is dying.

Shrewd of you, Doc. That's exactly what we say, in the profession. When a comedian's up there and he isn't getting laughs, we say he dies.

The symbolism is most interesting.

You think we're all sick then, Doc?

Again you are putting words in my mouth.

Disturbed then, Doctor?

Possibly disturbed.

You're sure it's not the audiences that are disturbed, Doc,

otherwise why would they be there? Why would they need us?

It is hard to draw parallels between group behaviour and the psychopathology of the individual.

What I need is a psychoanalyst with a sense of humour. But if he had a sense of humour, probably he wouldn't be a psychoanalyst. He'd be laughing at things all the time instead of breaking them down into their component parts, like Doc Weiss does. I can see that a sense of humour must be a terrible disadvantage if you're going to be a psychoanalyst. Dr Weiss never laughs himself, but he knows why people laugh. It's all a question of psychic economy, whatever the fuck that means. If people weren't inhibited, there'd be no comedians; like if people didn't get ill, there'd be no doctors. But he doesn't understand comedians. He admits it. *I* don't personally think Dr Weiss understands a fucking *thing*, though he's very good on why you wanted to butter up your father, or why you wanted to knock off your mother. They're both dead now, anyway. But he's right about one thing. I *do* divide the world into two parts; me and the audience.

Even when I joined Alcoholics Anonymous, it was the same.

'My name is Johnny Lucas, and I am an alcoholic.'

That's supposed to be a great step forward, the moment of truth, the beginning of the cure, when you stand up there in front of all the other dipsos and admit it; but for me, it was just one more turn. They were just one more audience. This terrible thing; they were there to offer sympathy, there to give support, and what I was looking for was laughs.

My name is Johnny Lucas and I am an alcoholic and I don't feel a thing. It was a line somebody else had written for me, like most of the lines I'd ever spoken in my life, when all that mattered was how you delivered them, how they were received.

And suddenly, of all things, I thought of Red Skelton doing his Guzzler's Gin bit, the commercial where he gets drunk: 'Guzzler's Gin – Smo ... oo ... oo ... th!' and it was me that started to laugh, something that had never happened to me professionally, and obviously something that had never, never happened to them, because then I got a reaction all right; like a preacher who'd farted in church.

'Mr Lucas,' said the Chief Alcoholic, or whatever the bloke called himself who was running the show, sitting beside me to give me support, 'this is not meant to be a comic occasion. If you don't take it seriously, we can hardly help you to help yourself.'

'I know, I know,' I said, but I was still laughing. 'I'm very sorry, I didn't mean it, it was something that suddenly just came to me.'

'We don't find alcoholism very funny, Mr Lucas,' another of them said, 'we're surprised that you do.'

'I don't,' I said, and then, so help me, another joke came into my head, and I told that, too. It was the expression on their faces that did it, all so bloody solemn. 'I don't know about Alcoholics Anonymous,' I said, 'but I know a producer who's in Alcoholics Unanimous. Anyone's having a drink, he joins them.'

'I think we're wasting our time, Mr Lucas,' they said, and of course they were right. Where they were wrong was thinking that I didn't take things seriously. I took it dead seriously: it was them I couldn't accept, them and the production they made of it.

So I had to try and kick the habit without them; I must have been to four or five places to try and dry out; it'd take for anything up to a month, then something would upset me and I'd be off again; whisky mostly, Ballantine's for preference, but if I couldn't get that, brandy would do, or gin, or rum; or anything, really, if it was in a bottle. It was June who got me off it in the end, but it nearly killed both of us. And seeing what happened anyway, Christ knows whether it was worth it. I'd seen all kinds and colours of reptile when I was on the piss, I'd had spacemen in my head and Nazis in jackboots coming out of the wall, but I'd never been a bloody computer.

Here at the rest home, there were plenty of people with a so-called drinking problem; the poor old Colonel was one of them, which was why he was here. 'I've always drunk. Got the habit in India.'

'Had your chota pegs, did you Colonel?' Mrs Casey asked.

'Yes,' he said, very patient, 'some of us used to call them that.'

'I reckon you must have put away a whole row of chota pegs to get like you are now, Colonel,' Mary Smith said, grinning all over her fat face. Then they got on to why, with the Welsh Twit leading them.

'Has it ever been suggested to you that the cause of most heavy drinking, Colonel, is repressed homosexuality?'

I thought the old boy was going to explode. The blood came into those nut-brown cheeks, those washed-out, pale blue eyes were full of fire. 'Has it ever occurred to you, Doctor, that people can get lonely?'

Sniggers from the women.

'Why do you put up with it?' I asked him one day, in the garden, and he looked at me like a poor stray dog and said, 'There's so little left to try.'

'What about you, Mr Lucas,' Dr Tomkins asks, knowing the answer perfectly well, obviously having been through my file till he could set it to music, 'have *you* had any problems with drink?'

'Yes,' I said, 'I had one great problem. I could never get enough.'

In this group we're all lushes, anyway, except for Tight-Arse and young Ivan, who's meant to have been on hash. 'You'll have a job getting enough here,' Mrs Casey says, and she's right; they practically hunt the stuff down with bloodhounds. They even search the visitors. Not that it's unbearable; that's the advantage of being gradually turned into a vegetable. It isn't that I still don't want it; it's that I don't need it. I'm back at the earlier stage of being a drunk, or a potential drunk; where when anything goes wrong, you reach for the bottle. Except that now, of course, the bottle isn't there.

The second stage is when you're hooked; the body takes over and you've no chance, it does your thinking for you. You've gone beyond misery and sorrow and forgetfulness. Your body needs it, your blood needs it, you'd kill your mother for it. I hope the Colonel isn't that far gone; except he wouldn't kill a fly, unless someone gave him the order.

The only times I almost wished I was back on the booze again was when Dr Weiss got on about my dreams; I could have had some fun with the spacemen and the boa constrictors.

What did you dream about last night?

I dreamed about Sid Field. *Which was true.*

Again about Sid Field?

Still my hero. Just as much as ever. In this dream, I'd somehow got in on his snooker sketch, only it wasn't taking place on a stage, it was happening in a real billiard hall, and he and I were both playing at the same time, potting away like crazy, sinking one ball after another, while Jerry Desmonde, his straight man, very tall, with the grey hair and that long nose, was hopping about saying Sid's line, 'What a per*for*mance, what a per*for*mance!' But Sid and I took no notice of him, no notice of each other, we just went on potting away until there was only one ball left on the table, the black, and we both went for it at once, from opposite ends, our cue balls hitting it together, bang. Sid looked furious, I'd never seen this expression on his face before, and suddenly I thought, what am I doing, my one chance really to get to know Sid Field, and here I am competing with him!

Let us talk first about the significance of this potting.

Doc, it was a sketch he did at the Prince of Wales. Jerry Desmonde was teaching him snooker.

Nevertheless, the symbolism of knocking balls into holes is not altogether obscure.

Which made me think of the other great bit he did; the golfing scene. Dressed in those plus-fours, ball teed up, lifting the driver. 'Slowly back,' Jerry Desmonde says, and Sid starts walking backwards.

'No, no, slowly *back*,' and again he goes backwards.

'*No!* When I say slowly back, I don't mean slowly back. I mean slowly *back*!'

Up there in the gallery, I'm falling about, don't even notice the hard seat biting into my arse, any more; people round me are crying with laughter.

'Oh, why can't we go and pick flowers?'

I am most interested in your identification with this Sid Field.

He was the greatest, wasn't he, Doc? He was out on his own.

And he, also, drank?

For Christ's sake, Doc, most of us do, unless we go the other way and become teetotal. There isn't any in-between, not for comics.

In your dream, the identification is particularly clear. Also for the first time your feelings of hostility and rivalry.

Rivalry? What rivalry? There'll never be another Sid Field. To me, he's still what he was when I first saw him as a kid. The funniest man who ever lived. Timing, personality, movement, everything.

Living on like a sort of legend. Like a fairy tale or something in the Bible. Forty years old before he got to London. All those years and years in the sticks, playing the local flea-pits, the end of the pier, because he'd signed this bloody contract that kept him and that great big talent tied down in the provinces; like Gulliver, tied down by the pygmies. Maybe I do identify, but nothing like that's ever happened to me, thank God. I've been a lot luckier than Sid. When you think how little time he *did* have when he eventually got to the West End; still only in his fifties when he died. Pathetic. A pathetic waste. And now: nothing left. Which is something else that's made a great impression on me. When a comic goes, he goes; our kind of comic, Sid's and mine. Maybe not the radio and television kind, though I've been that as well, but when what it's all about is you on a stage, you in front of an audience; you can't preserve that. There isn't a hope.

I've seen Sid on film, but it isn't the same. It doesn't work. I've even seen the golfing bit on film. Nothing. The electricity's missing. I own them all, the few films he made, and I project them now and then, but only to see his face, to be reminded of him. A great face, a real comedian's face, broad and gentle and flexible and kind. A country face, really, though of course he was a Brummy. Maybe too kind for a comedian, when you think what bastards most of us are; boozers, sadists, misers, egomaniacs. He drank all right, but I'm sure he never did anyone any harm. Intentionally.

I remember asking for his autograph, a snotty little nervous kid with a prison haircut, hanging about outside the stage door, with a pencil in my hand and a page torn out of a school exercise book. It was near Christmas, very, very cold, and I'd got no coat, I was shivering.

'You look cold, son,' he said, coming out with his great, wide smile, just like on the stage; a genuine smile. He put his arm round my shoulders and I couldn't speak, I was that choked up. I just held the bit of paper and pencil up at him. 'Here,' he said, 'I'd better sign it with a pen, it'll rub out,' and he took a fountain pen out of his pocket, I can still see it, it was one of the new American Parkers that everybody wanted, streamlined, the kind with a covered nib.

'What's your name?' he asked, and I tried to tell him, but it wouldn't come out. He stood there waiting, very patient, while I tried again, and the third time I managed it, in a kind of croak.

'John? John who?' he said.

'John Lucas,' and he signed the paper, 'For my friend John Lucas, with best wishes from Sid Field.' Then he said, 'Here, go and get yourself a nice hot Bovril,' and he gave me half-a-crown. I didn't even thank him, I was too choked up. Sid Field, the great Sid Field, giving *me* a half-crown. I was still standing there looking at it, after he'd gone. Spend it? Never in your life!

After that, I'd hang about the stage door quite a lot; even if I hardly ever had enough money to get into the show. But I'd hang about on the fringe, hoping he wouldn't notice me, and if he did turn towards me with those long, narrow cat's eyes of his, I'd scuttle away out of sight. He must have thought I was daft, but I was terrified in case he reckoned I was after another half-crown. So I never spoke to him again. Never. Getting into town didn't cost anything, not on the tube. It was a long old ride from Mile End to Piccadilly, change at Holborn, but if you were quick, you were past the fat old ticket-collector at the barrier before he knew what was happening; and he was never going to catch you.

How I found out about Sid was people in the pub, talking, when I was in and out, fetching things for Mother and the old man. He'd made a big impact, so big it had even reached as far as the East End; and don't forget there was no television in those days. As for the West End, to kids like me it was foreign territory. It took a lot of time screwing myself up to make the journey; like starting out on the North-West Passage. But the more I heard about him, the more I saw the Herberts in the pub trying to go through his routines, the more I knew this was for me. *Something* came through, even when *they* did it, though one or two were fair mimics, like they are down the East End.

At this time it seems to me perhaps that Sid Field was more to you of a father image.

He was the whole fucking world, Doc.

Especially with a father like mine. Belt you as soon as look at you. 'Where are you going? Where have you been?' Taking your life in your hands if you weren't back by closing time. A big, heavy man. Mum was big and heavy, too. When I think of either of them, I see them in the bar, the old man pulling pints with those huge, strong, hairy forearms, fingers like white sausages, signet ring. Nearly bald, just a fringe of black hair lapping his skull. Hard brown eyes; he never smiled much. Big white teeth; but not his own. He had this very special way of pulling the beer; I'd call it a resentful way.

'Pint of old and mild, George!' someone would say, and at first he wouldn't seem to notice them, wouldn't look at them;

he'd turn away with a sort of disgust, like there was no one in that whole pub but himself, and he'd work the lever, fill up the glass, put a nice head on it, and hold it out at the end of his big arm, still without looking at the fellow. 'That'll be nine-pence,' he'd say, or whatever it was, very flat and weary, then he'd cop the money in his other big hand and put it in the till.

He did talk to customers, of course, he couldn't very well have stayed there long if he hadn't, but always, as it were, reluctantly, putting this distance between them, which in a funny way they seemed to accept. Whether he believed it or not, there was no doubt he gave the impression it was all beneath him; though God knows what he would have wanted to be. He'd boxed a bit, I knew that, though he never talked much about it. It was known he wouldn't stand for any trouble in the pub, and he'd flattened a few people in his time. I never saw him actually do that, but when things started getting nasty he'd be out from behind the bar in a flash, 'That's enough of that, then,' and if they gave him an argument, out they went through the swing doors. Ted boxed, and Dad would give him a bit of coaching. I didn't, but he just shrugged his shoulders and accepted it. He'd given up on me. I admired him and I was frightened of him. Later on, the usual way, when I was coming up and he was getting old, I felt sorry for him. It's always harder for a man who's been strong and physical, whose whole life has been built on that, to feel himself getting weak and ill.

As for Mum, she had what he never had, a marvellous laugh, a tremendous sense of humour; any talent I may have inherited – and in my opinion it comes out of the air, you don't inherit it from anywhere – would have come from her.

Not that there was much to laugh about, most of the time; the pub to run, with hardly any help, Ted and me and my sister Betty, the youngest, now in Canada, to bring up. When she did laugh, though, it was great, like an explosion; you felt she'd rattle all the glasses off the bar. Brown hair that she wore in a bun, broad shoulders, big bosom and plump, very white arms, a tremendous cook. When she wasn't in the kitchen she was in the bar, and when she wasn't in the bar she was in the kitchen; and always so cheerful with it. When there was a sing-song in the bar, when someone got on the beaten-up old piano in the corner with the yellow keys, 'Knocked 'Em In The Old Kent Road', 'My Old Man Said Follow The Van', 'Bird In A Gilded Cage', or whatever it was, you could bet she'd be in the middle of it: 'You ought to of been on the halls, Peggy.' Yet always in a hurry; everything she did for you, she seemed to be doing on the run. You cut yourself, she bandaged the cut, she gave you a kiss, and she was off. You came back from school howling, because the tough kids had been knocking you about; she gave you a hug, she told you not to mind, and she was away, again. What she gave you was wonderful, but it was never enough. In fact just because it *was* so good, so human and so understanding, you wanted more.

It may even be possible that your whole career has had as its aim to gain the exclusive attention of your mother, and to make your father laugh at you.

Have a heart, Doc.

Though who am I to know? With my own kid, who I never see; bar that one night at the Palladium. Stabbed me to the heart, that did. Me and Sid Field all over again, except that Sid owed me nothing, I was just a stranger, whereas Bob's my son. My own kid, and I've never tried to see him, since.

In many ways, you have been acting out the behaviour of your father *and* your mother.

Come off it, Doc, I'm *me*. I didn't see him because I didn't want to hurt him. It was better for him.

For him or for you?

All right, then, for both of us.

Which may only be a rationalization.

I can't win, can I?

Psychoanalysis is not concerned with winning.

Behaving like my father? Like my father did when *he* came to the Palladium. The first time I ever played it, way down the bill, so early in the show, if you had trouble parking, you missed me. Mother and father in the second-row stalls. It's true: I was playing to them. Trying to make them out in the dark, seeing if she was laughing, seeing if *he* was laughing. Wearing the long, camel-hair overcoat with a tied belt, the wide-brimmed hat, little bit like Arthur English, but I didn't come on as strong; after all, he was a *radio* comedian, he had to lay it on a bit thick. More observed, mine; with maybe a little bit of Sid's Slasher Green in it. Just a little.

'Cars, I'm flogging cars, this week. Started with nylons, now I'm working my way up the ladder. Like it? I'm moving up the ladder. Tell you what I've got: a genuine Golden Ghost. Not a Silver Ghost, a Golden Ghost. Every time you press the self-starter, the engine dies. No, seriously.'

Mum was laughing at that, I could hear her, but was the old man? I couldn't see. Afterwards, they both came round the dressing-room and Mum said, 'Oh, I laughed that much, John, you were so funny,' but all the old man said was, 'Well, I'll say one thing; it's better than work.' He never changed his tune, either. 'Getting paid for making people laugh! Blimey!' For him, it was a kind of con trick, like flogging black-market butter or dodging around the street corners, running a game of Find the Lady. The farther I went, the more he shook his head; 'Well, *I* don't know.' Did *he* think I was funny? He never said so, and I never asked him. I never did, because I reckon I knew what answer I'd have got. 'You don't make *me* laugh, son, but if you make other people laugh enough to pay for it, good luck to you.'

Going to see Sid Field that first time, going to the Prince of Wales, I was honestly trembling. Talk about setting out for the North Pole. Piccadilly I knew about, though I'd never seen it; the middle of everywhere, the nerve-centre of London, where everything that was going to happen happened, where the big cars came and the people with money to spend and now, in the middle of the war, hundreds and hundreds of Yanks. If you went up to one and said, 'Got any gum, chum?' he'd give you a packet of chewing gum; but they never got as far as Mile End.

But a theatre; that was right outside my scene. I don't suppose any of my family had even been in a proper theatre; though my mother liked going to Collins Music Hall, over Islington.

When I came up out of the tube at Piccadilly, after dodging the ticket-collector, I felt like a mole coming into the light. Except that then there wasn't that much light, we still had the black-out; one of the turns at the Prince of Wales was Zoë Gail singing, 'I'm Going To Get Lit Up When The Lights Go On In London'. But never having seen them, I didn't miss them.

What bowled me over was the excitement of it all, the life crackling in the air, the feeling there was so much happening; because people *wanted* it to happen, where at home, things happened because they had to, always the same things, no avoiding them. There were Yanks everywhere in their khaki forage caps, the officers in olive jackets and fawn trousers, like the wrong ones had come back from the cleaners, all of them plastered with so many medal-ribbons you'd have thought they'd served with Custer, and most of them with a girl on their arm, staggering along, giggling, on wedge heels, their hair down to their shoulders, curled at the bottom.

They'd boarded Eros up for the duration, but people were still sitting and standing around the steps, Yanks again, mostly, chewing gum, chatting up girls. There were British soldiers and sailors, too, but it was like the Yanks had taken over, and they impressed me, they carried things off with a swagger, they didn't apologize for being there.

I saw the Prince of Wales right away, the opposite side of Piccadilly, with the name of the show up on the billboards: *Strike a New Note*, and when I saw that, it was like a great gust of warm air blew up from my stomach into my chest. I'd done it. I was here. But once I'd crossed the road, I got scared. How did you get in? Who did you ask? Did I have enough money? I'd been told that the gallery didn't cost much, and I'd been saving for weeks, the threepence pocket money the old man gave me, a few bob more I'd got from doing a paper-round, lugging that great satchel round the streets before school, getting up at six in the morning, fingers all numb in the cold.

There was still an hour and a half before the show began, and the foyer was practically empty. I hung about for more than ten minutes, trying to get up the courage to go in, till at last a bloke in a boiled shirt and a bow tie came up and asked me what I wanted. 'The gallery,' I said.

'Round there,' he said, pointing towards the corner, 'there's a queue,' very disdainful, like he wasn't used to dealing with the lower orders.

There was a queue all right, stretching all up one side and right around the back of the building, everybody sitting on little low wooden seats, uncomfortable as hell and somehow undignified, like they were determined to humiliate you for paying such a low admission. I've sympathized with people in the gallery ever since, I can understand it when they give performers stick, even if it's me; they've made a sacrifice to watch the show, not a sacrifice in terms of money but in terms of dignity and comfort. They've earned their right to disapprove if they want to, as much if not more than the people in the stalls.

It was cold as a witch's tit, so I sat there and shivered, next to a young bloke and his girl who laughed a lot, very loud, talking to each other in posh voices, obviously finding it all a bit of a giggle, giving me just one look, and then ignoring me. An old man came round busking in a ragged coat, playing the spoons, couple in each hand, whistling through his teeth, shuffling about in a funny little dance, then holding out his cap for money, his eyes watering, face red with the cold.

'How wizard!' they said, the two people next to me, 'how absolutely super!' and they gave him a shilling. 'Unbelievable,' the girl said, 'really unbelievable.' But at last the queue started moving, me dreading all the time that just before it came to my turn they'd say, 'Sorry, full right up.'

But no, I did get in, went up what seemed like a thousand stairs, till at last there we were in the gods, looking far, far down on the stage and the safety curtain. An usherette offered me a programme. 'How much?' I said. I'd have loved to have a programme. 'Sixpence,' she said. I couldn't afford it and I knew she knew it, the contempt she looked away with. I got as far down the gallery as I could, which was three or four rows from the rail, and I looked down at the people coming in below, the toffs, men with black ties, women in fur coats, and I felt like a monkey watching from a tree. Then the orchestra filed into the pit, the lights went out, the music started with a swing, and I forgot all about that. The curtain went up, and we were away.

It was magic. Nothing in the world existed but that stage and the people on it, like a cavern of light with these people singing, these people dancing. It was great, but I was waiting for Sid Field; and then, there he was. The singers went, the dancers went, and this big fellow came lolloping up on to the stage, wearing an enormous long dark overcoat with padded shoulders, a beaten-up black hat with the brim pulled down, and everyone around me was laughing and clapping, the applause broke out like an explosion, everyone was pleased, everyone was expectant, you could feel it in the air; he'd got the audience before he'd even opened his mouth. And it wasn't just his reputation, though obviously that helped; after all he was the new star, setting the West End alight. More than that though, it was his presence. Even where we were, that far away, it came across.

And that taught me something I've never forgotten; that either a comedian has this or he hasn't, and that without it, he's nothing. He isn't necessarily born with it, though I think he's born with the *potential* for it. It doesn't always come at once. One of the big reasons why the older school of comedians, the pre-television comedians, had it, for me, was just because they'd had to slog away so long at the seaside and in the provinces before they got to London; even if they didn't have to wait as long as poor Sid Field. Whereas now, with so many of them, they're manufactured. A big agent and a television producer get together and they say, 'Him, he'll be next.' The Tom Nana Show. Audience: sixteen million. Budget: a hundred thousand. And on comes this pitiful little bloke saying, 'Like me, please like me,' terrified in case they won't so he'll be back washing dishes in Bootle, smiling a nervous little smile, milking the audience like mad for laughs, whereas the real comedian, the one with presence, the one with authority, behaves as if he doesn't give a fuck.

Of course he does, he cares like hell, after all, it's his whole life. Like Dr Weiss said, and for once he was right, they laugh, therefore he exists. But he *looks* as though he doesn't care. He's an arrogant bastard. If you laugh you laugh, he seems to be saying, if you don't you don't, I still get paid, where the new lot, what I call The Nobodies, are begging, 'Please laugh, please laugh.'

Sid Field, Bob Hope, Fred Allen, Arthur Askey, Jack Benny, Tommy Trinder, Tony Hancock, Frankie Howerd, Will Fyfe, Ted Ray; all very different comics, English and American, but this they had in common. They had presence. I'm not saying it can't become too much of a good thing, that great comedians can't fall in love with themselves. Some of the most conceited, egocentric men I've ever known in my life have been famous comedians; they talked about themselves, on stage and off, with a sickening sort of reverence, as if even their shit was holy. Horrible.

Not that there was ever any arrogance about Sid Field. The moment he got on that stage, you not only laughed at him, you liked him. I think he was the most *likeable* comedian I ever saw. So many of them, as I say, are shits, and you can usually tell. They're funny, but there's a sadistic touch about their humour. They like ridiculing people, they like putting people down. You know that once they're off the stage, that smile clicks off like a light. Not Sid, though. He never said, love me, but you loved him, and he never hurt anybody in his humour. Maybe he did send up queers a bit in his pansy photographer sketch, and even in the golf and billiard scenes he was camping it up a bit, but again, there was nothing cruel about it. You couldn't imagine anybody being offended; there was none of that spite and viciousness you so often find in queer jokes on a stag evening.

He came on first as Slasher Green from Aldgate, the tough guy, the wideboy, shouting insults at a bloke in a box, above the stage. Of course he was sending up Cockneys, but it didn't matter to me, as a Cockney, any more than it mattered to the people who'd talked about it in our pub, no offence meant, none taken, even if he was really a Brummy, even if, as I can now see, it might have been a little bit patronizing; a Cockney character set up for the people in the stalls to laugh at.

I loved everything he did that night, I was crying with laughter; Slasher Green, the golfing scene, the fairy photographer when Jerry Desmonde, as the Mayor, comes into his studio to be photographed. 'Sugar?' he asks. 'Five lumps,' says Jerry, so he pours the tea into the sugar basin.

Naturally in those days I'd no idea how much work and technique went into these performances; and those later on like the snooker scene, and the lovely bit he did on his own, as the organist.

'Ladies and gentlemen, a fu-u-u-gue!' and every time he goes back to the organ, he trips over an invisible object; the classic gag built on repetition.

When Dr Weiss talks about identification, I don't have to tell you he's got no idea what he's on about, because in many ways we're two completely different types of comedian. Sid was never a stand-up comic; like Tommy Trinder was, then, just up the road at the Palladium. Later on I got to see him, too, he was the king of the Palladium during the war, a real London comic, very, very quick, terrific on his feet, but never the same to me as Sid; great ad-libber, but he hadn't the charity.

You are saying that you wanted to be loved.

I didn't want to be loved, Doc. I wanted to be laughed at.

But in your case it is clear that you equate one with the other. When people are laughing at you, then they love you.

I've told you, Doctor, there've been hundreds of comedians who've been bastards. Their own mothers wouldn't love them.

But for you one may say that if people laughed, then *your* mother would love you.

You're sharp as a tack, Doc, but you'll never understand.

# *Chapter 2*

June came.

I saw her belting down the drive. No coincidence; I'd been looking out of my bedroom window for the last two hours. Of course she was late. Three, she'd said in the letter; it was five to four by the time she turned up. Driving like a lunatic, as usual. Showers of gravel whirling off the wheels. And seeing the car, seeing her in the driver's seat, always in the driver's seat, with her long, red hair, I got a mixture of feelings; pleasure, anger, expectation and resentment. This seemed to sum it all up; she was making her usual entrance, and making it late. We hadn't seen each other for nearly three months, and when she did come, she still couldn't be on time.

Not that she hadn't wanted to come before. She'd written me a lot of letters, very good ones, and I'd written her a few. I wanted to see her, yet I was terrified of seeing her. I loved her, yet I blamed her. For the first month, anyway, Dr Weiss wouldn't budge: no visitors. After that, it was up to me. There were dozens wanted to come, June said, dozens kept phoning – I was meant to be having a 'rest' – but I didn't feel up to seeing any of them, her least of all, and anyway, visitors were limited.

'It is for you to decide,' Dr Weiss said, 'but my advice to you for the moment is that until you are quite sure, you should wait.'

Seeing her arrive, seeing that flash of white thigh as she got out of the car in a brown suede mini-dress and the usual boots, I thought I should still have waited. In fact I'd asked her just *because* I wasn't sure. I wanted to try myself. If she came and it was all right, then I'd be one big step nearer to getting well, again.

Your hostility towards her is because you blame her that she did not save you.

No one could have saved me, Doc.

Quite possibly. But unconsciously she was your talisman, and the talisman failed.

Maybe he's right. Christ knows. A lot of the time I think he probably is right, but that doesn't matter. It doesn't change anything. Explaining things doesn't cure them. That's where Dr Weiss and I will never agree.

When she came bouncing up the steps to the front entrance in that way of hers, all energy, I wanted to lock my door and have her told I wasn't here. In fact I actually flung myself on the bed and plunged my head into the pillow, praying that something would happen, that she'd go away.

A long time seemed to pass. I thought she really had gone, like people do in a dream, then all at once I heard her step, *tap*-tap, *tap*-tap, very brisk, quite unmistakable, and a knock at the door; not hers, the nurse's, Eddie. 'Mr Lucas! Visitor!' If I didn't answer, there was still a chance.

'It's me, Johnny!'

Door handle turning. No chance.

'Hallo, John!' her voice above my head. 'Is he asleep?'

'Are you asleep, Mr Lucas?'

Fuck off, fuck off.

A hand on my shoulder. Her hand. Smell of perfume. Balmain. Hers. I roll over. 'Must have nodded off.'

'Hallo, Johnny,' she says. She's smiling down at me. I know that smile. She isn't taken in.

'I'll leave you, then,' says Eddie, and he shuts the door.

'Hallo, Johnny!' she says, again, and bends down and kisses me, just quickly, on the lips. Now I'm glad she's here, I'm delighted she's here. 'June!' I say.

Her arms are full of gifts. No booze, of course. Chocolates, fruit, magazines and flowers. The room's already full of flowers and plants she's sent.

'*Well*, then, how *are* you?' That deep voice, that fantastic smile. Smiles a lot, but seldom laughs. A very inward smile, full of secrets, self-possessed and self-contained. Sensual. Knowing. That was what had hooked me, the smile.

'You *look* all right,' she said.

'Yeah, I don't feel bad.'

'Relaxed. And you've put on weight.'

'There's not much else to do but eat,' I said.

'Well, *that's* not bad.'

She wasn't finding it easy, either, I could tell, but she always carried these things off well.

'Oh, yes,' I said, swinging my legs on to the floor; it was ridiculous lying there, for one thing, and for the other, I'd had too much of people looking down down at me on beds and couches. 'Oh yes, they feed you up, all right; that's part of it all. They shock the shit out of you, and then they feed you.'

She went around the room arranging things, putting down the presents she'd bought. 'Are you making any jokes, yet?' she asked.

'There isn't much to laugh about,' I said. 'I'll start making jokes again the day I get out of here; if I can still think of any.'

She was by the television set, now, and she turned to me, still smiling. 'Do you watch this much?'

'Everything except the comedy shows,' I said. 'They sicken me.' Which was true. They sickened me because they were bad, or they sickened me because they were on at all; it sickened me to see anybody working. I was ashamed of that, but it was like sex jealousy; when you've got it yourself, you don't care who else has got it. When you haven't, then you hate them for it. Which reminded me of something else.

'You know we can't make love,' I said.

'Oh God,' she said, 'do they count your orgasms? It's like Big Brother, isn't it?'

'Not just Big Brother,' I said. 'Here, they're all fucking watching you.'

'Good!' she said, 'that's nearly a joke!' and stupidly enough, that seemed to encourage me. She'd always been able to do that; encourage me.

'Here!' I said. 'If Big Brother kept watching you, does that make him a voyeur?'

'Yes,' she said, 'that's a *funny* joke. Very good!' and she came over to me and kissed me, properly this time, and at last I felt the old stirrings down below, worrying but wonderful. She started pressing against me, she smelled marvellous, but I pulled away. I said, 'I'd better be careful.'

'Yes,' she said, 'if you can't be good ... Otherwise something dreadful may happen. A bomb will explode in your subconscious.'

'Or something,' I said, but I was trembling. It was ridiculous. It showed me how far away I was from getting better.

June sat down in one of the leather-covered chairs. The rooms were all like dentists' waiting-rooms; if those had had beds in them. I suppose the idea was that if you went berserk and started smashing things, they'd be either too solid to smash, or weren't worth much. Very restful paintings on all the walls, too; cornfields and fruit in bowls.

'I heard from Ethel,' she told me.

'Oh, God,' I said. That did it. I sat down on the edge of the bed. 'What does she want?' I asked. 'More alimony?'

'No. She's worried about you.'

'Her! Don't make me laugh.'

She lit a cigarette. She smokes a lot; I've never smoked at all, though sometimes I've wished I did, even though it meant risking cancer. Maybe life was a bit more bearable till it caught up with you; and smokers didn't get DTs.

'She wanted to know where you were,' June said. 'She wanted to know what had happened.'

'And did you tell her?'

'I told her you'd had a breakdown, but you weren't drying out, this time. That you were somewhere in the country. She wanted to come and see you.'

'Christ,' I said, 'that's *all* I need.'

'I didn't *tell* her. I said you weren't allowed visitors. But she's written to you. Here!' And out of her bag, a great blue leather satchel of a thing, you'd never find her carrying anything as compromising as an ordinary handbag, she took this letter. Same old lavender-coloured envelope, with Ethel's sprawling scrawl all over it. It gave me the usual turn. 'Well, take it,' she said, 'it isn't a letter-bomb.'

'I'm not so sure,' I said, and laid it on the pedestal by my bed. 'I'll read it later.'

Ethel and June. Past and present. Or were they past and past? The thing about women is they can't accept change, they won't let go, make a clean break, no recriminations. Love lasts forever. Marriage lasts forever. Like cavemen living on into the twentieth century, still wearing skins and carrying clubs. It isn't that I'm not grateful to Ethel, that I don't appreciate her loyalty, what she did for me. It's certainly not that I exploited her, like she kept on telling me: 'You use people, Johnny, and then you kick them in the teeth. When they're no more good to you, you ditch them.'

The truth was that for me, there'd been two eras; an Ethel Era and a June Era. In the Ethel Era, I'd never have looked at June, and in the June Era, I was wrong for Ethel. A lot of suffering's caused by this pretence of continuity; that people stay the same throughout their lives. They don't, especially if they're some kind of artist; Chaplin, Picasso, Orson Welles. After all, you go through life with the same body, but what comparison is there between the body of a child and the body of a full-grown man? In the same way, your whole personality changes. Like I tried to tell Ethel, 'If I *had* stayed with you, I'd never have made you happy.'

That was the time she threw a big, heavy vase at me and split my head open; I went on stage with a wig over the plaster. 'You bloody phoney!' she yelled. 'I can put up with everything except your fucking hypocrisy!'

But it wasn't hypocrisy. A snake changes his skin. A man, especially if he's a comedian, changes his personality. He has to grow. June used to send me up when I talked about that. 'And then, of course, there's your duty to the public!'

'Not my duty to the public,' I'd say. 'My duty to my talent. Don't you believe you've got a duty to yours?'

'I admit it can be a very *use*ful belief,' she said, but it's not like that. I've thought a tremendous amount about it, and though I don't believe in God, to me it's a religious feeling. There's something you've been given, and you've got to guard it.

'*I* see,' June said. 'Like the keeper of the sacred flame.'

Women don't seem to have the same conviction; even when they're as talented as she is. Very talented. A great voice, fantastic sense of rhythm and phrasing, more like an American Negress than a white girl.

I was top of the bill at the Talk of the Town; she was the singer. It wasn't my favourite audience; I'd rather have played it when it was still the London Hippodrome, like it was when I was going to the gallery of the Prince of Wales, just a few hundred yards away. Now, it wasn't a night club, it wasn't a theatre. It hadn't got the intimacy of one, or the audience participation of the other. When people are eating, they're eating. 'I won't stay long,' I'd say. 'I'll come back when you've finished the celery.'

June was the same about it: 'It makes me feel like a singing waitress.'

We'd never met before, though of course we knew about each other. I'd seen her on television, I'd heard she could be a bit of a cow, and to tell the truth, I wasn't too keen on working with her, especially with the state I was in, then. One of the really, really bad times, when you think it's leaving you, you're afraid it's never going to come back. Like being impotent.

That is a most significant analogy. You have talked before of 'dying'. Impotence, too, can be interpreted as a kind of death.

What I'm getting at is that they're both something you can't control. You're powerless.

When you had this sensation of inadequacy, were you also impotent?

Sex didn't even interest me.

So you turned to it only in the hope it would release you.

Anything to break the spell. Anything to get me going again.

Anything, in fact, to be reborn.

That's right. That's what I've been trying to tell you all along. To tell *her*; Ethel. To be reborn.

Like I've been saying, a comedian, an artist, *has* to be reborn, and when he's reborn, he leaves himself behind. That's why I understand all the comedians who suddenly leave their wives and run off with a dancer or a dolly-bird, in middle age. They're not just dirty old men. They're not monsters. It isn't sex they're looking for, or rather, it isn't really sex; they're desperate, and they turn to sex as a means to an end.

Things had been bad for a year, bad in my work and bad at home; bad at home because they were bad in my work, though for some time I'd been wondering were they bad in my work because they were bad at home, bad with Ethel. I'd been drinking like a bastard because things were going wrong, and because I was drinking, they kept getting worse. Twice I'd gone into clinics to try and dry out, but it wasn't the answer, any more than drinking was the problem; it only reflected the problem.

Naturally I hadn't been working much. I'd done a few things on television, in other people's shows, and hadn't been satisfied with any of them. I'd played Blackpool in the summer, and hated every minute of it. I'd changed writers three or four times. I'd been bad in Blackpool and I knew it; there of all places, just down the coast from Fairleigh, where it had begun.

I find most interesting this tendency of the comedian to become symbolically impotent, but it is not unknown elsewhere. For example, there is writer's block.

Most of the writers I've ever used had that, all right.

But the writer is a creator; the comedian, it seems to me, is an interpreter.

Don't you believe it, Doc. A great comedian's the most creative person you'll ever find. He's creating every moment that he's on his feet. He's sussing out the audience, gauging the temperature, changing his rhythm, cutting out some jokes, bringing in others, maybe ad-libbing. He never stops.

Until, as you have said, he grows impotent. But we still have not found why.

And never will. You think I haven't tried, God knows how many times? You think I haven't beaten my brains out, trying to explain it to myself, gone over and over the things I used to do when it was going well, every movement, every inflection, when people were laughing and the power was flowing through me? Do you think comedians haven't got together and chewed it over for hours on end, however competitive and suspicious we are; because it's the one thing that hangs over all of us, like a racing motorist knows he's going to crash? You might as well ask where our humour comes from.

All I know is that at that time, it wasn't coming to me. Every dressing-room I sat in was a prison; and they're strange places, dressing-rooms, they're either prisons or sanctuaries. Before you get into the profession, you imagine them to be like bloody boudoirs, very spacious, full of armchairs and sofas, thick carpets, clean and comfortable. Even when you're in the sticks, in a dressing-room with a cracked mirror with broken bulbs around it and a grimy dressing-table, paper peeling from the walls, coconut matting if you're lucky, and hardly room to swing a mouse, never mind a cat, you still think: wait till I get to the West End. Things will be different, there. Bags of space. Warm and cosy. Carpet. Then you get there and find the same old slums, maybe not quite so grimy, but slums just the same, up miserable flights of stone stairs – or down them – into more little cubby-holes. And when things are bad, the walls close in on you. Talk about claustrophobia. They never seem so small, dressing-rooms, as when you're frightened to go on, and want to cower there. They're your last refuge, but you hate them, because you know that what they really are is not a refuge but a trap; you've as much chance of hiding there as a greyhound has of hiding in his stall when they spring the doors. When the boy comes by and he knocks, it's like the Gestapo. You hear the music start, and it's for your funeral. The place reeks of sweat and make-up, and you want to vomit. That's when it's bad.

But when it's good, then dressing-rooms seem different. They're the chrysalis and you're the butterfly. You feel the power in you; you're totally relaxed. You take your time smearing on the make-up; like a ritual. When the boy knocks, there's a pleasant little fluttering in your guts; you know they're going to laugh.

When June came in my dressing-room at the Talk of the Town, the second night, I had a whisky bottle there in front of me. 'Secret drinker?' she said. 'Or can I have one?' which made her special, for a start. Most women in the same situation would just have been embarrassed; they'd apologize and go.

'Help yourself,' I said, 'if you can find a glass.'

She'd get one from her dressing-room, she said, and smiled at me. High cheekbones, grey cat's eyes, long red hair; real red. She came back, we had our drink, and I went out and was great.

'You *use* women!' Mary Smith. Blue eyes fairly glittering with glee, as they always are when she sticks the knife in.

'All men do,' says Mrs Casey, the sanctimonious bitch.

'Johnny does,' says Mary. 'Haven't you heard him talk? She did this for me, she did that for me, this one saved me, that one let me down. He thinks we're all only here to sacrifice ourselves to the great star.'

'They don't make human sacrifices like they used to,' I said.

'Why do you feel men use you, Mary?' Dr Tomkins asks.

Snap! Her face changes. Now she's feeling sorry for herself, again. 'Because they do.'

'Might it be because you're ready to be used?'

'Are you calling me a masochist, Doctor?' We all know the patter.

'Most women are masochists,' says Mr Stubbs, our friendly, tight-arsed bank manager. 'Either that or they're bullies.'

'I reckon yours would have to be a masochist, then,' I said.

'Well, at least she isn't a tart, like *some* people's visitors.'

'Jealousy,' says the Colonel, of all people.

'How *dare* you!'

'Saw her myself. Damned attractive.'

'Do me,' says Ivan. They're all coming out from under their stones.

'Dressed like a whore,' says Mrs Casey.

'Jealous,' says the Colonel.

'Do you think you might be jealous?' the Welsh Twit asks Mrs Casey.

'Certainly not!'

'Could you possibly be competing with her?'

'With *her*! I'd be ashamed.'

'Don't worry,' I say, 'you aren't in any danger.'

Round and round we go, clawing one another. Later on, the Colonel tells me, 'Damned good-looking woman; I envied you myself.'

I like the Colonel. I'd like to make the Colonel laugh.

I started on a letter to Ethel, but I tore it up, after half a page; like I'd torn up hers, afraid to read it, glancing at the scraps, 'still think about you', 'help in any way', 'despite everything', 'concerned'. All I was doing was justifying myself again; it was ridiculous, but that was all that was left between us, she accused me, I justified myself, which was why I preferred to keep away. You did, I didn't; you did, I didn't. Like two tape-recorders, playing to each other till Kingdom Come, because there was no present for us and no future. The only way to go had to be backwards.

To a great sound, the sound of the sea, coming in across the sands at Fairleigh, up to the bottom of the steep promenade, as tall as a cliff. Whispering over the seaweed. Nearly always a grey sea, looking cold, even when it wasn't. She could swim, I couldn't. Where would I have learned to swim? Even the old man couldn't swim, with that great, hairy carcass of his. I see him lying in a deckchair at Southend like a beached whale, old-fashioned dark blue bathing costume with straps, covering his big chest; blotched red here and there by the sun, there was never time to tan, great hands clasped behind his head, bushy black armpits, mouth open in a snore. Even *he* couldn't swim; we paddled. It must have looked ludicrous; this giant shuffling through the shallows like a little old lady.

But Ethel was from Fleetwood, up the coast, and she swam like a mermaid in her goose-pimpled white bathing cap and one-piece Jaeger. 'Come on,' she said, 'I'll teach you.' I was terrified.

The Fairleigh Follies. Happy days, those. At least they look like it, now. Maybe they were. The only drawback being ambition; the old termite, gnawing away in the wood. Denis

Jackson never suffered from that; so he stayed there, in Fairleigh. Met me that morning on the station platform: 'Welcome to the Fairleigh Follies!' Round about forty-five, five foot eight or so, looking up at me, stretching out his hand: 'You're taller than your photographs!' He talked with a Lancashire accent, which still seemed a bit comical to me, even after a couple of years in the Army, where you heard every accent; to us down the East End, provincials were still red-necks.

He had a round, friendly sort of face which you could see belonged to a comic, though maybe, knowing what I do now, it was a bit too nice for most comics; largish grey eyes, a strange nose that broadened at the bottom, wide mouth with several teeth discoloured, and a grey Homburg hat with a big black band. His gimmick; always wore it on the back of his head, through every show. When he did take it off, you saw he had black, wiry hair with a spreading bald patch in the middle.

He looked up at my green trilby, there was over six inches between us, and he said, 'That your demob hat?'

'That's right,' I said. It was my demob suit, too, and my demob raincoat, practically the only things worth a light I owned; there was fuck-all else in my broken down old suitcase. He took a great, deep breath, like an Army P T instructor, and he said, 'Sea air! There's nothing like it! We'll soon put a bit of colour in those white cheeks! We'll soon fill out a few of those hollows! I've got you good digs. Mrs Everson. Plain cooking but plenty of it.'

I liked him, but I couldn't take him seriously. It was the London thing again; Northerners were a laugh.

I was there for a month's trial, twenty-one years old, answered an advertisement in *The Stage*, sent him the few cuttings I'd got from appearances with E N S A, garrison theatres, and that, never expected to hear a thing, and *bingo*! the offer. Six quid a week, and eight if they kept me on. It sounded like a fortune after what I'd been getting in the Army; or since I'd got out of it, come to that.

'You don't have to go on tonight if you don't want to,' he said, 'but I thought you might like to give it a try, and we can have a look at you. It's a good night, Monday; plenty of people just arrived for their holidays. Of course, you won't be able to join in the sketches.'

I hadn't expected to go on for about a week, but I said okay, wanting to show willing. We got into a little beaten-up black Morris Minor outside the station; it looked at least five years old, and I remember thinking as we drove along, with him constantly waving to people, there can't be much money in this. Oh, yes, I had all the ambition.

'We've got a family audience,' he was saying, 'so nothing blue, nothing that'll offend them, though they don't mind the odd little cheeky bit.'

That didn't encourage me, because my act then was very, very blue. You can't play to Army audiences without blue gags, double meanings. But it discouraged me for another reason, too, because to me, if you stop a comedian making jokes about sex, it's like castrating him. Sid Field never did, I know that, but Sid was on his own. However much I admired him, I'd already found out I could never be quite like him. The stand-up comedian who relies on nothing but dirt is to my mind contemptible, but if he's doing his job properly, he can't *exclude* sex, because the whole world is in a conspiracy to put down sex; vicars and magistrates and parents and policemen and mothers-in-law. So the comedian has to stand up for sex because he's a rebel, he's an individualist; what he makes fun of isn't sex itself, though I know some comics do, he doesn't want to sneer at sex, he's having a go at the people who try to shove it out of sight. In fact one of the most successful songs I used to sing to Army audiences was one I put together with another bloke doing his conscription, a musician: 'Don't Give Me That; I Want The Other'. I couldn't see myself singing *that* to a family audience.

One great thing about starting out in Forces entertainment, you're all on your own, with whatever you can invent or pinch or remember. No gag writers. You can't even afford to send off for those 'Jokes – Five Shillings Each' you see advertised in *The Stage*. Later on you turn to writers, but you need never be a slave to writers, like a lot of comics; you need never get the feeling of being nothing more than a ventriloquist's dummy, mouthing other people's lines. So when you want, so to speak, to purify your act, to make it you and only you, the way somebody like Lenny Bruce made his, then you've got something to fall back on.

Not that any joke's good enough to stand on its own; it still needs the comic to deliver it. Frankie Howerd could say, 'I was a-*mazed*!' and make it sound the funniest thing ever written, when the line itself was nothing. And just as comics often get round to writing their own material, so writers quite often try and turn themselves into comics, so they can fire the bullets themselves, instead of just making them for other people. Writing gags without delivering them is a kind of premature withdrawal.

Not that I only relied on verbal gags; I *looked* funny, too. I had a funny face and a funny body. My face was what I'd call plastic; like one of those little rubber faces you could buy before the war, and squeeze into any shape. Thick black eyebrows, big brown eyes, a large mouth with a thick under-lip, and a long straight nose. I found I could sometimes get the biggest laughs just with a grimace; eyebrows raised, mouth wide open, all shocked, a little like Frankie Howerd, though if I'd learned it from anyone, I'd learned it from Sid Field.

As for my body, I wasn't a Chaplin, I hadn't got that incredible grace, but I was funny *because* I was clumsy. I never forgot Sid Field always tripping on the stage in that great organ scene; there were a million variations on that, and I was always finding them. Sometimes I did the gormless bit, a little like Nat Jackley, the rubber-necked comedian, who was very tall, like me; other times I was stiff and solemn; it's amazing what you can do with a dead straight face and awkward movements, like the two men in that sand-dancing act, Wilson, Keppel and Betty. For years and years they came on dressed like Ancient Egyptians and shuffled about with poker faces, nothing more, nothing less, and they brought the house down. I could lean forward to adjust the microphone and get a laugh.

Besides, you've got to exploit your physical oddities, not try and hide them. If you're tiny, like Arthur Askey, if you've got buck teeth, like Ken Dodd, a big nose, like Jimmy Durante, you make a thing of it. If you're lanky, like me, you use that, too.

It was a nice day, that first day in Fairleigh. The sun was out and the streets were full of cheerful-looking people carrying spades and buckets and shrimping-nets. 1949 this was, before the holiday camps really got going; they were still the days of long-sleeved open-necked white shirts, rolled-up grey flannel trousers, and men in deckchairs wearing knotted handkerchiefs on their heads. As a matter of fact, this became one of my most popular acts, after I'd been at Fairleigh a little while. I'd come on wearing all this clobber, knotted handkerchief, trousers rolled up to the knee, carrying a kid's coloured bucket in one hand, an iron spade in the other, a loopy expression on my face, and say, 'Ladies and gentlemen, a little song entitled, "I Do Like To Be Beside The Seaside, 'cos there's no one up my castle but me".'

He wasn't sure about that, Denis, but he let me try it in the end. It got the loudest laugh of the show, and it stayed in from then on. It was a good bit, too, because I really had observed it, I'd spent hours just strolling along the sands, watching the people, how they sat, the way they moved, how they talked to their kids, what happened when they went into the sea, plus a little bit of my old man paddling.

Another thing I did up there, which I'd worked up in the Army, was my sergeant-major act. They're always fair game, but I'd observed this one very, very closely, too, so it wasn't just the usual parade-ground thing, the bawling at recruits, but the sudden change of tone when he's talking to a superior officer, all obsequious, from bellowing to cringing, the 'sar'nt-major posh' talk, aping an upper-class voice but dropping g's and h's; switching from one to the other so abruptly that he gets confused and starts shouting at the officer but buttering up the men, the right words with the wrong tone. I'd wear a Guards cap with the peak pulled down so far over my eyes that I had to lean backwards to see straight, a little waxed moustache, and I'd carry a swagger-stick. The trick was to treat the audience as if they were the squad, so rather than doing it in a vacuum, you get the extra dimension. Audience participation shouldn't just mean chatting up the front three rows and getting everybody to join in the choruses; which of course is one of the great things in any seaside concert party, including ours.

Anyway, Denis drove me into a little street of red-brick Victorian villas, semi-detached; number fourteen was Mrs Everson. My first theatrical digs. The first of God knows how many hundreds. How many doorstep slices of bread and margarine; always margarine at that time, there was still food rationing, the excuse for everything. How many cups of tea so strong you could have stood a knife up in them; Woolworths knives with blotched blades and wobbling handles? How many congealed poached eggs with palsied whites and yokes as hard as stones? How many damp, darned sheets on narrow beds in rooms that smelled as if they'd never had a window open; windows with broken sashes, windows with leaded panes and always, always net curtains? How many landladies with mouths like slits and chests like boards, measuring out the coal in thimbles? How many randy widows ready with a late cup of coffee; and how many married ones that drifted into your bedroom when their husbands were out: 'I just brought you up a clean towel?'

Mrs Everson came to the door wearing the landlady's uniform; a flowered apron. Fat, fair hair, face like a friendly pig, chin falling away. Bosoms like footballs. I'd find they were always a fair guide to landladies, bosoms; the ones that had them were by and large better news than the ones that hadn't, though I've known some mean bitches with big tits and some saucy ones without them. When she folded her arms, Mrs Everson, they looked like a couple of pillows.

'Here we are, then, Mrs Everson,' Denis Jackson said, 'another victim.'

'We'll do our best, Mr Jackson,' she said.

In fact she was a widow, there was no we, only her, but she always used the royal plural. She looked me up and down like she was buying me in a market. 'As long as he doesn't smoke in bed,' she said. 'The one thing I'll not stand for, that is.'

'I never smoke at all,' I said, and she nodded and stepped aside, as if I'd said the password.

The first thing I smelled inside that gloomy little hall with its lino was cooking cabbage, and it would be with me all the time I stayed there. Great on cabbage, Mrs Everson was, it was what you might call the speciality of the house. Lukewarm, pale green, very watery, and the smell of it followed you everywhere like a Mountie. It was like the old story of the starving regiment with nothing to eat but camel dung; there was tons of it. In fact I will give her this, she never stinted you with anything; what it lacked in quality it made up for in quantity. Yorkshire puddings and chunks of suet roll you sunk your teeth in and had to send for help to get out. Plates of tapioca you could sink in and never be heard of again.

There's a lot of sentimental crap written about theatrical digs, but for my part, I'm glad that when I play the provinces now I can afford to stay in a decent hotel. You *do* get your good landladies, the kind ones, the motherly ones, the encouraging ones, but for the most part these are sad places run by sad people. I look back and I see a great, long line of henpecked husbands washing up and stoking the boiler, of nagging wives, locking the door at eleven sharp, of anything-but-merry widows. People in the profession like to get together – when they've made it – and talk about good old Grandma This and mean old Mrs That, but it's like schoolteachers; it's all right to laugh at them when you've gone a safe distance.

'Bruce and Marlene here?' Denis asked.

'They'll be back for lunch,' Mrs Everson said, and for my benefit, 'one o'clock sharp.'

'Banjo duo,' said Denis, 'you'll like them, won't he, Mrs Everson?'

'Very reliable people,' said Mrs Everson, making it sound like another dig at me. 'I'll show him his room, then.'

My room? My cupboard. If you stood up, you felt like a broom. Turn over in bed, and you were nearly out the door. I'd find out in time that if theatrical landladies were special, then seaside theatrical landladies were double-special; and the same went for the lodgings. There was a shilling-in-the-slot gas fire and an electric lamp hanging from the ceiling under a great pagoda, with a bulb the size of a torch bulb.

The bathroom was about the same size as the bedroom and you had to share it with the geyser, which was bigger than I was and a lot noisier. Two bob a bath, and don't forget to wash it out when you've used it, though why anyone should bother when it had been stained more brown than white was beyond me.

Later on, of course, I'd develop my seaside-landlady routine, with a bright red wig, two enormous falsies, a flowered apron, carrying a mop – not to mention the pantomime dames I played – but not in Fairleigh, not in the Follies.

Naturally there was a parlour downstairs that no one ever used, a sort of shrine, with everything polished till it shone, including an upright piano you could see your face in but couldn't play, and the silver frames of photographs of Mrs E. and hubby. Thin, he was, and going bald, with a little moustache, just half the size of her, like the characters in the seaside postcards come to life. The whole room stank of polish.

Meals always in the dining-room – Bruce and Marlene showed up that day at five to one sharp; I had a picture in my mind of Mrs E. standing at the door with a stopwatch in her hand, pressing the button at one o'clock dead and saying, 'No dinner for *them*.' She only served us, she never sat down herself. In fact it was a bit like the angels, it was a mystery when she did eat, and we used to wonder about it. Maybe in the kitchen, while she was dishing up for us. Maybe in the afternoon or evenings; she'd eat it cold when we were doing the shows. Or maybe in the dead of night, creeping down the narrow little stairs when she was sure we were all asleep. Eating for Mrs E. was a bit like sex; she seemed to be ashamed of it.

As for Bruce and Marlene, they played the banjo and they smiled. What's more they smiled even when they weren't playing the banjo; it was the first thing that struck me about them, their smiles. They had a sort of a desperate quality, like if they let them go even for a moment, even off stage, they'd never be able to get them back for when they went on again. He must have been in his late forties, she was a bit younger. 'Delighted to meet you,' he said, when he arrived. 'Ever so pleased,' she said, very ladylike. He was a Geordie, she came from somewhere in the Midlands, I think. He was quite tall and broad, with a brick-red face that might have come from drinking, though you seldom saw him take more than a beer – and jet-black hair so heavily brilliantined and brushed that it lay on his skull like patent leather. She was thin with fair hair in a permanent wave, they were still very big then, perms, and huge front teeth. She never said an unkind word about anybody, but that in itself could drive you mad: 'Oh, I don't think he's reely as bad as that,' 'Oh, you *are* being a little hard on her, surely.' You got the impression she wasn't like this by nature, but as a matter of policy.

Bruce didn't often speak at all, except to say things like, 'Pity the poor sailors,' if it was a stormy night, or, 'Let's see what's for chow, then,' before dinner. I sometimes wondered what they said to each other when they were alone. On stage, they sat side by side strumming the banjos, him in a dinner-jacket, her in a long, red dress, strumming like crazy; and smiling. They weren't bad – if you liked banjo acts, and banjos were still well in around that time.

After lunch, Denis picked me up again in the Morris and drove me down to the theatre. He was obviously very proud of it. Open-air, a couple of hundred yards from the promenade, rows of green chairs sloping down to the foot of the stage, which was wooden, painted white, maybe thirty feet by fifteen, with a thick brown curtain that ran along a rail, dressing-rooms round the back.

'What happens when it rains?' I asked him.

'Don't say that!' he said, quite upset. 'We never mention the word rain.'

When he'd showed me round what there was to see, we stood together on the stage, he put his hands in his pockets, and he looked about him like the king of the castle. 'This is it, Johnny,' he said. 'Never less than two-thirds full all season. Most appreciative audiences you could hope to have. I wouldn't swop it for the Palladium.' I knew I would and all, but I didn't say so, I just tried to look impressed. Then he went to the mike and turned it on, he said, 'Okay, show me what you can do,' climbed down from the stage, and sat himself in the front row.

That left me struggling, all right. There was he, smiling up at me, all encouraging, and me wondering what the hell to do that would make him laugh and wouldn't offend a family audience; whatever that was. In the end, I decided on the sergeant-major routine, cleaned up a little bit; I hadn't got the props, but I made what I could of it, treating *him* as the platoon, till in the end, thank God, he started laughing.

When I'd finished, he said, 'Fine, fine, you'll do; as long as you can make them understand you.' Which was a reference to my Cockney accent. It would still have been pretty thick, then, and the way I spoke was pure London, East End, with a lot of double negatives, a fair amount of effing and blinding, and not too many h's. But I could take off most accents by then, largely through being in the Army and having to hear them; Scotch, Welsh, Irish, Northern. I never used to think, when I lay in those stinking barrack rooms on those horrible beds, that it was all going to be grist to the mill.

They did two shows a day, the Follies, and I watched the afternoon show. As a young, randy bloke, I'd naturally been wondering about the birds, and there were three. They turned up together; high heels, permanent waves and a lot of lipstick. 'Here they are,' said Denis, 'our three soubrettes.' But the one that I went for was Ethel. She was blonde, with a very pretty face; huge blue eyes, a slim, straight nose, a rather full-lipped, sexy mouth, with beautiful teeth. She was wearing a sleeveless print summer dress, and you could see she had a terrific body; fine, firm tits, arms bronzed and slender, but nicely rounded, like what you could see of her legs. Do for me, I thought, but although she was friendly, and came across as really very nice, she seemed extremely self-assured; and I wasn't.

I may have come over fairly strong with all the jokes and the repartee, I may have had this London superiority thing, but underneath it I was still very self-conscious; self-conscious about how tall I was, self-conscious about how thin I was, self-conscious about the way I looked, my ridiculous face. It's all very well to say these things become advantages; they were still becoming. It was only the Army that had made me into a comic, and even in the Army I'd had a hard time at first, just like at school.

Naturally I was 'Lofty', naturally there were all the jokes about being awkward and skinny, especially when we had to do P.T. 'All right, Lofty, don't try too hard, son, or you'll tie yourself into a knot.' Just like at bleeding school, I kept on clowning, and the end of it was I clowned my way into camp entertainments, I clowned my way into E N S A; and now I'd clowned my way into the Fairleigh Follies.

The other two birds with Ethel looked a bit easier, but hard, both of them. One, Cynthia, was a peroxide blonde, you could spot them a mile off in those days, face caked with powder, pale grey eyes, about twenty-seven, obviously very experienced. The other, Doreen, was a thin brunette who giggled. They were all from the North, they all seemed a little bit amused by me, but I was used to that. Later on, like I've said, when you've made it, when you've turned all these drawbacks to your own advantage, and you're getting birds because you are who you are, you tend to forget that's what they originally were; drawbacks, that they never seemed like advantages, not then.

The show was like nothing I'd ever seen before, never having been to the seaside on more than a day trip, but the place was full and everybody seemed to enjoy it like mad. Besides the girls, who danced and ogled and sang a few songs, and Denis Jackson himself, and Bruce and Marlene strumming and smiling like their life depended on it, there was a young tap dancer called Charlie Roach, and a couple of big, hefty singers, married; a soprano called Doris Ames and a bass called Roger Potts, sometimes doing solos, sometimes duets, in the fruity old Webster Booth-Ann Ziegler style: 'We'll Gather Lilacs', and that.

Everybody joined in the sketches, which were a little bit cheekier than I'd been afraid they might be. The first one had the soprano taking a gold watch, dropping it between her big Bristols, and saying, 'I shall keep it *here*.'

'Ah,' says Denis, 'there's gold in them thar hills!'

Denis, in his way, was really very good, quite confident, very lively. He was the gaffer, all right, and he knew it, and he had the audience eating out of his hand. They seemed ready to accept anything, even the busy bee sketch that Denis did with Roger Potts and Charlie Roach, that unbelievable sketch which for all I know seaside concert parties are doing to this day. If I ever have nightmares about the Fairleigh Follies, my mouth's full of water and I'm doing that sketch.

You may know it. It starts with Charlie coming on with Denis and asking him, 'Do you know how to play Busy Bee? All you have to do is sit in that chair, I come flying in as the bee, and *you* say, "Busy Bee, Busy Bee, give me some honey".'

So Denis sits in his chair, Charlie comes back flapping his arms like wings, with his mouth full of water, Denis goes, 'Busy Bee, Busy Bee, give me some honey,' and Charlie squirts the water into his face.

Denis then tries to pull the same trick on Roger Potts, but while Denis is off and Roger's sitting in the chair, he fills his own mouth with water. Denis comes bouncing on with his mouth full, flapping and flapping, making little noises at Roger, but Roger won't say a word, till at last Denis can't hold out any more. He swallows the water, says, 'You were meant to say, "Busy Bee, Busy Bee, give me some honey",' at which Roger blows water into *his* face. Very basic, but everybody loved it, especially the kids.

There was a sing-song, of course, with the words of the chorus being let down from the flies on a sheet of cardboard. The favourites that year, as far as I can remember, were, 'I Like A Nice Cup Of Tea In The Morning', and 'You Are My Sunshine, My Only Sunshine'. Then the girls did a high-kicking routine – well, fairly high – and Ethel's legs looked very good, and she herself came on alone and sang, 'Ma, He's Making Eyes At Me', with a lot of finger on the chin and wide-eyed stuff, but she put it over with plenty of vigour, and she seemed far the best of the three to me.

To be honest, though, I think I knew right away that although she might be good, she was never going to be *that* good, she'd never be a threat to me.

While I watched, I wanted to be on that stage, I wanted to show them. Those are the great days; when you're keen and you're beginning, when you can't bear to see a stage with anyone else on it but you, though the time will come when you'll thank God somebody else is there instead, and you pray you'll never have to be on one again. I knew I was better than all of them in the Follies, funnier, more talented, with much more potential. If Denis Jackson could get laughs here, then I should have them rolling off their seats.

Which I did, that evening. The sergeant-major act went like a bomb – they'd rustled up a cap and stick and false moustache by that time – but so did the ad-libbing; I was chatting up the audience, and they loved it.

Denis came on himself and announced me: 'And now, ladies and gentlemen and kiddies, we are very, very proud to announce a new member of the company I know you're all going to like and laugh at. All the way from London, everybody, and straight out of the Army where he's been rolling them in the aisles with ENSA, a comedian who can *really* spin a tall story – Johnny *Lucas*!'

The pianist, a nice little old fellow called Bobby Reynolds – there wasn't an orchestra – struck up 'Knocked 'Em In the Old Kent Road', and on I came; as the sergeant-major. 'Right, you 'orrible lot, sit up straight on them chairs, wipe those silly grins off your faces, get your thumbs down by the seams of your trousers, and PUT THAT CIGARETTE OUT IN THE FRONT ROW, THAR!'

It had the effect it was meant to have, they weren't sure at first how to take it, the aggressiveness of it shook them, so that when, after thirty seconds or so, they realized it was all just a con, the laughter was twice what it would have been otherwise.

This, of course, is quite consistent with Freud's theory of a psychic economy; with the lifting of fear as well as the original inhibition, the economy is doubled, so therefore also the laughter will be proportionately increased.

Something like that, Doc.

I'd naturally been worried at first how I'd feel in front of an audience like this, when all I'd been used to, other than a few turns in East End pubs after my demob, was up to several hundred hairy-arsed soldiers, with maybe just a sprinkling of A T S; stag audiences, in fact. Plus the fact that now I was in the North. But with that first laugh, I knew I was away. I was enjoying myself. The laughter was fabulous; each fresh laugh was like a charge, giving you power, making you want to go on and on, surpass yourself, excel yourself, till they were laughing so hard that they were right out of control, and you couldn't hope to make yourself heard.

I started improvising, I did a little strut up and down the stage for half-a-minute or so, without saying a word, then, when they were really pissing themselves, whirled round on them, pointing with my stick; which made them laugh louder still. ''Oo's that laughing, there? 'Oo is it?'

When I came off, Denis grabbed my hand, really excited, saying, 'Lovely, lovely!' They all seemed to be looking at me in a different way, smiling at me. Ethel, too. Ethel, too. I knew, then, that I could have her. I went up to her after the show, moving straight in like a real London boy, and asked her, 'How about a walk, then?'

'Walk?' she said, looking at me a bit amused, though not unpleasant. 'Walk where?' which shook me a little.

'Anywhere,' I said. 'Along the beach,' and she laughed. 'The beach?' she said. 'But the tide's in!'

'Tomorrow morning, then,' I said, just blundering on, and it seemed like a million years before she answered, very cool, 'All right. Tomorrow. Pick me up at my digs, at eleven.'

She shared them with the other two, and I had this nasty picture of them all pulling back the window curtains as I came along the street, peeping out and giggling. It felt like a fair old walk, that, when I actually went down it – it was very much like my street – but when I got to the house and looked, there wasn't a curtain moving. She came out before I could even press the bell.

She walked very quickly on those dancer's legs of hers, quite easily keeping up with me, though my stride was so much longer. As we walked, I took hold of her hand, but she tugged it away at once, saying, 'Not in the *streets*, stupid!' Though again in a way that didn't destroy me. And very soon I realized what she meant, because people were smiling at us, people were nodding at us, people were pointing us out to one another, till I realized: we were celebrities. It was the same when we got on to the sands; children looking up from digging their holes, people stopping in the middle of throwing quoits, others staring from their deckchairs and saying, 'It's them! Them in the show!'

She was wearing sandals. I hadn't got any sandals, in fact I hadn't got any other shoes at all than what I was wearing, and the sand came crunching into those; which amused her, too. 'You've no idea how to look after yourself, have you?' she asked.

No girl had ever said anything like that to me, before, and it suddenly seemed to me that maybe Northern birds were more human. I'd only known one or two in the A T S, and those were really just slags. As for the London girls, they were sharp and hard. It was a question of your wanting something and them knowing what you wanted and seeing that you didn't get it; or not before they'd put you through the hoop one way or another. What Ethel said confused me, too; it seemed to set everything on a different basis; it wasn't just the usual business of getting it or not getting it.

There were other things I got from her I'd never had from birds before, like admiration. She'd take the micky quite a lot, about my big head, the plans I had, and that, but now and then I'd catch her giving me these looks, like she really reckoned me; though for a long time I couldn't be sure if she fancied me. 'No!' she'd say. 'Not here!' she'd say. 'People are *looking*!' she'd say, till I started wondering whether she wasn't a virgin. She'd turned twenty-two, but those were the days when you could still wonder that about girls her age; though not down Mile End. I could always make her laugh, though, that was one thing, and in my experience it was a big step along the way.

I'd lie in that diabolical bed of mine thinking about her, of maybe having her up against a breakwater. Night, it would be, a bit of a moon, low tide, not much wind, a tang of seaweed, barnacles, and as I fucked her, we'd hear the sea; I'd fuck her to the rhythm of the sea. Quite romantic I was, then. In fact the first time she let me kiss her was by a breakwater, one night after the show, tongue in her mouth at last, a great, great feeling, but as soon as I put my hand on her tit, she pushed it away. 'That's enough,' she said.

She'd been going around with Charlie Roach, so I was told, before I came, but there was nothing in it, I could tell, though he wouldn't speak to me for quite a while, and kept giving me dirty looks, till in the end he settled for Cynthia and started looking happier. He was obviously getting it, there. He was a Scouse; dark, round about twenty-seven, stayed out of the Army with some chest complaint, and I suppose quite good-looking in a dance-hall gigolo way; which was what he'd been at one time.

What *was* happening was that for the first time in my life, someone was inspiring me. Everything I was doing up on that stage, the new gags, the ad libs, the variations of business, were for her. All right: they were to impress, but it wasn't just that. There were girls you could try to impress forever, you could fly through the bleeding air, but it wouldn't do a thing, while in *her* case, she was interested, and I loved to see her laughing. She'd be in the wings, there, where I could turn and see her, and in fact – I loved her.

First time ever. I didn't just want to screw her, though of course that was there as well. I was in love.

'The thing about Johnny is he's in love with himself.'

Bloody Mary Smith again. Our group cannibalism session.

'He falls for people who admire him, so he can worship himself through someone else's eyes.'

'I think, to be fair to Johnny, there's an element of this in every love relationship. Putting it technically, one projects one's ego into somebody else, so one can love it there.'

The Welsh Twit: at his worst.

'Not me,' says Mary, the Human Sacrifice.

'Nor me,' says Mrs Casey. 'Women aren't like that.'

'Oh yes, they are,' says Mr Stubbs, the bank manager.

'They're not,' says Mrs Casey, till the Welsh Twit says, 'We mustn't let this degenerate into a battle of the sexes. Johnny, do you think there's any truth in what Mary just said?'

'Maybe,' I said, I was well into the swing of it by now, 'but she's right, it isn't true in her case. She's looking for people to despise her, isn't she?'

'*You* never would,' she says, her eyes switching on the malice. 'As soon as they stop admiring you, or you find somebody who admires you more, you're on to the next one!'

'Look,' I say, 'you've never been an artiste, you've never been a performer; and I mean that in *every* way.'

'That's bitchy,' Mary says.

'All right,' I say, 'you've never been an entertainer, so how can you know what an artiste wants? How can you know what an artiste needs?'

'There we go again,' says Mrs Casey. 'Because you're on the stage and tell jokes, you seem to think you're different from everybody else.'

'We are,' I say and there's a great big jeer from all of them, except the Colonel. But it doesn't worry me. It's what I expect.

This question of your differentness, this question of your separateness, it complicates very much your analysis.

Doctor, I *am* different. If I wasn't different, I couldn't make anybody laugh at me.

All of us are certainly different from one another. Artists especially. But at bottom, the fundamental experiences of the human race are held in common.

Then why am I a comic while you're a psychoanalyst?

I did not say that the reaction formations were the same. It is only when you cease to believe that you are something unique that I shall be able to help you.

The day I stop thinking I'm unique, Doctor, is the day I stop being a comic.

When it happened, it didn't happen on the beach, it didn't happen up against any breakwater, it happened just almost casually, at *her* place, which was the last place I'd ever have expected it to be.

It was run by a married couple, somewhere in their fifties. She was a skinny little woman who always wore a scarf around her head, and gave out with a ten-minute spiel if anyone dropped cigarette ash on the carpet. Houseproud wasn't in it, though how anyone could have been proud of that house, God knows. He was retired from something or other on a disability pension and spent most of his time in the front room, snooping on the visitors, listening to the radio, and doing the football pools. He had brushed-back, thin brown hair, which looked as if he'd creamed every separate strand, horn-rimmed glasses, and a bushy brown moustache. Dead against any sort of screwing, he was. 'The one thing we will not have on these premises,' he used to say, 'is illicit sex.' You got the feeling that he and his old woman hadn't had it that way or any other for the last thirty years, though I heard he was a bit of an illicit drinker, on the quiet. Great Christians they were, too, Catholics; which was really how it all happened.

One Sunday morning, I turned up there with a sketch I wanted to discuss with Ethel. We'd been talking about it for the past few days, we were going to play a couple of kids on the beach, coming on with buckets and spades, I hadn't even thought about it being Sunday. Normally what happened when anyone went round there and wanted to speak to one of the girls was she had to come down and see him in the front parlour, with the door open; a room that stank of polish even worse than Mrs Everson's front parlour, while on top of that the walls were plastered with suffering Christs and texts from the Bible. If you'd *wanted* to have it off in there, you never could have got the erection.

So I rang at the door, expecting the old crocodile to answer it, when who should open it but Ethel. 'I don't know but whether I ought to let you in,' she said. 'I'm on my own.'

'On your own?' I said, thinking she must be joking, but it was true; the crocodile and her husband were out at church, Doreen had gone home to Runcorn for the day, and Cynthia had taken off somewhere with Charlie Roach; which was one turn I owed him.

'It'll be nice to be alone in the parlour,' I said.

'As a special privilege you can come upstairs,' she said, 'as long as there's no nonsense.'

'Anything but the parlour,' I said.

And upstairs, one thing led to another; which in a funny way I think we both knew it would, as soon as she opened the door. She had a room of her own; Doreen and Cynthia shared one. Ethel's was even smaller than mine, if that was possible, but to be honest, that didn't worry me.

She sat on the bed, I sat on the only chair, a plain, hard, varnished, wooden one like a kitchen chair, holding the script between us, our knees touching. Her knees were round, not at all bony, and her legs were bare, just nicely flecked with little golden hairs. We talked for a while, speaking lines, but we were both very distracted and suddenly, spontaneously, we bent forward and kissed each other; then we were on the bed, and the script was God knows where.

She was saying, 'No, no, Johnny!' but they were only words, and we both knew it. I put my hand on her thigh; it was cool and full, then farther up, till I could feel the crisp hair underneath her panties, could feel her getting wet.

It wasn't a seduction, though, that was what was best about it, because we both wanted each other, now she had hold of me, we were kissing again, till suddenly she pulled back and said in a very practical voice, 'Let's undress.' It's amazing how down-to-earth women can suddenly become at moments like that, as though having gone through all the preliminaries, the refusing, the resisting, they've accepted what's going to happen, and they suddenly change gear completely. They take over. I knew then, though, that she couldn't be a virgin.

So we did make love, and it was tremendous; she went down on me, too, which was the first time any woman had ever done that, and it seemed the most beautiful thing that had ever happened to me. Then, when she'd come and I'd come, the bell rang downstairs and she said, 'Oh, God, it's Cynthia,' and she'd changed gear again, she was off the bed and throwing on clothes, hissing at me to hurry up and dress, and while we were dressing the bell rang again, longer and louder now. She went down the stairs first – I can still remember the drugget over the carpet, the shiny stair rods, the polished, knobbly bannisters – she deliberately making a lot of noise, me tip-toeing behind her like a big fairy, trying to make no noise at all, then slipping into the parlour when she opened the door: 'Oh, *hallo*, Cynthia; we've been reading this script, Johnny and I,' and Cynthia, 'Yes, I'm sure you must have been enjoying it.'

That was how it started, then, and afterwards it was a question not so much of when but where. We used to take all the obstacles a bit for granted then, like you would the weather, but looking back, what a poxy, hypocritical thing it was that two young people who loved each other couldn't find anywhere to go to bed. Our lodgings – hopeless, unless some hundred to one shot came off, like it did when everyone but her was out, that Sunday. The beach – very dicey. Even old Denis used to say, 'Look, boys and girls, I'm not a moralist, I'm not a kill-joy, I'm broad minded, but remember the show that's all; remember the Follies. They admire us in this town. They recommend us to one another, year after year. It's a family show. If word gets around that you know what; well, we'll all suffer, and I'll suffer more than anybody.'

He was married, himself; his wife was quite a pretty little dark woman called Jane, who kept the books and helped with the costumes. They had a couple of grown-up children, and in summer they lived in a flat in Fairleigh, in winter they went back to Manchester where Denis had a pub, like my old man; except his was a free house and a bit of a hotel, too.

I enjoyed working with him, doing the sketches, but at the same time it convinced me of one thing: I was a solo turn. A lot of people start off as double acts, then break away; others you couldn't imagine without their partners: Laurel and Hardy, Abbott and Costello, the Western Brothers, Morecambe and Wise. Even Sid Field used to feed off Jerry Desmonde, though it wasn't quite the same thing. In most double acts, one bloke's funnier than the other – though Laurel and Hardy were an exception – but a straight man's different; and he never gets joint billing.

You're very unlikely, anyway, to run slap into your perfect partner. The best double acts come together almost by Fate, and there's a kind of chemical reaction involved. Suddenly two blokes find they're on the same wavelength, and not only on the same wavelength but that they somehow complete one another. I've never felt that, not with anybody, and certainly not with Denis. Our ages were too different, our rhythms were too different, our backgrounds were too different. What was a joke for him would often be only the beginning of a joke for me; of what I'd call a firecracker, a joke that you set off and it keeps exploding, with the biggest bang at the end.

I had trouble with this rhythm thing when I was on my own, too; with the audience. They were mostly from the North, and I was an out-and-out Cockney. I was quick myself, I expected other people to be quick, and if they didn't get a joke, bad luck, they'd have to wait for the next one.

There seem to me to be two styles of humour in English comedy, London and the North, with most of the Northern comics coming from Liverpool or Manchester, and in the days before television, the difference was more obvious. I don't think it was so much they were different in themselves, because when Northern comics came to London, and when they started doing radio, they soon seemed to speed up; it was more down to the kind of audience they'd been accustomed to. After all, it's no use being fast and sophisticated if your audience can't keep up with you. As for Sid Field – well, for me he was what you might call an honorary Londoner, even if he did come from Birmingham. Certainly his style was much more London than it was Northern.

So there were times, standing there at the microphone, smelling the old sea breezes, when I knew I was being good, because you always know, yet I could feel the audience slipping away. I'd left them behind. They were struggling. An old comedian once said to me, 'Never underestimate your audience, son. You won't be able to, even if you try,' but I never felt like that; well, certainly not at the beginning, or if I did, what I wanted to do was educate them, bring them up to me. I believed I'd got something new to give, and there was a public for it. And I was right to think like that, because what a comedian finds, if he ever breaks through, is that he takes the public along with him. When he's on his way up, he can never be quite sure of himself, whether he's really funny, or whether *people* think he's funny, so in a way, though he must never show it, he's a supplicant, he's asking them to laugh, because if they don't he's finished, he's back down the pit or on the factory bench, swallowed up again in the mass. But once he's established, once people *accept* that he's funny, then it's him that's calling the tune. He'll still have difficult houses, of course, audiences that sit on their hands, but by and large they'll come ready to laugh. He's the king, and they're his subjects. Beforehand, it's more like running for Parliament, when he needs their votes; and he can't let on that he's running for King.

Which brings me to something else; that in Fairleigh, I started cutting down on the imitations. It was an instinctive thing at the time, but now I realize why I did it. It was to do with being King, again.

Imitations were very popular, then, a lot of comics used to do them; film stars, mostly, Jimmy Cagney – 'Ya dirty rat!' – Humphrey Bogart, James Stewart. They went down very, very well with Army audiences. But they're dangerous, imitations – unless a mimic's *all* you are – because you finish up not being you. Look at the really great comedians; Chaplin, W. C. Fields, Groucho Marx, Sid Field. They were themselves. Could you imagine W. C. Fields ever imitating anybody? It would have been beneath him. Sid Field did sketches, he invented characters, Slasher Green and the photographer, but they were *his* characters; like the seaside landlady and the sergeant-major were mine.

Denis noticed it, he'd say, 'Haven't heard much of the old Cagneys, lately, Johnny; I like that, your Cagney,' but I'd laugh it off. Even then I knew what I was doing, and I think he knew that, too. 'Johnny,' he told me one day, after a show when I'd been really good, exceptional, 'it's been wonderful to have you here, and I'll watch for when your name goes up in lights down

South. You'll always have two loyal fans in Jane and me.'

I said something about hoping I'd work with him again, but he shook his head. 'You're too good for us,' he said. 'We couldn't keep you here. It wouldn't be fair, anyway. You'll have your troubles, but you'll go bloody miles. Mind, I don't envy you a bit. I'm happy where I am, me. It's a nice backwater, a good, healthy life. There may not be much money in it, but there's peace of mind.'

Which tells you, really, why he could never have been a great comedian. A real comedian not only won't ever settle for peace of mind, I don't think he can ever hope to achieve it. A comedian's basically hurt by the world, and humour is his response, just like a cuttlefish gives out a cloud of ink. A fellow asked me once, a night-club owner, 'Excuse my saying this, but why are all you comedians such miserable bastards?'

'Because we spend our lives trying to get laughs out of miserable bastards like you,' I said, but later on I thought about it a lot. It's not true that *all* comedians are depressed when they're not performing, or that those who are, are down all the time, but a lot of us *do* get depressed at certain periods. All that on with the motley stuff has got some truth in it.

What you are implying perhaps is that most comedians are manic-depressives.

How many patients you got in this hospital, Doc?

In the sanatorium? At the moment I think forty.

How many of them are manic-depressives, then?

It is hard to say. You cannot always so narrowly categorize. Perhaps twelve. Maybe only ten.

And how many of those are comedians?

Very interested in manic-depressive comedians, Dr Weiss is. What boosts us up, what pulls us down. He's great on the old patterns. He wrote a book, I can see it in his bookcase from the couch, if I roll a little to the left: *Patterns of Anal Fixation in Paranoiac Schizophrenia*, fat gold letters on a fat blue book. One day there may be another next to it, all based on me: *Patterns of Mania in a Depressed Comedian.*

It makes me think of Maurice Franks, the first person I ever heard this sort of talk from. He'd lean back in his armchair, big nose tilted at the ceiling, and he'd say, in that weary, weary voice, '*All* comedians are melancholics, even if they don't start as melancholics, and they turn their scriptwriters into bloody psychotics.'

Maurice had a lot of books, too; *he* read Freud, and God knows how many books on the psychology of humour, the analysis of laughter. If you asked him about them, he'd sound as bored as he was by everything else. 'Don't ask me,' he'd say. 'I only read them for encouragement, to see that great brains like those knew even less about it than I do. You're better off with Joe Miller's Joke Book,' which he had, as well.

He'd say things like, 'There's nothing new in comedy. Nothing. You know what the first recorded instance of repartee was? When one caveman threw a club at another, and the other one picked up the same club and threw it back.'

He was writing my radio show, then, *Johnny Come Lately*, and if comedians were depressives, then he must have been the gloomiest bloody comedy writer in England. If you saw him smile, it must have been Christmas, and as for laugh ...

'Why should I laugh?' he'd ask. 'In a comedy writer, laughter's a weakness. A comedy writer's got to be the toughest one-man audience in the world.'

He was different from some of these American gag writers, though. They look all jaded, as well; heavy, middle-aged blokes in short-sleeved shirts and horn-rimmed glasses, sitting side by side behind their typewriters, throwing ideas backwards and forwards to each other like they were cooks, or engineers. They didn't seem bored; just so professional that they'd dried up inside.

Maurice, then, could only have been about twenty-five, but he gave you the impression he'd been alive a thousand years, hating every minute. He was a Yiddisher, originally from round Hackney, and his father had been a mouth-organist on the halls, The Fabulous Franks, so he'd been brought up in show business. Maybe this was part of his trouble; he was browned off with show business, but at the same time it was all he knew.

He despised what he wrote, what he believed the business and the audiences demanded, he despised the audiences for laughing at it, yet at the same time he'd never take the leap. He liked the comfortable life, Maurice. He wrote lines like, 'I'm not saying she's mean, my mother-in-law, but she's the only woman I know who carves the joint with a cut-throat razor.'

Personally, I got on well with him. He was from my part of the world, even if his background was a lot different, so we understood each other pretty well. He lived then in a big, white block of service flats near Regent's Park, couple of rooms and a bath, famous knocking-shop, which I used to get on at him about. 'Listen,' he'd say, 'if they don't bother me when *I'm* knocking, why should I care when *they're* knocking?' which was fair enough. The place had long, narrow corridors with doors all the way down either side, like prison cells, and if someone had died there, I don't suppose anybody would have noticed till the maid came round to clean the flat. Later on, Maurice went on to fancier places, posh blocks round Baker Street and there, but even then, he still seemed very prosperous; expensive suits, handmade shoes, television set when not that many had them, cupboard full of drinks that he seldom drank himself.

Coming, like I said, from the East End, he dug my kind of humour, even though he never gave me quite what I wanted, I felt constricted by him, and we'd argue a lot, sometimes for a couple of hours over a single line. 'I can't say that,' I'd tell him, 'it sticks in my gullet.'

'So swallow hard and say it,' he'd tell me. 'If you don't get a laugh, then come back and complain, but you'll *get* a laugh, believe me; and it'll be *your* laugh, not mine,' which was shrewder than it may have seemed. The old, old comedian's dilemma. Any line that gets a laugh is a good line, any line that doesn't must be a bad line. Which of course, like I say, ignores the whole question of your delivery and your audience – W. C. Fields could say, 'Quite so,' and have them falling about – but it still can't be denied. Like Dr Weiss said, they laugh, therefore you exist.

It was no coincidence, Maurice Franks being a Jew, because

as soon as you come into London showbiz, you find it's full of them, my agent was a Jew, but I'd known quite a few of them at school, and I'd always got on with them okay; maybe because they were being persecuted and I was being persecuted, them about their names and their noses and their money, me for being so big and awkward.

It was a strange thing, this radio comedy; strange to think how big it was then, and had been for the past twenty years, before television came along and swept it out of sight. Myself, I'd grown up on radio comedy, in the war; Tommy Handley and *It's That Man Again*, all quick-fire gags and funny accents, and then, on the American Forces Network, Bob Hope and Fred Allen and Jack Benny. It was an important experience that, being able to hear these people at that age, and I still reckon I was very lucky. You couldn't see them, yet it didn't seem to matter. Their personalities were distinctive, they were still *there*. Of course, they weren't what you'd just call radio comedians, like Handley was; they were great comedians who happened to be working on radio because then it was the big medium; Fred Allen always so morose, Jack Benny always so mean, Bob Hope so brash. They were in the room with you.

When I came to do it myself, I found it wasn't so easy. I made my name on radio, I suppose, like everybody had to, then, but you were caught betwixt and between, between the studio audience and the radio audience. You need the studio audience to spark you off, but you stand or fall by the radio audience. To begin with, it seemed ridiculous, just standing around a microphone with a script in your hand, everyone in their ordinary, everyday clothes, jerseys and suits and dresses, making believe we were in an aeroplane or at the North Pole, to a studio audience that could see the most energetic thing we did was to turn over the pages. It embarrassed me that, at first, and it frustrated me, too, because I've always relied a lot on gesture and movement and expression. I don't think there's ever been a good comedian that hasn't. But when you hear it all played back, *on* the radio, then it makes sense, and I reckon in the end you benefit by it, because it forces you to use your imagination. You've somehow got to believe you're in a studio but you're not in a studio; you're actually in the areoplane, you're actually on the ice floe.

Can those be penguins, over there?

Either that, or the Eskimos have started dressing for dinner.

Maurice, again. Not one of his best. On the other hand, he didn't have any best; he never fell below a certain level and he never rose above it, which was probably why he was so successful, and why when television came along, with the same sort of demands, the same sort of standards – or lack of them – he did well there, too. And why I felt constricted, even when I was getting audiences of eight or nine million. The only time I really felt myself was doing the warm-up before the show started, just a straightforward stand-up patter act, a lot of it ad-libbed, sometimes throwing in a bit like the old sergeant-major. Though I'd lie if I told you I didn't like it at the time; the fame, the listening figures, the laughs, the money. Plus when you're as young as that and it's all suddenly started happening to you, it's like being carried along by the current; all you have time for is to wave now and then to the people on the bank, then you've gone past them, and though the water's coming into the boat and your arse is damp, you're frightened to stop it, in case you capsize. That was me, on radio.

It's amazing how it can get in the way, success. I'd never have admitted it then, on the crest of the fucking wave, but I reckon I was more me when I was with the Follies. Money's very dangerous till you're used to it, though, and if you've been poor, you never really get used to it. Not that you're greedy, or want to be flash, but in some way it seems to be *proving* you. The money's rolling in because you're good, it proves that you must be funny. Maurice understood this; he was a clever bastard. If I told him about some line he wrote, 'It's not me,' he'd say. 'Who's me? A *schlapper* at the seaside earning ten pounds a week, or a comic with an audience of millions?'

What you're doing, of course, is selling out, though you'd never formulate it, then; you just go on getting this uncomfortable feeling. It's harder for a comedian than almost anybody else to admit this to himself, especially when he's starting out, because he tends to be so insecure. Like I've often said, he never knows where the next laugh's coming from. However big you are, however successful, it's always like a little miracle when you're up there again in front of an audience, and the first laugh comes. In a sense, a comedian is always starting from scratch.

Each laugh could always be the last one.

So now you are saying that a comedian is not only subject to pain, he is reacting to pain.

Yeah, I think he is.

But that it is not the same pain.

The pain that makes him *become* a comedian isn't the pain he feel *as* a comedian.

But a man's unconscious does not change because he becomes a comedian. It is more likely he becomes a comedian because he is that sort of man; with a compulsive necessity to make people laugh.

Not back to manic-depression again, are we, Doc?

I am suggesting only that the resemblances in his pain may be greater than its difference.

Look, Doc, he laughs because things hurt him, then he's hurt because he worries about getting laughs.

Can this not be a logical progression? If people do not laugh with him, then he fears he may return to his loneliness and to his pain.

Doctor, I'm not a psychologist; but you're not a comedian.

(They've got the text books, they've got the old patter, but they haven't lived it, they don't know how *being* changes people. In that way, they're almost as bad as women.)

We are prepared always to accept and analyse the here and now, but psychoanalysis by its nature cannot be only existential.

You've lost me again, Doc.

'What's so *special* about being a comedian?' Bloody Mary Smith, again. 'You talk as though you had a mission.'

'It's just a job, like any other.' Tight-Arse, the bank manager.

'You're paid to make people laugh; I'm paid to look after their money.'

'And a housewife probably works twice as hard as either of you –' Mrs Casey jumping in '– and she isn't paid at all.'

'No, but really,' says Mary Smith, with that laugh, 'what *is* so special about being a comedian?'

'Well, Johnny,' says the Welsh Twit. We're all on first-name terms now, though we don't like each other any better. 'Aren't you going to tell us?'

'If you can't see it,' I say, 'I can't tell you,' and for some reason I feel terribly choked up, almost in tears.

'It's your *feelings* about this I want to get at,' he says.

'You mean why I should believe such a lot of cobblers?' I say. I've got his fucking number by now, all right.

'Not necessarily, not necessarily.'

'If I told you a comedian was like a priest,' I say, 'you'd all say I was out of my mind.'

Which they did. A great bloody outburst of jeers and laughing.

'George Robey used to come on as a priest,' says the Colonel. 'All that stuff about dry rot in the pulpit.'

'I've told you,' I say. 'If you can't see it, I can't bloody explain it to you.' And I get up and leave.

Better than a priest, in fact, more important than a priest, because what's a priest, today? A priest is a phoney. He's like an agent representing a firm that's gone bankrupt. People go to comedians and priests for the same reason. They're saying, 'Help us. Ease our pain.' But a comedian's more honest than a priest. He promises nothing. All he'll try and do is make you laugh, and while you're laughing, you'll forget yourself. After that, you're on your own. As for psychologists, they're con-men, too. They make out that if you let them dig up your past, they'll change your future, when the only time we any of us live in is the present; which is where the comedian scores, because that's all he's concerned with, the present. He knows the past's dead and the future can't be controlled, that what it comes to is jam yesterday, jam tomorrow but never jam today. So he tries to give you a bit of jam today.

From a Messiah, you have now become a priest.

That's an improvement in your book, is it, Doc?

I would agree that the new identification is closer to reality.

I was a megalomaniac but now I'm just a maniac, is that it?

The analogy between comedians and priests is quite suggestive. It is very possible that one has even derived from the other.

I'm bloody sure it has.

Though the priest's ministry, of course, is regarded as holy.

Maybe a comedian's inherited that, and all.

So we return again to your sense of a divine mission.

I don't believe in God, Doctor.

Then let us call it a vocation.

I'll buy that, yes. See he's the last one left, Doc, the comedian is.

Because they're closing in on us from all sides, organizing us, controlling us, cutting the ground away from under us, with tower blocks and concrete and computers, with cops and bugs and motor cars, with fucking capitalists and sodding Communists. Every day a little bit less choice, a little bit less space, a little bit more interference. It's too much for psychoanalysts and priests; so we're the last, we comedians. At least we can make people laugh at them.

# *Chapter 3*

Lou Gold came to see me. My second visitor. My agent. They're encouraging them now, visitors. Nothing that's liable to upset me, though. I'm still very fragile. Overtax me, and I could easily turn into a computer again.

He was one of the few that knew where I was, Lou; him, June and Sid, my dresser. They'd written, him and Sid, they'd sent things; chocolates and plants and flowers. Now Lou turned up in his Jaguar, XJ140, grey. He'd had a Jaguar of some sort ever since I'd known him; the Jews' Rolls-Royce, we used to call them in the forties. You saw Lou at the wheel, now or then, soft black hat, big brown conk, horn-rimmed specs, thick lips, thicker cigar and jowls. Caricature of grasping agent. I thought so myself when I first clapped eyes on him, I admit it. When he asked me out to lunch at Isow's – where else – and said, 'I've seen your act at the Windmill, son. I'd like to represent you.'

Another one that hardly ever laughed, Lou. Smiled a little, when he found enough strength to part those big lips, but no apparent sense of humour, bar the wry, world-weary stuff. Yet he represented more top comics than any other agent. To be approached by him was meant to be an honour.

'So what are you making there?' he asks. He's eating chicken soup, with matzoh balls, and when I say eating, I don't know if I mean eating or drinking, or maybe both, because believe me he's enjoying all of it, he's gulping down the matzoh balls and he's swallowing soup out of his spoon like there's no tomorrow. I've noticed since then that they've got a special way of eating, Jews, when they're in Jewish restaurants, as though each mouthful's going to be their last.

Everywhere you looked that day in Isow's, there seemed to

be big men with heavy shoulders and expensive suits shovelling soup into their mouths. It was the most expensive-looking restaurant I'd ever been in; not posh, not elegant, just expensive. A long, large room with several rows of tables, each of them with tall leather-covered chairs, some of which had names on the back in gold, mostly of film and showbiz producers. It was in Brewer Street, only just down the road from the Windmill, up a high pavement and through glass doors, but once you were through them, you seemed a thousand miles away.

I remember how I just watched Lou eating, I was fascinated. There were great, long silences – he's always been big on silences – but they didn't worry me at all that day. Then suddenly he looked up and asked me this question, and I told him. It was twenty quid a week, I think, and it seemed like a fortune to me.

'You should have come with me,' he said. 'I could have got you fifty.'

Come with him? At that time I hadn't even heard of him, and if I had, I wouldn't have dared.

'You like it there?' he asked.

'Yes and no,' I said.

I liked the money – though I couldn't tell *him* that – I liked the idea of being in the West End, with the Palladium and the Prince of Wales so near they suddenly seemed in reach; but the audiences, the actual working: terrible.

'If you can make them laugh at the Windmill,' Lou said, 'you can make them laugh anywhere,' which I'd heard I don't know how many times before. Sometimes it was the one thing that consoled me. They say never act with children or animals. They ought to add nudes to that. Never tell jokes on a nude show. Outside the Windmill they put up a list of all the famous comedians who'd started there; Peter Sellers, Tony Hancock, me. I reckon it ought to have been a roll of honour, conspicuous courage in the face of the enemy. Or rather you were an enemy to them. To all the blokes – which meant practically the whole audience – for who you were just something standing between them and the crumpet. When you came on, the crumpet went off. When you went off, the crumpet came back. I hardly dared to look at those audiences. To me, they seemed like a pack of wolves. Youngish, a lot of them, and nearly all men.

As soon as the nudes came on, and that was what the Windmill was famous for – standing nudes, because the Lord Chamberlain wouldn't allow them to move – they'd come swarming across the seats from the back, like troops going over the top, a bloody great wave of them, with short haircuts and tan raincoats. And if somebody moved out of a seat in the front few rows, they'd literally fight over it, punching each other like animals.

One afternoon – the show ran right through till night-time; too right they were to say, 'We Never Closed' – I looked down at this from the stage and I said, 'One thing about the cunts in the audience; at least they're allowed to move.'

Show after bloody show, day after bloody day. No wonder they got through so many comedians, and no wonder quite a few made it; it was sheer law of averages.

I haven't forgotten that audition, how nervous I was, how anxious I was waiting to hear from them, Ethel and me in this little dump of a hotel in Paddington, how nothing could have been less like the real thing. Not that auditions ever can be. A theatre without an audience is a body without soul; a great, cold cavern, and a terrible, sour smell in your nostrils, just two or three people listening to you in the front stalls. If they *do* laugh – and it's a hundred to one against; they're pros, you see – it sounds like something in an echo chamber, *ha*-ha! – and you're better off without it.

So you stand up there like a spare prick at a wedding, making these jokes, which are just going out into space. It destroyed me, I admit it; it's a bad experience for anyone, an audition, but most of all for a comedian, because he lives off laughter, and if no one's laughing, then he must be bad. On top of that you're not even on your own, you're one of a queue, it's like being back in the Army again, 'Next! Next!' I remember the bloke before me was a little red-headed Scotsman with the thickest Glasgow accent I'd ever heard. He came on in a kilt and did a sort of Harry Lauder act. He may even have been very funny, if you'd understood what he said. On top of that, he shouted every line like he was trying to reach the back of the gallery. There was one joke about haggis, I remember that, but the main thing was he was so bad he encouraged me, I thought, whatever happens, I *can't* be as bad as that.

I started with a bit of patter, the kind of thing I thought they'd want in a place like that, but I was struggling. Then in desperation I got on to the sergeant-major, but I was hardly into that when they stopped me, 'We'll let you know,' and thank God they did, a couple of days later, two of the longest days in my life.

So it was back to stag audiences again, only they were different, these, they weren't the stag audiences I'd been used to in the Army, just wanting a bit of good, honest dirt. This was a real stag audience – even if most of it wasn't listening to you – so what it wanted was crumpet jokes and queer jokes, which were what it usually got. Crumpet was what brought it together, queers were what it felt superior to. Instinctively you feel this with a stag audience, you feel the vibrations in the air, whether it's at the Windmill or in a room at the Hilton. There's this frightening electricity, which has nothing to do with you, this throbbing violence – like if they can't fuck, they'll fight – this aggressive, baying laughter. It tends to make you coarsen your act.

On the face of it, I had twenty times the freedom I'd had in Fairleigh with the so-called family audience, where tits were in but twots were out, yet in fact it was just as limiting in its way, and maybe more dangerous, because you weren't so aware of it. You tend to think about an ideal audience, but in fact there *is* no ideal audience. I suppose for a comedian the ideal audience would be the one that laughs at everything he says or does; but then it could easily be a studio audience, which as everybody knows can be the lowest. Maybe it would really be somewhere between the stag audience and the family audience, with a bit more sophistication than either. All I know is I'd been happier at Fairleigh than the Windmill; on stage, at any rate.

Off it, at least I was in London now, I could stroll about and dream things, I was that much nearer what I wanted; or so I thought. It was a marvellous, bubbling feeling, getting familiar with the West End at last, belonging to it. Soho and Leicester Square and Piccadilly Circus; all that part that had seemed the Promised Land when I was a kid, slipping in to watch Sid Field, and that I never even saw by daylight.

I'd wander up to Argyll Street just to stand outside the Palladium, looking at the coloured placards and the stills. It was a time when they nearly always had an American over to top the bill; Danny Kaye, Bob Hope, Jack Benny, Danny Thomas, and when Bob Hope went on, he went on with Jerry Desmonde as his straight man because he was dead, Sid Field.

I couldn't believe that when I heard it, I was still in the Army, up in Catterick, square-bashing on the parade ground, route-marching round those horrible bloody moors, because I'd always felt inside me I was going to meet him again, and that he was going to approve of me. I'd imagined it in a lot of different ways, very sentimental really, but then comedians *are* sentimental, even if they don't sing, 'Tears', or, 'My Mother's Birthday'. Sometimes I'd have made it, he'd come backstage to congratulate me, and I'd tell him, 'Mr Field, you'll never believe this, but when I was a kid I got your autograph, I came up specially, and you gave me half-a-crown.' Or I'd be doing a spot on the same bill as he was, much lower down of course, and he'd tell me, straight up, 'One day you'll be a bigger star than I am, Johnny,' to which I'd say, 'Than you? Never, Mr Field!' Only now it would never happen.

I found out, of all poxy places, in the latrines. I was having a crap, someone had left the *Daily Mirror* on the floor, and when I picked it up, there it was: SID FIELD DEAD. Still only middle-aged. I started crying, I just couldn't stop, and then I was glad I was in the latrines, where at least no bugger could see me. More than anything I wanted to talk to somebody about it, but who the hell was there to talk to? Which of the bloody swede-bashers I was surrounded by would ever even have heard of him, let alone seen him?

That afternoon we had a route march, and I honestly fucking welcomed it, the misery of it took my mind off Sid, trudging over the moors, bandolier biting into your shoulder, boots rubbing your feet raw, sodding great pack on your back, fingers sore with chilblains. Who cared? 'Cheer up, Lofty!' said the Sergeant. 'You're not bloody dead yet, but you soon bloody will be.' Who fucking cared?

To see the Prince of Wales now, without his name on it, was terrible, a reminder every time I passed the place, which now was practically every day. I'd no idea then, at Catterick, how it had happened, the drink and that, but when I did find out later on, it made no difference, he was still my idol. He hadn't destroyed himself, like some people said; he'd *been* destroyed, they'd made him wait too long, and I think I knew then, when I was still wet behind the ears, what a comic was up against if he was really original; how everyone would try to do him down, even inside the profession.

One day in a pub – the Salisbury I think it was, the Victorian one; I was always round pubs in Soho then, sandwich bars, anywhere that things might happen – I stood right next to Jerry Desmonde. I was close enough to touch him. I could easily have said, 'Excuse me, Mr Desmonde, but what was it really like working with Sid Field?' but I never did it. To tell the truth, I was frightened of the answer, not that he might rebuff me, he seemed a nice enough bloke, just like he did on stage, but in case he'd say something that'd shatter me, like, 'The times I had to carry him through those sketches,' or, 'He never bought a round,' I wouldn't take the chance.

I asked Lou Gold about him that day in Isow's, though, and he looked up at me from under those heavy eyelids, lizard eyelids, that seemed to take so much lifting, looked up from the roast chicken, and he said, 'Sid Field? A wonderful comedian. But he should have come to London sooner.'

'Him?' I said. I couldn't believe it. 'But they *stopped* him coming.'

'Listen,' he said, 'if you want to do a thing enough, you do it,' and he went on eating, like a Jewish Buddha. There was never any arguing with Lou, but I still wouldn't believe him. Sid bottling it? Sid *wanting* to stop in the provinces?

Now he sat there in my room, Lou, same old Jewish Buddha, kept all the brushed-back hair he had, though a little bit greyer now, and he said, 'So when do I start booking you, again?'

It was the same question he'd asked me before, when I was drying out in those nursing homes, or when I'd staggered out of them, and it always made me feel better, like there wasn't any doubt he *would* be booking me, because *he* didn't doubt it. Nothing changed him, nothing threw him, he was one of the most unimaginative men I've ever met, and that was his strength. He was a great agent, and he'd never had any idea of what I was up to than he had of flying an aeroplane.

'God only knows,' I said to him, yet I was still pleased.

'Madge sends her love,' he said, 'made you this cake,' and he gave me a round biscuit tin with a rose on it. She was his wife, Madge, not Jewish, a right surprise when I'd first met her, little plump red-haired woman he'd married out of the chorus. Two daughters, both at Roedean or somewhere, married, now. 'Kids all right, Lou? Grandchildren all right?'

'Wonderful, don't worry.'

Then a silence. One of his Buddha silences. If he'd nothing to say, he said nothing, he could do it, no trouble, but I'd had enough of silences with Dr Weiss, brooding there behind the couch, waiting for me to fill them in. I didn't see why I should speak now, just because Lou wouldn't, why I should have to spend the whole of my life playing to audiences, so it became a kind of contest – on my side, anyway – of who was going to speak first. In the end it was Lou; the words suddenly came rumbling up like lava out of a volcano: 'I saw June the other night at the Savoy. The cabaret. Terrific, she was.'

I was pleased, and yet I wasn't pleased. For me, June was always terrific, but she was working and I wasn't. It also made me wonder, was she knocking it off with anybody, something that I brooded on a lot, which I'd very nearly asked her when she came, just stopping myself each time, knowing just how she'd answer.

'What did she wear?' I asked, punishing myself.

'Green,' he said, 'a lovely dress, strapless. Satin, it looked like. Lovely.' He seemed like the craftiest man you'd ever met, Lou, but with his clients anyway he was dead straight. He looked like the most lascivious, yet he was a family man. He spent his life surrounded by birds, ravers some of them, but when he praised them, it was in a remote sort of way, like he was their uncle.

'Food good?' he asked.

'All right,' I said. 'What do you expect from a hospital?'

'The Caprice it isn't.' That was as close as he'd ever come to making a joke. 'Isow's it isn't,' I said. Then another silence, like after his joke, he was exhausted. I was glad he'd come, and yet I wished he'd go. He was the outside world, and I was living in my guts, in my skull.

'You've got an original act,' he said to me, in Isow's. 'You put it over well. A little bit like Max Miller. Maybe a touch of Frankie Howerd. Who's writing your material?'

'I am.'

'So we'll find a writer. That shouldn't be hard. Blue gags yours as well?'

'All of it.'

'You'll have to clean them up a bit. *I* don't mind, but they'd mind on a lot of the halls, especially the provincial ones with the watch committees; they'd mind on radio. Is that yours too, the one about the nancy boy and the umbrella?'

'Yes.'

'You'd never get away with it. *Double entendre.* You know what that is?'

'No.'

'You say one thing, you mean another. Like Max Miller. He meets the girl on a precipice, and he doesn't know whether to block her passage or toss himself off.' Very subtle, I thought. 'It's just an example, that. In fact it got him banned. You've got to know where to stop, even a man as experienced as he is.'

So he became my agent.

'But it won't be quick,' he said. 'Don't expect miracles. I can open doors, but I can't move mountains. All I'll promise you is this. If you stick at it, you'll make it.'

I didn't walk back to the Windmill for the afternoon show, I flew back. I flew back to Kentish Town, and all, when the last show was over, tube from Leicester Square – who thought of cars in those days? – back to the flat I was living in with Ethel. If you could call it a flat. One room with a carpet in ribbons, paper peeling off from the ceiling, furniture that wobbled if you touched it, kitchen the size of a cupboard, and a stench from the bog on the landing below, that you had to share.

Three at a time I went up those narrow, smelly stairs, opened the plywood front door, flung my arms round Ethel and said, 'I've got an agent, I've got an agent!'

'Well, isn't that good?' she said, smiling like she always did when I brought her good news; a wonderful, pleased smile.

Like a mother?

You *could* say that.

But did you feel that?

Maybe.

Later, perhaps, more and more, until her role becomes that of the mother, rather than the wife.

Like I've said, Doctor, things change, people change.

Or become more totally themselves.

That's cobblers, Doc. If I ever saw her as a mother, it was because she *became* a mother. In reality.

But I am talking about reality.

They were great days for us, those. Everything was right, except that lousy flat, and at least we were there together. Sexually, it was marvellous, the best I'd ever known. We'd fuck in the morning, we'd fuck when I got back from the Windmill, we'd fuck into the night, making up for all that frustration up in Fairleigh, where every fuck took a week to plan.

We'd been married in Fleetwood at the end of the summer, in church, would you believe it; parson, white wedding-dress and all. Her parents wanted it, my Mum was pleased about it. She'd always reckoned herself a Christian, my mother. She was the one who'd take us if we ever went to church, my brother and me, she was the one who'd pack us off to Sunday school, or try to, she was the one who'd talk to the Vicar, if he ever came round.

A funny old bloke, the Vicar; Ted and I used to hide round corners laughing at him, and as for the old man, he wouldn't even give him the time of day. I never found out what he was, my father, what he believed; I got the impression that for him, things like God were left to women, he had other things to be getting on with.

Very tall he was, the Vicar, greying-bald, somewhere in his sixties, gold-rimmed glasses, high, posh voice, for ever putting his fingers together like a steeple. God knows why they'd sent him to a manor like ours. He'd no chance. Later, when I ever wanted to take off a parson, it was always him, poor old bugger.

The parson up in Fleetwood was a lot different, broad Lancashire, beetroot-faced and stocky; he came on a little like a turn, himself. 'I'll tell you this much, bride and bridegroom, Ethel and Johnny; you're both on the stage, we hope you'll have success, but you will never, never appear before a more appreciative audience than this one.'

Little, ugly church. Organ music. Me in tails, feeling ridiculous, like I was appearing in a bad sketch someone else had written. Love, honour and obey. Till death us do bloody part. I meant all that, I *felt* all that, but it came from inside, it was just between us two, I didn't have to be told. Ethel fantastic in her white veil, breasts two lovely hillocks in the satin, walking very gracefully, dancer's walk, giving me these happy smiles. My brother Ted best man, with his copper's haircut and his copper's posture, given the day off from Poplar police station. Her parents and mine getting on well, whispering to each other in the front pews.

He was a chemist, her old man, little tubby bloke with wavy grey hair and glasses. The looks obviously came from her mother who must have been a cracker once though she was lined now, and her hair had lost the life that Ethel's had. There were a couple of swede-bashing brothers, an older, married sister – pretty, too, blonde, too, but heavier – and all in all it could have been much worse.

At the reception, her father got a little pissed. There was a lot of beer, not too much champagne, and the women were on port and sherry. He took me by the hand and said, 'You'll look after her, won't you? She's a lovely, loyal girl, is Ethel. Bloody worships you. Don't let her down.'

Those days in Kentish Town, all I needed was Ethel, and all she needed was me. Idyllic, really, and I couldn't have had more temptation round me than I did, not at the Windmill, crumpet everywhere, tits and thighs, dancers slipping into things, nudes slipping out of things, pretty birds, sexy birds, birds that went past looking at you like they'd eat you. Except it wasn't a temptation, because I had all I wanted, which was what I'd got, and that was Ethel.

We knew every little thing about each other's bodies, every little thing the other wanted. It's a beautiful thing, monogamy; as long as it lasts.

She'd been looking for a job, too, Ethel, but with neither of us earning when we got to London, she'd had to take one as a waitress in a café near the Marble Arch. When I got the Windmill I wanted her to give it up, but she got bored in the flat alone, she said, so she went on doing it, still looking for things in her spare time, still not finding anything she wanted. She'd been in the chorus line and she didn't want to go back to that unless things got desperate – which they would, all right – and there wasn't any call for her type of soubrette, not in London. But whatever she did, she did of her own free will. I didn't ask her. I didn't force it on her. I never told her, 'My career matters. Yours doesn't.'

But such things do not always need to be made explicit. What you shared was a belief in *your* vocation.

What's so terrible? What if we did?

Only that things do not occur by accident.

Always looking for someone to blame, Doc, aren't you?

Not to blame; simply to interpret.

'You, you, *you*!' she said to me, at the end. 'It's all been *you*!' Like I'd put a pistol to her head. '*Your* career, *your* talent, your bloody *mission* in life!'

And you continue to believe in your mission.

Don't you think you've got a duty to a talent, Doc, whatever it may be?

To develop it, certainly, but this may also be used as a defence mechanism.

Defence from what?

From one's responsibility.

Greatest good of the greatest number, isn't it, Doc?

To make many laugh, one may sacrifice the few?

Even in hospital, I've got scriptwriters.

It would be interesting to know if *all* comedians think as you.

They may not think it. Inwardly they feel it. The real ones.

One that didn't feel it, or not by the time I knew him, was a little bloke called Ernie Pockett. I'd run into him occasionally in the sandwich bar where I had lunch, round the back of Leicester Square. Very clean place, food quite good, salt beef and that. You'd sit on high stools along a shelf round the walls. It used to be full of street photographers, a right bunch of chancers, and it was run by a big, silver-haired, retired copper who'd have booked them as soon as look at them if he'd still been in uniform. 'Brother on the force?' he'd say. 'Well, at least one of you's earning an honest living.'

'Depends on whether you want to make jokes or be one,' I told him, and this little fellow laughed.

He was a Yorkshireman, forty-five or so, little bit down at heel, little bit watery-eyed, red bow tie, green trilby hat. He'd played the Windmill too, he said. One of those that was forever pulling out his Press cuttings: 'Look; see what they said about me up in Middlesbrough.' Now and then he'd take me for a quid.

One day he came in a little pissed, doing the good advice bit: 'I've been in the business longer than you.' He said to me, 'Johnny; I saw your act. I went in there. Very good, you were. Real funny. And now I'm going to tell you something. Seriously. Stop now. I mean it. On your way up; that's when it's best. Quit while you're bloody well ahead, lad. It's not worth it, all the rest. The misery and the worry. When you're going up, it's great. When you're there it's a bloody dog's life.'

'Yeah,' I said, 'thanks, Ernie. I'll remember that.'

'No, you won't,' he said. 'You're an arrogant young bastard, just like I was. You'll find out when you're there, though; if you don't get out in time. Go and keep hens. Open a sweet-shop. Be a bookmaker. It's a life, that. A comedian's isn't.'

Pissed out of his mind, I thought, the poor old bastard, but he read that, too. 'I may be drunk,' he said, 'but I know what I'm saying. *You'll see.*'

I told Ethel; we laughed about it. 'Poor old man.' She was like me. You've never any doubts, then. When you're young, you're going to make your own rules, no one can tell you. It was sad about Ernie, but he hadn't had what it takes. As to what had happened to Sid Field, I was in London already, wasn't I?

It was a funny London, that, looking back on it. A subdued London, though I wouldn't have thought it then. It had come out of the war, but it still hadn't quite come into the peace. Things were still a bit short, they were still a bit shabby. There was rationing; people queued for things. There wasn't any pride in being young. No swagger.

Great days for hats they were, though. Comics still wore them. Lots of birds wore them. Most men wore them; not just in the City. Max Miller came on with the famous high-crowned white hat with the broad band; I don't think I ever saw him when he didn't wear a hat. Arthur Askey had that little curly-brimmed one he wore like a forage cap. Tommy Trinder wore his boater. I even wore one myself, blue snap-brim trilby; it went with the personality I was putting across; London boy but not the spiv type with the big, wide brim, the Slasher Green hat. It was dated, that, it had gone out with the forties. Arthur English was still doing the routine with the hat, the broad ties, the fast spiel, but it belonged to the past, to history.

Ethel went in for hats, too. That summer, it was a hot one I remember, she used to wear a broad-brimmed, dark blue straw on the back of her head, a good shape for her, a good colour, making her look about eighteen, especially when she was happy.

But she wasn't always happy; she was homesick, then, although she'd never say so. She didn't get the charge from London I did; the theatres weren't shrines to her, the West End wasn't Mecca. It was all too fast and big; I could tell. 'They're *cold* down here,' she said, once. I knew what she meant, even if she was wrong. She'd got no friends. There wasn't even my family to fall back on, though she and my mother got on. They were still right over in Mile End, and I'd put that behind me. Just to go there depressed me, and I'd nothing to say to the old man, even now, the pig. 'It's got such *character*,' she said, when we did go down to the pub, but to me, looking around all that heavy Victorian brass rail and varnished woodwork pressing in on me, its character was what it always had been, like a tomb; except that tombs are quiet.

Nights, that's when things were good between us; nights and Sundays, when I wasn't working, when we'd go to places. Speakers' Corner, and study the nuts. On a fine day, take a steamer down the river. All those square old things; everything we did together was fun. Tower of London, where I'd march about like a Beefeater, all stiff, or be the Headsman on Tower Green: 'Perhaps you'd prefer our off-the-shoulder effect, Your Highness?'

At Madame Tussaud's, down in the old Chamber of Horrors, I got into the tableau with Burke and Hare, the body-snatchers, standing dead still, holding my breath, big snarl on my face, arms outstretched, with fingers crooked. A little old lady came past and said to her husband, 'Never realized there were three of them; and *he* looks the worst of the lot.'

Humour, then, was never something that I switched on and off, it was something I carried over from life into my act; observation, funny voices, quick reactions. My act was *me*, and I think you'll find that's true of most stand-up comedians, making allowances for exaggeration. Later, when things get to us, when we start to worry and we don't know where the next laugh's coming from, this is when we may become morose in private life, but how can a comedian start unless he starts by being funny?

We were perfect for each other then, me and Ethel. She loved my jokes, I loved making her laugh; much more than any audience. I didn't need anyone sophisticated, anyone with a big talent; like June. I wasn't ready. It could even have destroyed me. And I wasn't ready for someone whose career meant as much to them as mine did to me; like June's. For that, you have to be on top, you have to have arrived.

I was so grateful to her then, Ethel. I wanted so much to get her things; a big house, a big car, dresses, servants, so she wouldn't have to do things; and eventually I got her all of them. She asked for nothing; she was wonderful. I knew it then, I know it now.

'Too bloody good for you.' That's Mrs Casey, of course.

'Bloody men.' That's Mary. 'Candles on your silly altar.'

'But what if she was happy?' Ivan asks. I like that kid; I've warmed to him a lot, and part of why it is he reminds me of Bob, my boy. They'd be almost of an age. The Welsh Twit's noticed that, of course: 'Playing out a father-and-son fantasy.'

'That's typical of Johnny,' Mrs Casey said. 'He'll do it when there's no responsibilities. When he just has to be nice for an hour.'

'Do you think that's fair, Johnny?' asked the Welsh Twit.

'There's nothing fair about Mrs Casey, Doc,' I said, 'including her hair.' Which is dyed blonde.

And then he came, Bob. The most amazing thing. As though thinking about him, remembering him through someone else, had somehow brought him to life. I'd noticed this kind of thing before, though I never told Dr Weiss, because I knew he'd have a name for it. You could have turned the water into wine in his glass, and he still would have given you an explanation.

If I'd not been walking through the garden then, feeling like a crazy gardener again, I'd never have seen him; they'd have pounced on him and sent him away. As it was, I set eyes on him just as he came round a corner of the drive, and a male nurse started moving towards him; Jimmy, a big fellow in his white coat. Though it took me a moment to recognize him; what with the long hair and the jeans and the beard and the bullfighter's hat. When I did, I was so pleased and excited that I shouted his name, 'Bob!' and ran over to him, heart fairly banging against my ribs, got in between the big, bloody nurse and him and said, 'It's all right, Jimmy, it's my son, it's Bob!'

'I don't know about that,' he said. 'Has he got permission?'

'Leave it to me,' I said, holding him off, 'I'll straighten it all out,' and I took Bob by the arm, I led him up the steps into the house. 'My son!' I shouted, as we passed the office, 'Down in a minute!' then went on with him up the stairs, two at a time, panting like hell, into my room and locked the door.

'What's the hurry, man?' he said.

I stood back and looked at him, what a scarecrow he was, but I was so happy, I could have cried. I wanted to ask him as much as I could, tell him as much as I could, before *they* were there, banging on the door, dragging him away, and from their own point of view perhaps they were right because I *wasn't* ready for him, he *was* upsetting me, there was a bloody great earthquake going on inside me, joy and guilt and misery and excitement. As for Bob, he seemed very cool, though I suppose that was the style, all 'together' and that.

There were so many questions in my mind, they were knocking one another out of the way, and the one that came out in the end was a nothing one: 'Where have you come from?'

'St Ives,' he said.

'Cornwall,' I said. 'On holiday, are you?'

'Like I live there, now,' he said.

'You've got a job there?'

'No,' he said, 'just living.'

'On what?' The last question that I'd meant to ask, but out it came.

'On chicks,' he said, 'on what I get from Mum. On jobs I sometimes take in cafés and that.'

And suddenly, as though someone was controlling me, the whole conversation was swinging out of my grasp, I was speaking someone else's lines, wasting the minutes we'd got, saying, 'You're nineteen, where's *this* going to get you? You should be at University,' doing the heavy father bit, like however hard we tried, the two of us were frozen forever in the same positions, me reproachful, him defiant – 'University was a drag, man' – except he'd never been this cool before, this passive, and suddenly I found myself putting my hands on his shoulders, looking into his eyes, dull as a cow's, and shouting, 'You're on drugs, aren't you? You're on drugs!'

'We all turn on,' he said, and ducked from under my hands; he was nearly as tall as I was, now. 'You were on booze, I'm on grass. So what?' and I sat on the bed, my head in my hands, torn to pieces, too strung up to say anything. And a terrible thought came into my head, that he'd come to beg money, because what had we got between us? It was four years since I'd seen him.

'What do you want?' I asked, looking up at him. 'Money?' and as soon as I'd said it could have cried, done anything to take it back, thrown my arms round him, asked him to forgive me. But his face didn't change, nor did the tone of his voice.

'I always need bread,' he said, 'but that's not why I came. Mum wrote to me. She was worried about you; things she'd heard.'

'So it was her you came for?' That jumped out, too. Jesus, I was sick.

'I came for both of us,' he said.

Then the footsteps, the knocking at the door, the handle being turned. Two or three of them, by the sound of it, the Welsh Twit included. 'Open up, now, Johnny!'

'What's this?' said Bob. 'The heavy mob?' He still didn't seem to be worried. As for me, I was drained, I hadn't even the strength to get off the bed. I motioned him to unlock the door, which he did, and the three of them burst in like a police raid, the Welsh Twit and two nurses, Jimmy and Eddie. 'My son,' I said, 'Bob.'

'Well, he's no right to come sneaking in here without permission,' said the Welsh Twit.

'He didn't,' I said, 'I brought him up here.'

'You know the rules,' he said. 'No visitors without specific permission.'

'Certainly, Herr Doktor,' I said.

'You'd better come downstairs,' he told Bob, who looked at me and shrugged, then he went out between the two nurses like he was under arrest.

'It's for your own good,' Dr Tomkins said. 'Look at the state of you!'

I started to answer him, but I felt myself choking up, I knew I'd cry. So I just linked my fingers tight, bowed my head, and gently shook it.

'I'll bring you a tranquillizer,' he said. I still couldn't trust myself to answer, but when he came back with a glass of water and the usual red bomb, I was able to ask, 'Can I see him before he goes?'

'For ten minutes only,' he said, 'and under my supervision,' and I laughed then and said, 'Like prison,' which it was. Sitting down there in Tomkins' office, facing each other across a table with him presiding. 'Want us to put our hands on the table, then?' I asked.

So now, of course, there was another reason for not asking all the questions I wanted to ask; him being there, the Welsh Twit. Anything you say may be taken down and used in group therapy against you. In fact for five minutes or so, Bob and I didn't say a word, though he'd never been one for saying much, and now he said less than ever. In the end I started off as clumsily as I had upstairs: 'How did you get here, then?'

'Hitch-hiked,' he said; just that and nothing more.

'Your mother all right?'

'Don't see her a lot. She's okay, I suppose. Doesn't go out much.'

That made me feel good and bad; guilty yet, in a childish way, pleased. 'Going to see her now?' I asked him.

'Yeah. I'll spend the night there.'

Out of the corner of my eye, I could see the Welsh Twit looking from one of us to the other, *greedily* is the only way you could describe it, feeding off our relationship like a bloody vulture.

'Give her my love,' I said. 'Tell her I'm getting better – *slowly*,' and I glanced at the Welsh Twit, but he was making a great production out of looking through the window.

What I was groping for, I suppose, was contact; we hadn't made any upstairs, and it had been my fault, leaping on him like I did. Now, the way we were, who could make contact, even if things had been easier between us? I asked him when he'd walked out of University.

'March,' he said. 'I couldn't take any more of that competitive crap.'

'And you'll never go back?'

'There?' he said. 'You're joking,' and I wondered what he'd really come for, if there was something that he wanted to ask, something that he wanted to know; like the time he'd been shown up to see me at the Palladium.

Very different, then. Short hair, no whiskers or medallion. A knock on the door of the dressing-room. Sid, my dresser, looking out, then saying, 'A boy at the stage door. Says he's Bob, your son.'

'If it's Bob, bring him up,' I said. Bang, bang, bang, the old heartbeat. Eighteen months since I'd seen him, and it *was* him, Sid with his arm round him – known Bob since he was a baby: 'Look who it is, look who it is!'

Drooping his head, shy as a deer, mumbling, me hugging him: 'Where did you sit?'

'In the gallery.'

Straight to the heart. 'Why didn't you let me know? The gallery: you *paid* to see your father; I'd have put you in the front row of the stalls.'

'Didn't want to bother you.'

'What do you mean, *bother* me?'

I was overjoyed to see him. Just like I was overjoyed when he was born. In fact if I look back over the years, that's what I see, those marvellous meetings, wider and wider spread it's true, with me being overjoyed, every time.

And was your son overjoyed?

He was pleased, he was always pleased, but he's been shy from the very beginning.

And in between these reunions?

In between I didn't see him, did I? I was away. I was working. That's a comedian's life.

But for a young child this may be hard to understand. Was

this again your policy of the greatest good for the greatest number?

For Christ's sake, Doc, what chance did I have? You're beginning to sound like my wife: '*I'm* the one who's had to bring him up. You've never taken your responsibilities.' Diabolical!

What she meant, presumably, was that your priorities were not the same as her own.

In other words I had to sacrifice my whole career.

The conception, then, was unexpected?

I'll say it was bloody unexpected.

Like a thunderbolt. A right kick in the knackers. I was in Wolverhampton, playing the Palace, looking for laughs like a prospector looks for gold. Hate at first sight it was, between Wolverhampton and me. Worse than bloody Birmingham. While I was waiting to go on, in the first house, a message: ring her in London, and I did. Trembling little voice at the other end: 'Johnny, dear, I'm pregnant.' *Bang!* 'Johnny? Johnny?'

What could I say? I knew what she *wanted* me to say; wonderful, fantastic, to make *her* sure it was wonderful and fantastic, but all I managed in the end was, 'You're sure?'

'Quite sure,' she said. She sounded like she was almost crying. I'd never heard her like that before; it had all been so happy and so good. 'Are you angry?' she said.

'Of course I'm not,' I said, but I *was* angry, I don't know when I'd been so angry, not with her particularly but with it, with what had fucking happened, smashing everything before we'd had a chance to plan. *I* didn't want it, *she* hadn't wanted it.

Are you sure she did not want it?

Doc, we'd *talked* about it. I'd never excluded children. It was *when*, that's all. We just weren't ready. I was only starting. It would be like tying on a ball and chain. I knew about women and kids. That's their function. That's what they're in the world to do; but there was plenty of time to do it.

If I'd been with her it would have been different, touching each other, seeing each other's faces, but standing where I was, at the stage door telephone, behind the old boy looking out of his glass box, with his big, hairy ears pricking, how could I come up with the right words? Get rid of it! I was shouting inside me, get rid of it! though in those days it wasn't like now, National Health, all on the level, book a bed, in and out, and all for nothing. Then it was illegal, then it was risky, then it cost money.

'Ethel,' I said, 'you'll have to let me think about it. It's a shock. I don't know how I feel, yet,' which again was the last thing she wanted to hear. 'I'll phone you later,' I said, then I went back to the dressing-room.

I shared it with a bloody snake-charmer, Abdul El Harid, who was a Scotsman from Dunfermline; he was sitting at the mirror in his green turban, creaming off the pancake from his face. The snakes were in their basket in a corner; maybe they were Scotch, as well, but I never asked him. 'What's the matter, son?' he said.

'I'm going to be a father,' I told him, and sat down on the only other chair.

'That'll be expensive,' he said.

'It's my wife, you twot,' I said.

'Och, then it'll cost you more.'

That was all I needed, humour, but he did have a bottle of whisky, and he poured me a good one. I drank very little those days, and I remember the way it went down, the heat of it. Ten minutes later I was on stage, bloody Pagliacci, the first time in my life I'd wanted to tell an audience to get stuffed. I was savage. I didn't give a damn. I came on to the Maybe It's Because I'm A Bloody Londoner music, which was a bad thing for a start, because they loathe the Londoners up there, in fact they loathe everybody.

'Good evening,' I said, 'and let me thank you all right away for being such a wonderful audience; that's just in case I happen to forget at the end. Blimey, if silence was really golden I could retire at the end of this week. They tell me Wolverhampton's the only place where a comedian comes on and says, "A funny thing happened to me on my way to the graveyard".' Which of all things started the bastards laughing, and this taught me something; that audiences can run true to life, true to individuals, all bullies being cowards. Stand up to a bullying audience, give it some stick like I did that night, and it'll probably get nervous and start laughing. The more I got stuck into them, the more they laughed at me.

'I'm not saying you sit on your hands up here,' I said, 'but there was one comedian wandering about in the market square. Twelve o'clock at night, he's down the market square, being propositioned by the ugliest old slag in Wolverhampton. Pockmarked? If a fly crawled over her face, it would break a leg. So anyway, a friend of his sees him, a fellow in the show, and he says, "What's the matter with you, cock? Good-looking bloke like you, getting off with a terrible old bag like that", and the comic turns round and he says, "Listen, it's the only way I can get a clap in Wolverhampton".'

That night, I had it off with a girl in the show, a dancer called Louise, a London girl, red hair, freckles, nice knockers, always used to giggle at me. Before, I'd left it at that. I could have fancied her, but I was still like I had been at the Windmill; monogamous.

As I came off stage after my act, she was waiting to come on with the rest of the line, the old plumes and sequins bit, big, white dumplings squeezing out of her shiny blue cups. 'Ooh, didn't you have a go at them!' she said, with a real come-on smile.

'Yeah,' I said, 'I'll have a go at you later on, and all,' it just leaped out, but when I realized what I'd said, I still felt glad I'd said it, I was still savage, and that night, after the second house, I took her home. Big production she made of it, too; giggling like a lunatic as we got into the taxi, looking back at all her mates. She was up there for the winter and she was sharing a flat with another of them. As soon as we got through the door she put her face up to mine with her eyes closed and her lips pursed, all sex, nothing but sex, kiss me, fuck me, and I did, the whole night we went at it, like animals. 'Oh, God, you're good!' she said, 'Oh, God, you're good!' she was panting and sweating. It wasn't love, it was a caricature of love, a caricature of what I'd had with Ethel, but that was what I'd wanted.

What Ethel wanted was the kid, it was obvious when I got back to town that Sunday; she did, I didn't but she wanted me to want it. We walked miles that afternoon, all over Hampstead Heath in the rain, water dripping off the trees, water shining on her face; very pretty she looked, very upset, so you couldn't tell half the time whether it was rain or tears. 'You're *blaming* me; it's not my fault. I'll have it done away with if you want me to.'

'No, no,' I said, 'I don't want that, I don't want that.' Of course I wanted that, but how could I tell her, if she didn't? I hated that fucking kid for doing what it had to us, spoiling something perfect, never an argument; too good to last, I supposed.

'I'll work when I'm able,' she said.

I wouldn't look at her, I squelched across the grass, there was water in my shoes, just like that day on the beach. 'You won't have to,' I said. Bloody Nature had put a pistol at our heads. It was the unfairness that got me more than anything. No chance to wait and do things like we'd wanted.

Like *we* had wanted?

Yes, like *we'd* wanted. We both had our careers, didn't we?

*You* had your career. By then it must have been clear to her that her own was quite secondary.

You mean she was getting back at me?

I mean only that unconsciously she may have revised her ambitions.

You saying that she had the kid on purpose?

In the sense that you intend it, no. Unconsciously it is quite possible, just as you at the time unconsciously believed.

Yeah, but you don't have an unconscious baby, do you?

I was away a lot that year she was pregnant, and I fucked a lot, I admit it. To be honest, the bigger she got the more I resented it, the more I couldn't stand the sight of her; that bulging stomach was a physical reminder of what had happened to her, what had happened to us, what was *happening*. When a woman swells up in pregnancy, she's literally putting up a barrier against you. The nearer she gets, the bigger she gets, the more she's saying, keep away.

We'd left Kentish Town, we'd got a flat off Haverstock Hill, bigger now, more expensive, our own bog and telephone, but when the kid was born we'd probably have to move again.

When he was born, I was away again. It wasn't my fault, that; I'd planned to be at home, I'd turned down an engagement, but he showed up a week early. I was in Portsmouth this time, not so far away, naturally playing to audiences with a lot of sailors, which took me back a bit to the old Army days. You knew what they'd laugh at; I had this exit line: 'Oh, well; "Full speed astern!" as the fairy said to the admiral.'

The message came to my lodgings, just after I'd got back from doing a matinée: 'Mr Lucas, Mr Lucas! The hospital on the phone!'

What hospital? I felt terrible, like I was going to be punished; I came down that miserable staircase, past all the pictures of stags at dawn, like the clappers. But it was the maternity hospital, the one we'd booked in at: 'Mr Lucas? Many congratulations! Your wife has had a boy!'

It was the relief, probably, but I felt great. I started babbling on about when was it born, what did it weigh, how were they? I was just going to ask what its name was when I caught myself. I wired flowers to her right away, I couldn't get out of doing the show that night, but next morning I was on the milk train.

Now it had happened, after all this time, it was a tremendous feeling, like beginning again, and I was right pleased it was a boy. When I came into her ward, clacking across the lino, like Father Christmas with the flowers, the fruit, the chocolates, she had the baby in bed with her; little, tiny red-faced thing with its eyes screwed up as if it was in pain, and black hair like a hearth brush. As for Ethel, she looked beautiful, so calm, like a saint, kind of fulfilled, her skin very clear, like a young girl's skin, all happy and exhausted. She might just have won a race. She turned her head to me on the pillow in sort of an appeal, are you sure it's all right now, and I felt like shit. All right? It was wonderful. It was the best thing ever. I was mad about that kid. Terrific. Just as it was great when he turned up in my dressing-room, great when he turned up here, round the corner of the drive.

Each time it is a tableau. But when the tableau starts to move, you are no longer so happy.

You're talking like my wife again, Doc.

'*Love* him? You don't love him! You *pose* with him! You use him, you always have, but he's not your mirror, Johnny, he's not your audience, he's your son!'

'Who changed his nappies, then? Who took him for walks?'

'And who hated every minute of it? You've never talked to him, you've never understood him!'

Out on the Heath again, pushing a pram, feeling like a prick. What could I look like? A great tall bloke like me, poncing about with a pram. Trying to send it all up a bit by suddenly belting down a slope, then up the other side like a tank, Bob laughing his head off.

I could always make him laugh – then, anyway. Not now. God only knows what makes him laugh now, him and the rest of them. Bending over the pram, pulling faces at him, putting on daft voices; fall about, he would. At least I can make *you* laugh, I'd think. Not knowing where the next laugh was coming from, because if you're not working how can they be laughing and it may be *because* they're not laughing that you're not working. Every day, five or six times a day, on the phone to Lou Gold.

'Don't worry, when there's something, I'll tell you.'

Wondering every minute I'm on the Heath, every minute I'm out doing the shopping – feeling an even bigger cunt in the little streets, among the Mums – will the phone be ringing? Will *she* sleep through it? Will I miss something? Because she had to sleep, getting home at five in the morning, going straight to *his* room – '*How* are you, love, *how* are you?' – falling into bed too tired to fuck. 'What was it like tonight?' 'Oh, same as usual,' then how's his tooth, how's his nappy rash, how did he eat?

Not that I much want to fuck, either, it doesn't go with the act; male nanny, ponce, living on his wife's immoral earnings. Or that's how she makes it seem, dancing on the line at the Mountjoy, ten pounds a week, routine after routine, and a dressing-room, she says, like a cattle-pen.

Lou, I want to ask him when I ring him, aren't I funny any more? Won't they ever laugh at me again? Am I out of bloody fashion already? All questions that I don't dare ask. He's not a man to ask personal questions, Lou. Besides, how would *he* know if I'm funny, seeing he's as cheerful as a bloodhound? How do you ever make *those* jowls shake?

'You think this never happened to other comedians? Believe me it's happened. It happens to all of them, doesn't matter who they are.'

Jack Benny, Bob Hope, Sid Field. All of them. Very reassuring, that. Lou wasn't worried, so why should *I* worry? I could be out of work five years and he'd still sit there in Isow's, swilling his soup and munching his matzoh balls, not worrying. What did he have to worry about? Sometimes this did reassure me, just for a little while, immediately after I'd finished talking to him. After all, look at him, a top agent, been in the business thirty years, and *he* wasn't bothered. What right had I to be? Push the pram, change the nappies, live life to the full, and suddenly it would happen. 'Long distance here, a call from Hollywood.' Hollywood? Just then I'd have settled for a call from Hendon.

'But how do you *explain* it, Mr Gold?' That much I did ask him.

'I don't explain it, son. These things happen.'

Like drought. Like tidal waves. Like a total eclipse of the sun. Like not being funny any more. Fashions do change, every comedian knows that, even if I'd hardly had time to be fashionable. *Where Are They Now?* You open a newspaper and they're interviewing some poor bastard, down on his luck, living on the dole, just made bankrupt, a national name five or ten years back. 'I don't know why it was, but suddenly no one seemed to want me.'

Or you're driving through outer London on your way to somewhere, through South-East London maybe, through all that jungle of car-dealers and traffic snarls and grimy little shops and mouldering brick tube stations, where suddenly you pass some theatre that you've never heard of with a name on the marquee that you *have* heard of, George This, Terry That; I thought the bugger was dead. Remember him on the radio, week after week, couldn't go wrong, never very funny but always in work. Now he's here; a fate worse than death. Dying Tonight. Every night he's dying on stage. And a shiver goes through you, like you've seen a ghost, maybe your own ghost. Please God not me, never me, spare me God from dying in this jungle.

I didn't even like to talk to Ethel about it; she was always so tired. 'Funny? Of course you're funny, darling, you'll always be funny!' Shrugging it off, almost. Shrugging me off.

'Okay, then why aren't I working?'

So tired. She looks up at me with her tired eyes. 'You're resting, Johnny, that's all. Everybody rests at times. Never rains but it pours. Suddenly they'll want you everywhere.' Now run away and play, John.

Get me something, Lou, any bloody thing. A stag dinner, a Masonic evening, anything.

Yet some comedians go on and on. They work until they're seventy. Look at Jack Benny; he's been thirty-nine for the last twenty-five years. Look at Groucho Marx. They could work till they came on in wheelchairs. And look at me; I make my son laugh. Fifteen months old; I lean over the cot, only have to pull a face, and he's falling about. A baby. At this rate, I must have fifty years ahead of me. You bet I can wait; but can my wife keep dancing fifty years?

'Hallo, Mr Lucas, still pushing the pram around, then?'

'Still pushing the pram, Mrs Wilkins.'

As a matter of fact, I'm studying a new role. I'm studying what it's like to be a nanny. Like Old Mother Riley. In a few months' time you'll see.

It would have been better if only I'd been able to get up to Soho, to hang around the Salisbury and the sandwich bars, talking to the other pros that were resting who'd tell you that there's nothing strange about it, that it happens to everybody. If showbiz people live in one another's pockets, that's part of the reason; reassurance. As time went on, I'd find out that all over London there were these little pockets of actors and writers and comedians, this one in Hampstead, that one in Putney, the other one in Islington, all propping one another up, all taking in one another's washing, but then, when I needed it, I didn't know. I was alone.

Wheeling the pram down to the Labour Exchange once a week to draw the dole; that was another great experience. Queueing up with a lot of shuffling layabouts that looked as if they'd never worked at all, never mind working again, was bad enough, but to have the pram with me too, to hear the remarks; that made it diabolical.

'Sending the wife out to work, then?'

'Gone off with the milkman, has she?'

'Blimey, what are you, unmarried father?'

'No,' I said, once, 'but I bet yours fucking was.' There was nearly a punch-up.

Things got so bad I even thought of going back to Fairleigh, though I never mentioned it to Ethel because I'd got a nasty feeling she might jump at it. After all, she'd be near her home, she'd be back doing something she really enjoyed, not dancing in some poxy night club. Just for the season, I started telling myself, just till something turns up, I started telling myself, but I knew that for all the slogging round Hampstead, all the changing nappies, all the going down to the Labour Exchange, it was wrong, it was surrender. I could see us staying up there forever like a dear old couple, the two most popular people in the town, me coming on in a hat like Denis Jackson's:

'Under the spreading chestnut buff,
A maid sat with a hacking cow.
She asked her mother for some duff.
Her mother said, "You've had enow".'

Like Denis said, it was a lovely, healthy life, no worries. Not much money, but so what? What sort of money was I making now? And no more fear. Wasn't that worth something? Where could you buy that?

You are talking now, it seems to me, of two quite different kinds of fear; the fear of not working and the fear of no longer being laughed at.

It's all the same to a comedian, Doc. Like you said, either they laugh or you're dead.

But not to work is a fear you share with others than comedians. The fear not to be laughed at becomes truly irrational only when work itself is not a problem.

It's the same old fear, Doc. Stand on me.

Perhaps in the beginning it is two fears, the rational fear masking the irrational.

Backing it each way, are you Doc?

I am trying only to make a connection between the need to make people laugh and the fear that they will not. The common motivation may be guilt.

There's the title for your book, then, Doctor, eh? *Guilty Laughter*.

Bob in the dressing-room that night.

'Did you laugh, Bob? Did you like it?'

Do I still make you laugh?

'Yeah, I did laugh, Dad.'

If I could only have seen him, stuck him in the front row stalls and watched his face. Played to him a bit. Looking at him now, I couldn't imagine him laughing, so I tried to make him laugh, I needed to, I started making jokes. 'You heard the story of the bent copper? Went on duty at Leicester Square toilets and he got stuck in the slot.'

Usual big burst of laughter from Sid, but Bob just looked embarrassed. I wished we were alone, but in another way I was glad we weren't alone, because I had an idea it might be worse, we might just stand there like we'd been turned to stone. What was the password? How did I get to him; put things back to what they had been? I shouldn't have told him the joke, West

End joke, Soho bloody joke. He wanted something from me, I could feel it then, too, but it wasn't a joke he wanted.

I sat down at my dressing-table, wearing just the red silk dressing-gown and got on with creaming off the make-up, looking at him now and then in the mirror. Blue sports jacket, narrow trousers, school tie but no uniform; it was a progressive school. My hair, his mother's mouth and eyes, and the way his mouth moved worried me, tautening and twitching at the corners. I wanted to put my arm round him, but God only knew how he'd take that. What did they say about me, the two of them? What had she told him? Whatever it was he'd come, hadn't he?

Then June came in; which I hadn't expected. In her usual way; two short knocks then bursting through the door, I could see it in the mirror, but he couldn't; then he turned and did and his whole body went stiff; stiffer still. I wanted to tell her to tone it down, go easy, but she came on the way she always did, uninhibited: 'Fucking taxi driver! I told him to keep out of Oxford Street!'

'Bob,' I said, 'this is June.'

'*Oh,*' she said, in that deep voice of hers, giving him a long look. 'Hallo. I won't bite you,' because he was staring at her like she'd hypnotized him.

I got up and I did put my arm round his shoulders, but I might have been putting it around a board. I could understand it, her effect on him, a kid, even if she hadn't been who she was. She was wearing a bright green trouser suit with a very low cut white blouse showing off her lovely big boobs, and the colours were a knock-out, the green, the white, the red of her long hair. She looked fantastic, and I wished she hadn't come.

'I'd have *known* you,' she said. 'You're just like Johnny. Same colouring, same features, even the same posture. Are you as funny?'

'Bob's serious,' I said. 'One clown in the family's enough,' and Sid joined in from the background, the old chorus, 'Got the brains in the family, Bob did.'

'Just this minute walked in,' I told June. 'Watched from the gallery; didn't even know he was there.'

'The *gallery*,' she said, in that way of hers, that dark brown voice, but she'd got it all summed up, I could tell. 'Very *hard*, wasn't it?'

'Bit uncomfortable, yes,' he said, very quick and quiet, then, 'well, I'd better be going.'

'You can't go,' she said, thank God; I wouldn't have known how to stop him. She was standing right between Bob and the door and there was no way out unless he pushed her.

'Like me with Sid Field,' I said. 'I'd watch *him* from the gallery. Remember me telling you, Bob?'

'Yeah,' he said, but he wouldn't look at me; I'd lost him.

'I'd rather *be* in the gallery,' said June, and he gave her a glance, a very quick one, startled, like he couldn't quite believe in her. 'At least they're real,' she said, 'at least they react, not like the bloody stalls,' and she spread out her arms, tilting back her head, put on a blasé expression like she was bored to death, and that did it, suddenly he laughed, something I could never have done, at least not there, not then, in the dressing-room, and I loved her for it, I loved both of them.

'Did *they* laugh?' she asked him. 'The people in the gallery.'

'Yes,' he said, 'they laughed a lot,' and now he did look at me, a marvellous look, one I hadn't seen from him for God knew how many years, one I could never, never have given my old man; a smile like he was really proud of me.

'Remember him coming round the dressing-room before?' Sid asked. 'Tiny little kid, he was. Was it here, or was it the Met, Edgware Road? Or maybe it was Finsbury Park. Sat on your knee, he did, and said he didn't like the jokes but he enjoyed the music.'

'Good critic,' I said.

'Couldn't have been more than about six,' Sid went on. 'His mother brought him.'

Silence, then; we were right back where we'd started. Sid looked choked; he asked us if we wanted any tea, but no one did. A drink was what I needed. June went wading in, doing her best; I could tell the whole thing irritated her, Ethel lying across us like a shadow, she wouldn't have it, but at the same time, what could she do about it?

'Let's all go and have dinner, then,' I said. 'Ever been to The Ivy, Bob?'

He shook his head. I knew it was a lost cause. 'Got to get home,' he said, which was in Hampstead Garden Suburb, the house I'd left her with.

'I'll drive you home,' I said.

'No, that's all right,' he said, and went, leaving me with just one thing; that look.

'*Sorry*,' poor old Sid said, when Bob had gone. 'I'm that sorry, John.'

'*I'm* sorry,' June said, 'I'm sorry for arriving, we're all sorry for everything, but it was a bit like dancing on eggshells, and at least he came, darling.'

'Yeah, at least he came,' I said, and sat down at the dressing-table with my back to them both, wanting to be on my own. She was quite right, it was all that really mattered, and if he came once maybe he'd come again; though I knew it could only be like this time, off his own bat.

'I think it's the biggest compliment he could have paid you,' June said. 'Bigger than the one you paid Sid Field.'

And this, this coming to the sanatorium, was another compliment; four years later, and even harder now than it had been then, because at least the dressing-room was *my* dressing-room, at least I didn't have a bloody psychiatrist hovering over us like a gaoler. Another thing, I was a star there, I was a hero, he'd come down from the gallery, where they'd been cheering me and laughing at me, he was entitled to be proud. Now what was I? A poor bloody nut-case who wasn't to be trusted alone with his own son. June had got through to Bob that night by making him laugh; how could *I* make him laugh? It had felt impossible even then, in the Palladium, where I was the king, let alone now when I was in the sanatorium and he was on Christ knows what drugs. They spoke their own language, anyway, hippies, and if they had any jokes, which I doubted, they'd be their own.

I needed some kind of a bridge, though, something that would connect him to what he had been, to somebody I'd known, so that he might still, please God, be that again one day. So that I had a try, I said to him, 'Don't worry if the Doc here keeps on eyeing you. He's a psychiatrist, he's after your mind, not your body.'

And Bob laughed. It didn't happen all at once, like it used to; it was as if the message took longer to get through now, and then get back again; there were layers to penetrate before it could bubble to the surface, but then it did, it bubbled, he was laughing. I'd reached him, we were in contact; the Welsh Twit was there but he might have been out in the garden, and I almost felt grateful to him now instead of angry; after all, he'd made it possible.

I started remembering things with Bob, then; remember this, remember that; when you came to the Palladium, when we all went to Paris. It was better, the past, safer, because what had we got now, how did you build a bridge from him to me, from St Ives to this sanatorium?

'The Metro,' I said. 'Us getting lost, me trying to speak French,' and he smiled, slowly again, like he was seeing it all, re-living it, then spoke.

'You had your gestures all right,' he said, 'the way you waved your arms around. You had the accent. The only thing you didn't have was the French.'

'Dead right,' I said. It was fabulous, this; the only thing I was frightened of was that suddenly we'd dry up, no more memories, nothing I could touch in him. It was hard; I had to do it all. He'd smile, he'd even laugh, but he'd hardly speak at all. I felt like asking him, do you take vows of silence, then, you hippies?

I could feel Dr Tomkins just itching to come in and interpret, ask me what I meant by this, ask Bob why he laughed at that; it was almost like radio or television, playing to two audiences, one in the studio and one outside, but the only one you bothered about was the one you were looking at.

'Maybe I ought to be down there with you at St Ives,' I said. 'Sea air, no worries, plenty of birds.'

'They don't like us,' he said. 'They've put the dogs on us.'

'Bastards!' I said, I was that furious. Setting dogs on my kid. Just like they'd set dogs on us if they could, on comedians. A load of fucking shopkeepers, hotel-keepers, bank managers. I felt even closer to him, it was something more that linked us, even if his lot would probably never laugh at me, might never laugh at all.

'I think that's enough,' said the Welsh Twit. I was getting excited and we couldn't have that. I wasn't pleased, but I accepted it, we'd be leaving each other at a good moment, even though I still felt angry, in fact *because* I felt angry. 'What are they?' I asked. 'Alsatians?'

'Yeah,' he said, 'Alsatians.'

'Bastards!' I said again, and then he'd gone. I'd like to have kissed him, but I didn't. All that hair. 'Come again!' I said, as the Welsh Twit saw him off like a copper. 'Give your mother my love.' Why not? It cost nothing.

'You hide behind laughter,' said Mary Smith. 'No, I mean it. When anything embarrasses you, you throw up jokes like a smokescreen.'

Would I care to comment? Thank you, Doctor.

'Why do you hide behind tears?' I ask. 'When someone has a go at *you*, you break down and cry.'

'That's spiteful.'

'No more than what you were.'

'But you do tend to use laughter as a defence, Johnny,' says the Welsh Twit. 'I've noticed it outside this group as well.'

Said with a lot of emphasis, this, 'The question is, what are you defending?'

'My honour,' I say.

'There you are!' cries Mrs Casey. 'You're making jokes again!'

'I think Johnny has problems in relating,' Mary says, 'and he uses laughter as a way to get through to people.'

'That's an interesting perception,' says the Welsh Twit.

'Maybe you ought to tell Dr Weiss,' I say. 'Go well in his next book, that would.'

'I think people who need to make other people laugh are insecure,' Mary says. She's leaving the field behind, today.

'Hear, hear!' says Tight-Arse.

'How would *you* know?' I ask him. 'The only time you've ever laughed is when you've turned someone down for an overdraft.'

'Damn good thing to make people laugh,' the Colonel says. 'Noticed it in the war, especially in action. Stops you thinking about being killed.'

'That's the best way to die,' I say, 'die laughing.'

'There you are,' says Mrs Casey, 'another joke. You're running away again.'

'I'll cry if you prefer that,' I say, 'as long as there isn't a copyright on it.'

'What a bitch!' says Mary.

'Depends what you go to the pictures for, doesn't it?' I ask. 'A good laugh or a good cry,' and Ivan laughs at last, it's the first time he's opened his mouth, *ha*-ha, a great, bellowing laugh he's got. The three witches look daggers at him, but I like him better than ever. Three against three, him and me and the Colonel on one side, them on the other with the Welsh Twit in the middle as referee, a little bent.

'Laugh and the world laughs with you,' I say, 'weep and you bloody weep alone.'

'But *you* don't laugh,' says Mrs Casey, 'you just make other people laugh.'

'Or try to,' says Old Tight-Arse.

'Not you,' I say. 'Talk about flogging a dead horse.'

So round and round we go, the same old round the mulberry bush. I'm insecure because I try to make people laugh. Mary's insecure because she cries. Ivan's insecure because he says nothing. The Colonel's insecure because he gives away nothing. Tight-Arse is insecure because he admits nothing. Mrs Casey is insecure because she's aggressive.

'And you're insecure,' I tell the Welsh Twit, 'because you're a psychiatrist.'

'What do you mean by that?' Bristling. Doesn't like it when the worm turns.

'It's something to hide behind, isn't it?' I say. 'No one asks a psychiatrist questions. He's always in the driver's seat.'

'Ask me what you like!'

Like why are you such a cunt? There's nothing I want to ask him. I'm not interested. As for Dr Weiss, there's still a million things he wants to ask me. I fucking fascinate him. The Colonel had cheered me up a lot, though, because he was right. Laughter is life. If you're laughing, you don't think about death. I'd always wished *I* could have done all that, what people like Bob Hope did in the war, flying here, dropping in there, just behind the lines, making the troops laugh, instead of doing it in peace-time like me, when it didn't matter, when it didn't have the edge. Oh, death, where is thy bloody sting? I'd always envied him that, Bob Hope, even if later on he seemed to get his wars a bit muddled. And thinking all this led me on to something else, something Dr Weiss wouldn't half do some chewing on. Because if laughter is life, then people that want to prevent it are *against* life, and God knows there are thousands of them, everywhere; all the dictators, from Hitler and Stalin on, all the miserable sods behind leather desks, like Tight-Arse; and maybe even all the psychiatrists, too, like Dr Weiss, who only want to analyse laughter, not to experience it, and analysing it, after all, means taking it to pieces. What's left of anything once you've measured it and analysed it?

The purpose of psychoanalysis is not to destroy but to re-create.

Unconsciously, I mean, Doc, unconsciously. *Bit of my own back*. I know you *mean* well, but when you've taken everything to pieces, how do you know you can put it back together again?

Usually we *find* things in pieces, and we try to integrate them.

Well you found me in pieces all right, Doc, I'll give you that. Lying about all over the bleeding place, I was. Mind you, from your point of view, I was probably never much different.

Normality and abnormality are a question only of degree.

Yeah, but I'd been wanting to make people laugh, hadn't I? According to you and Dr Tomkins, that's a sympton, isn't it? So if you *do* put me back together. I won't *need* to make them laugh. And then I'll be unemployable.

All this, of course, is greatly oversimplified.

I'm a simple bloke, Doc, remember? If people don't laugh, I ain't even here.

So?

So why are you trying to abolish me?

Why should you *think* I am trying to abolish you?

Joking, Doc; you know me by now. False Messiah, that's what I am. They'll follow me into the Promised Land, laughing. That's an improvement, though, isn't it? I'm only a False Messiah, now. Still, you know what they say about Messiahs?

What?

They rise again from the dead, Doc. After three days.

Only this time, I was serious. It was something that had been in my mind since Bob came, and I'd started to feel better; still persecuted, but not hopeless. 'Rose again from the dead, rose again from the dead,' the words kept going through my mind. They could knock the nails in, leave you hanging there, but they still couldn't always stop you.

Before, when things were really bad here, all I could think of was the comedians who'd cracked up, the comedians who'd killed themselves, directly or indirectly, poor Sid Field more than any of them, because after all, he was my inspiration. But now I began to think differently, of the comedians who'd dropped out then come back again, like Frankie Howerd and those, and it seemed to me that maybe I was groping towards something; that if you were really funny, you were always funny, that the only important thing was not to die; who wanted to play a lot of one-night stands at seances?

And after all, I'd come back a few times myself. I could understand comics losing hope, I could understand them getting suicidal, it had all happened to me, but if we just stayed alive for long enough, the wheel would come round again. I didn't tell Doc Weiss; he'd have a term for that, too: manic-depressive. So what? As long as I wasn't just depressive.

Like I said, I'd come back every time, hadn't I, however low I'd felt, however bad it had got? A comedian, he's like Houdini; he has to be. You tie his arms, you put chains round his legs, you stick his head in a bag, you leave him in a locked room; yet every time, he escapes. Why not this time?

The first time of all, it was *Workers' Playtime* that saved me, though I can see now that if that hadn't come along something else would have. Not then, though. It was manna from Heaven then, and Lou Gold was God. God sat in his little Heaven off Shaftesbury Avenue in his swivel chair, and sent his commands by telephone. If he didn't send any, it must mean he was displeased; you were treading on the wrong cracks in the paving stones, you'd come last night before you'd counted to five hundred, you'd walked under a ladder without crossing your fingers. It's amazing how superstitious you get at times like these.

Then one day I was feeding Bob out of one of those tins of strained apples, he'd got apple all over his cheeks, I was pulling faces at him, making him laugh so that then he'd eat, my first experience of cabaret, when the phone rang. I was off like a gun; I don't think I've ever had such fabulous reflexes in my life as what I had in those days. They could have entered me for the Olympics and if the race had been over five yards, I'd have beaten the world.

'Mr *Loo*-cas?'

How well I knew that nasal voice, that bored North London whine, bored to tears whenever I rang *her*: 'Nothing, Mr Lucas, I'm afraid ... I'm sorry, Mr Lucas, Mr Gold is in conference.' But now, 'Mr Lucas? Mr Gold to speak to you.' Talk about the bloody tongues of angels. And then ... him.

'Johnny? I've got you *Workers' Playtime.*'

*Workers' Playtime!* He'd got me *Workers' Playtime*! If he'd said he'd got me Hackney Municipal Baths I'd have turned somersaults. Who needed the Palladium or the Hippodrome? I've got you *Workers' Playtime*; it was like saying, I've got you into Paradise, where when *I* was working it was, *Workers' Playtime*? Christ, switch it off! just as it would be later, and what are *you* in? *Workers'* Play*time!*

'Ladies and gentlemen, we present: WORkers' PLAYtime!' Always the same big boy scout announcing it, always the same great screech of glee, like the animals had been let out of their cage. Poor bugger, I'd think, playing *Workers' Playtime*. How fabulous, I thought, playing *Workers' Playtime*.

'Workers' Playtime comes to you today from the canteen of a French-Letter factory in Dagenham!'

Five days a week, at lunchtime. They'd cheer anything, laugh at anything. It used to make me wince to hear what some of the comedians got away with; every show had one. For years I'd been listening to it on and off, cheering myself up; at least I can do better than *that*, but now if I listened – and I'd have the radio on a lot when Bob and I were alone together – it was different. However bad they were, at least they were in work, so maybe they were better than I was.

All they wanted from me was five minutes to wind up the show. I told them I'd write my own script – who could afford a writer? – and I must have spent hours on it, polishing it, re-writing it, trying it on Ethel. My chance of a comeback; after three whole years in the business and three months out of work, except it seemed like the other way round. My big chance in radio. My first bloody broadcast.

I went along to the Aeolian Hall in Bond Street to see the producer. Big men they were then, the radio producers, emperors, with the largest audiences of anyone; till television came along and swept them into a corner. They didn't even work in Broadcasting House with all the riff-raff; Mayfair for them.

The bloke I saw wore a sports jacket with leather patches. Later on I found they all did, it was like a uniform, poor but powerful. They smoked pipes, as well. He was a little, toothy fellow, my one, glasses and a posh accent, very polite, very enthusiastic. 'Wonderful!' he said, like I was doing him a favour. 'You're going to be on our show! I'm so pleased! Now, what exactly will you do?'

To be on his show I'd have dived ninety feet into a glass of water, but so far as I could tell from listening it didn't matter what you did, you could read a page out of the telephone directory and you'd still get laughs; who needed canned laughter? But I told him more or less what I'd worked out and he told me that he didn't want to sound all prudish, but it was the BBC, which took me back to Fairleigh and the family audience, plenty of good, clean filth, but I was very serious and said I understood and naturally I'd take out the joke about the left-handed scoutmaster and he said, 'Absolutely splendid, marvellous,' and we were away.

A pickle factory in Walsall I think it was, or maybe that was another time, because eventually I did quite a few of them. We went up by train, the whole lot of us, the producer, a fifteen-stone soprano, a mouth-organist, the compère and me. I don't think I've ever been on a longer journey. The closer we got, the worse it became, till by the time we were actually going through the Black Country, through all the back-to-backs and factory chimneys, I was sweating, I could hardly speak, I was trying to remember lines but forgetting them, and I think he sensed this, the producer, he wasn't such a bad little bloke, while the compère was a big, noisy bastard, nothing to him but a voice, like so many of them in films or radio or television, who wouldn't have noticed if you'd suddenly sprouted horns.

I told myself it was a doddle, that they'd fall about at anything, those audiences, but it didn't work, there was too much riding on it. Ridiculous, it seems now, but if I had to do it again today, it could easily be just the same, like going up in an aeroplane the first time after you've crashed.

There were two things I could imagine happening, and I don't know which was the worse. One, they'd play the music 'Maybe It's Because I'm A Londoner', they'd got a little band. I'd walk on, to the usual screaming; and nothing would happen. Not a word; like I'd been struck dumb, paralysed. I'd had dreams like that. Or else it would come out all right after the screaming had stopped, my first joke, and then: silence. Just row after row of blank faces.

What I hadn't thought of was that as our taxi drove us through the gates of the factory, a lot of low, white, concrete buildings, the producers would say to me, 'Of course you'll do the warm-up, won't you Johnny?' It stabbed me like a lance, the warm-up, I'd never even thought about it; not only hadn't I prepared anything, but it meant I'd have to go on almost cold, no time to get myself together while the show was going on.

But I couldn't refuse: who else could do the warm-up?

I said, 'Yeah, okay,' and maybe it was a blessing in disguise, not having to sit through that whole show waiting to go on, half an hour of tension, shitting myself off stage, if stage was what you could call it. Just a platform, really, built in the canteen, them all sitting at their wooden lunch tables, women mostly in overalls and head scarves, which would account for the sort of noise they made during the show, the noise you were used to hearing on the radio, this banshee screaming, like they were ready to tear you apart or rape you, maybe both. Walking through the canteen to the stage, this was the impression you got, them all pointing and squealing and nudging one another.

A few fruity words from the compère then I was on, facing them, sweating; trilby, double-breasted grey suit with wide-apart chalk stripes, two-tone brown and white brogues, into that howl of noise that I just tried to ignore, or swim through like a sea. The one good thing was, being a warm-up, not yet on the air, you could get away with more and I walked straight up to the microphone and gave this joke out cold, dead-pan, just spoke it, like diving off the top board into the dark.

'Factories,' I said, 'very dicey places, factories, got to be careful in factories. Like this girl, she got off with a precision grinder and before she knew where she was, she was on the production line.'

And they were laughing. Laughing? They were all going spare. Shrieking, screaming, hollering like a lot of savages, but it was marvellous, it was all I needed, it was like adrenalin. I was off again, I could feel the confidence come flowing through me; I relaxed, I stood up straight, I shot my cuffs, I thought, now then.

'Walsall,' I said, 'it's wonderful to be up here in Walsall. Only city I know where you wake up in the morning and hear the birds coughing.' They went mad again.

*'And from that moment,' said the lanky Londoner, 'I can honestly say that I never looked back.'*

Did I say that? God knows if I said it. I must have given a thousand bloody interviews in my time. Half of them I needn't have bothered to turn up; it came straight out of their heads. Very flattering it was at first, to be interviewed, even if it was just some paper in the provinces. Then, the fourth or fifth time you told them something off the record and they printed it, all friendly over a bottle of whisky or a lunch on expenses, the hundred and fifth time they made you say something you never had, you turned sour. You couldn't live without them, journalists, but they were a necessary evil, and you soon got to classify the types.

The drunks – there's not so many of them now as there used to be. They were the kind you'd read about and seen in pictures; faces like a sunset, dead cynical about everything, very nosy, jealous, always sticking little knives in, especially when they were pissed. 'Pinch a lot of your gags, though, don't you? ... Of course, you can always slip a blue one in, when things aren't going well.' Or, always with a mean little look out of the corner of their eye, 'What are they paying you? Five hundred a week?' hating you for making more than they were.

Then there were the girl interviewers, you had to be very careful of those. Sat and smiled at you, showed a lot of leg, very sweet, gave you a bit of come-on, then turned you over properly in the paper. You couldn't blame *them* for misquoting you, you blamed them for quoting you, for getting you to say things under false pretences; like they fancied you, like they were fascinated.

What I called the Old Pros went in for that as well, the being fascinated bit. They were everybody's friend provided you were on top, or even if you were down, as long as you could give them a good story, though if their editor told them to screw you, they'd screw you. They'd been around for years, they knew everybody, and this was what they lived on; that they were nobody yet they knew everybody, they dropped names in and out of print like used matches, so-and-so told me this, such-and-such told me that, very, very intimate, ever so insinuating, trying to weave this web around you till they'd got whatever they wanted from you, worse even than the gossip columnists because they pretended to be better, whereas for me all they ever were was parasites.

And then there were the Intellectuals. There weren't many of them about while I was starting, they seemed to start coming up round the late 1950s, very intense, very serious, seemed to smoke a lot, asked all kinds of funny questions, then wrote things about you that you couldn't understand, how I stood for this, how I personified that, how the real meaning of my humour was the other, complicating everything.

Ethel kept a scrapbook, cut out all the articles, stuck them all in. I could never be bothered. After a while, I often wouldn't even read them, it saved me aggravation, though like Lou Gold said, 'Listen, the time to worry is when they never mention you. What they write, nobody remembers. Your name, they do remember.'

He didn't hear that *Workers' Playtime* show, I'd never expected him to; it came on at lunch, didn't it? I reckoned that about the time I began he'd be on his third forkful of chopped liver. After all, he wasn't worried, was he, and now, nor was I. Because it all started happening. More radio, back on the halls again, then the break-through, my own show, *Johnny Come Lately*.

It happened so fast I could hardly keep up with it, like being caught up in a hurricane and whirled across the sky; I hardly had time to wave to myself. Would I do this, would I do that? You're wanted here, you're wanted there.

Did I enjoy it? I loved it. I don't think there's anything quite like making it, when it all seems real and like it's going to last forever.

'Son,' old Lou used to say, 'it doesn't matter whether you're rich or poor, so long as you've got money,' and he was right. It was a marvellous thing to have, money, when you'd lived nearly all your life without it. Later on, when you were used to it, you could despise it, but for the moment, it was great. Buying a house. Buying a car. Buying new suits made to measure. Eating at the best restaurants, The Ivy, the Savoy Grill, The Caprice, so bloody near all those old pubs and sandwich bars; so near but yet so far.

It wasn't greed, though I suppose it was materialism. But what it was above all was reassurance, that you *were* funny, that people *did* laugh at you, not only that but that they'd *pay* to laugh at you. Every time you drove down the road in your Riley, long and black with the hard top, every time you got measured for a suit, every time the wine waiter came slinking up beside you in his poncey apron, asking what you'd like to drink, you were being told, you're funny.

The other side of it was that you couldn't quite believe in it all because it was new to you, because it had happened so suddenly; it was like the old crock of gold, somebody could wave a wand and the whole lot would disappear. So there'd be these moments, sitting in The Ivy or somewhere, watching the *crêpes suzettes* go up in flames, ordering another brandy, when I'd wonder, what am I doing here? They'll rumble me and throw me out; Joe Lyons for you, they'll say. Or standing like a prick with my elbow bent, the tailor measuring me, Mr Finkleberg, Tailor to the Stars, 'And I'll hope you'll be as successful in everything you do this year as I've been with this suit,' wondering, when's he going to realize that I can't afford it? Except that I *could* afford it.

Giving things to Ethel; that was marvellous, the best part of it, making up for what she'd had to do for me, all those months in poxy night clubs, crawling home in the morning, looking like a ghost. Making up for that, and what she didn't know about. It was good again, our marriage, different now but good. We could never go back to what it had been, what I'd call the perfect days, the Fairleigh days, even the Windmill days, when there was no one but us and what we wanted for each other, and neither of us wanted anyone else. I suppose you'd say the innocence had gone. Now Bob was there. I'd had it off. There'd been quarrels. You couldn't change all that. But with the tension going, with the money coming in, it was fine again; in bed, too. We were making love like we both wanted to make up for what had happened, what we'd said to each other, what we'd missed. 'I *love* you, I *love* you!' she'd say when I was screwing her, and I loved her, too. There was room for Bob *and* me, I could see that now; she was as pleased as ever when I had success, when there was any good news and there was good news all the time.

I didn't have to ring Lou any more, he was always ringing me, and if I did happen to telephone him, it was, '*Yes,* Mr Lucas,' and I'd go straight through.

'You've got to have a writer,' he said.

We were in his office, he was smoking a cigar, a huge Havana; I used to think he got them custom-made, as status symbols, because you never saw a bigger one, not even in Isow's. I could imagine him using them like animals do in this ritual display thing, peacocks with their tails and that, whenever there was a deal to be made. The producer would light up his cigar, Lou would light up his and that was that, they'd do it *his* way.

'I've done all right,' I told him. I didn't use a name, then; it was the period between 'Mr Gold' and 'Lou'.

'Of course you've done all right,' he said, 'who's criticizing you? But now you're doing more than all right. You're going to be a star, and a star needs writers. If you want a suit, you go to a tailor, don't you? If you're ill, so you go to a doctor. If your car breaks down, you go to a garage. It's hard enough to put over a joke. If you've got to write it as well, what chance have you got? You'll burn yourself out in a couple of years. Bob Hope, Jack Benny, you think they'd have lasted this long without writers?'

'W. C. Fields?' I said, but I admit I was struggling. It wasn't easy to give him an argument when he got you in there and blew that cigar smoke in your face.

'Since when was W. C. Fields a stand-up comic?' he asked. 'He began as a juggler.'

'Yeah, but how do I know these writers will write lines I can say?' I asked him.

'Don't worry: they'll write them. It's a question of finding the right ones, that's all. In a little while they'll be writing lines you'll think you wrote yourself. There's a word for it.'

The word was osmosis, but it was Maurice that told it me.

'Osmosis,' he said, the first time I met him. 'Rhymes with Grandma Moses. You don't share each other's bodies, but you're meant to share each other's souls. That's the idea, anyway.'

The writers I'd had up to then I wouldn't have shared a

safety razor with, never mind a soul. Some radio shows you had to have them, and all you could do was grit your teeth and get the lines out as best you could without puking. You could never make them yours, you wouldn't want to make them yours, but maybe you could take the curse off them. A script would arrive, I'd open it, I'd read it, and my guts would twist. Later on, I'd learn how you could build on scripts, use them as launching pads, turn a word here or a phrase there, modify a punch line, make them yours, but that would come later, and you had to be big enough to swing it. Starting out, in other people's shows, you had to take what you were given, and a lot of it was crap.

'You don't think it ever happens, this osmosis?' Maurice asked me. 'It happens, believe me; and that goes wrong, as well. Comedians don't like it in the end, they think they're being taken over, so they sack their writers for that, too. They never win, writers. Either they're not good enough or they're *too* good.'

For me, like I've said before, Maurice would never be too good, because he took the easy way out, the *cliché*, rather than what was original. He was clever all right, he was very professional, he knew more or less what I was getting at, but only I could get there, all he could do was follow me, and by the time he'd caught me up, I was on to something else. His idea of me was something like a cleaned-up Max Miller with maybe a touch of Tommy Trinder and a little bit of Arthur English, the wide boy. He was a Londoner himself and he'd got his idea of what a London comic ought to be, whereas to me the fact that I was Cockney was incidental, it was a beginning, that's all, something to grow from.

The great comedians weren't local, they were universal. Chaplin was a Cockney, anyway a South Londoner, and he'd conquered the world. Sid Field came from Birmingham, and what did it matter? Bob Hope was the most American comedian you ever heard, yet he was born in England. Jack Benny was Jewish, and who cared? You couldn't call him a Jewish comedian, not like Max Bacon or Issy Bonn.

I admit it, I wanted to make the world laugh, and I believed I could make the world laugh; like Chaplin. The first step was to make England laugh, the next was to make America laugh; I'd be the first since Chaplin to do it, because since then it had all been one-way traffic. They'd come here, Bob Hope, Jack Benny, Danny Kaye, the Marx Brothers, W. C. Fields, in shows or in films, and they'd set us alight; when were the Yanks going to start laughing at us? They were international, we were local. I'd spend hours thinking about this, puzzling about this; why we dug them when they didn't dig us. You could understand it all right if we spoke a different language, but we didn't. They'd laugh at the Marx Brothers in Blackpool. Why wouldn't they laugh at Will Hay in New York? Who was provincial, them or us?

I'd talk to Maurice, who was as hung up on American humour as I was, who even ended up working on television shows in Hollywood. 'We're too parochial,' he used to say. 'That's our strength and our weakness. We're only concerned with one small island. They have to span a continent. The only way an English comedian can succeed in the States is like Bob Hope did, go there when he's three or four years old.'

'Wait and see,' I told him.

All through my career I've been fighting that, and I've never beaten it. I've never even had the chance to beat it. We're an island, they're a continent, but when it comes to insularity, I reckon they leave us standing. 'Too British.' The number of bloody times I've heard that, when in England, who says, 'Too American?' Humour is universal, you can't chop it up and label it, this one for London, this one for Las Vegas. A really funny comic's funny anywhere; all he needs is the opportunity. If Sid Field had gone on Broadway, they'd have fallen about.

I've had this argument with June, as well; she's always singing in the States, and was brought up in Bermuda. 'Are you saying you could go to Tokyo and make a Japanese audience laugh?' she asked me, once.

'If they understand me, yes,' I said.

'But they'd never understand you, that's the point,' she said. 'Their assumptions are different. Their whole culture is different. It would be hard enough even for a visual comedian to get across to them, let alone a verbal one, like you are.'

'I'm visual as well,' I said.

'But not like Tati, darling, not like Chaplin. They don't have to open their mouths; *you* do. You're *better* when you're seen, but it's still what you say that matters.'

'Then why won't they have me in the States?'

'You're English, darling, you're a Cockney,' and round and round we'd go.

'Don't *you* think I'm funny?'

'Yes, of course I do.'

'Then why wouldn't they?'

'Because they're parochial.'

'Then why do we laugh at *their* comedians?'

'Because we've been conditioned by the cinema.'

'So I'm too local; is that what you're saying?'

'Not too local, darling, too local for *them*.'

You believe, in fact, that your message is for the world.

I've always believed that.

Which again is Messianic.

All right, it's Messianic.

Even Christ is not accepted by the whole world.

He's accepted in America.

'You need a writer,' Lou Gold said, 'and you need a dresser,' and the dresser that I got was Sid Green. He'd been in show business twenty-five years; he'd been a juvenile, he'd been a dancer, for a little while he'd been a merchant seaman, and now he was a dresser. He'd been dressing another of Lou's clients, a comedian called Jimmy Childs who'd practically retired, a bit of an old dipso I'd heard, though Sid never said anything but good about him. That was Sid; he was like a dog, dead faithful, yours for life. Lived with his mother in Clapton and gave you a wonderful massage. The only thing you'd never get from him was an argument. He was the world's greatest audience and the world's worst because he laughed at everything, not only laughed but laughed like he'd do himself an injury, fell about saying, 'That's terrific, Johnny, that's fabulous, really. Did you know that? Fantastic!'

To look at he was a little bit like a monkey, smallish, slim, though bigger in the legs than you'd expect, having been a dancer, with one of those typical London faces that you get such a lot around the East End, a bit Jewish, a bit Italian, curly hair, big brown sort of questioning eyes, flattish nose, prominent ears. He was very emotional yet he never lost his temper. He got on well with Ethel, and when I left Ethel, he got on well with June. Bob he was always nice to, giving him sweets, sending him toys on his birthday. I once told June how pleased I was he'd taken to her so quick, after he'd been so attached to Ethel.

'Attached?' she said. 'It's you he's attached to. Of course he took to me, he was glad to see the back of her. It meant that he stayed while she went. When I go, he'll be nice to the next one.'

'Do you mean he fancies me?' I asked.

'You're his bread and butter,' she said. 'Everyone fancies his bread and butter.'

I don't think she was entirely right, though it's true there were times when he could drive me up the wall, the bad times particularly, always agreeing with me, always laughing at every little joke I made – 'Marvellous, that. That's marvellous!' – while I lay face downwards, listening, being massaged. 'He's a *masseur*,' June said. 'Verbal and physical. While he does it with his hands, he's doing it with his voice as well.' But he'd stood by me through all my troubles and I could think of quite a few who hadn't. I *was* his meal ticket, but he could always get others, he was a good dresser and a good masseur.

To my mind, what happened was he got dependent, he'd no confidence in himself, Sid, and so he became *you*, the old osmosis thing. He had to have somebody to *be*.

When he came to see me at the sanatorium he came like Father Christmas, loaded with parcels: boxes, bags, chocolates, plants, magazines. He must have spent a fortune, and I didn't pay him that much. He was nearly in tears when he saw me, in fact he *was* in tears, they welled up into his eyes, then he got hold of himself. 'Marvellous, John, marvellous,' he said, then took my hand in both of his, small hands but very strong.

'Wonderful to see you. Now when are you coming back?' Then *I* felt like crying.

'God knows,' I said. 'Let's go for a walk.'

It was late autumn; there weren't too many patients about, or nurses, come to that. The lawns were soft and slippery, you crunched through brown and yellow leaves from the chestnut trees, the sky was a miserable swollen grey and it was drizzling. Sid was very smart, as always, though he didn't look quite right for here. Buckled black shiny shoes, tapered blue slacks tight around the crotch, white silk jersey, blue Continental-cut light raincoat.

The Colonel was out walking; walked in all weathers, the Colonel, swinging his stick. 'This is Sid Green, Colonel,' I said, and Sid grabbed him by the hand like he was afraid he'd run away.

'A very great pleasure, Colonel,' he said. 'I'm his dresser; to the very best comedian in the world. I mean that, Colonel. The finest anywhere.'

'Yes,' said the Colonel, 'he's a very funny fellow.'

'I'm glad you think so, Colonel,' said Sid, looking up into his eyes, still holding his hand like a prisoner. 'And I tell you something; he'll be back. My life, Colonel, he will be back, I promise you.'

'I'm sure he will.'

'We'll all be back,' I said.

'*I* hope so.' Stiff upper lip. I don't think he believed it, but I had to say it. Then we walked our way, he walked his; always on his own, poor old bastard.

'Fine type of man, that,' Sid said. 'Could do with a few more like him, believe me.'

'Yes,' I said. It was funny feeling closer to the Colonel than to Sid, but I did, though as far as background went, mine was Sid's and the Colonel could have come from Mars.

He rabbited on a lot, Sid; who was earning what, who was screwing who, who was on the bottle, who'd died in cabaret at the Astor, who'd come back and started playing the Northern clubs; all the old gossip, the kind of stuff you heard day in day out in show business, which in fact almost *was* show business.

Before, when I'd been drying out and that, I'd liked to hear it, it kept me in touch, but now it had a funny effect on me, it all seemed so miserable and trivial, the kind of world you'd find under a stone, full of nasty little creeping creatures, eating each other and living off each other. And if I was one of them, then what was I? Someone with a talent, someone with purpose in life, or just another insect, maybe a bit bigger than the others, which only meant it had more insects living off it?

It came over to me very strong, seeing Sid, listening to him chatter, how incestuous it all was, all the little cliques and groups, promoting one another, boosting one another's egos. It disgusted me. Not Sid, it wasn't his fault, it was what he'd been brought up to. If anything, I was disgusted with myself, and I was depressed as well; disgusted because I'd been part of it all these years, depressed because there was no way to escape it. If I wanted to work again I'd have to go back in; yet why *should* I go back? Why should making people laugh involve you in so much crap? Why couldn't you just stand up on a stage or in front of a camera and be funny? Why couldn't humour be pure? Not clean, pure, something that stood up on its own, instead of being what it was; more like a flower growing out of a shit-heap? And I'd probably never have felt this myself if I hadn't cracked up and been slung into the bin. After all, I'd accepted it all those years.

It was a kind of protection, I realized that, we were all frightened and we all needed each other, even when we resented each other and disliked each other. You saw someone like the Colonel, side by side with Sid, and you realized how phoney it was. It frightened me to feel so much alone, no way back yet no way forward, and no one you could even tell. Tell Sid, and he'd think you really were mad. Tell the Colonel and he'd never understand, you might be talking about Eskimos. Dr Weiss would only want to know why I felt this. Nothing exists for Dr Weiss, only the reasons for things. June was the one person I might tell, but June wasn't here, and besides, she was part of it like I'd been, she saw through everyone, she slagged off everyone, but she was still part of it.

We were sitting on a wooden seat, Sid and me, one of those

that look like they're built out of branches, and he was still rattling on: 'So they got together, these young dancers, three of them told him they were in the club, one of them said she'd got a dose, and he believed it. Terrified they'd tell his wife.'

I could see what was happening to me. I was frightened to leave the sanatorium, like a bloke that's spent half his life inside, so as soon as they let him out he throws a brick through a window so they'll nick him again. The longer I stayed, the more hooked I'd be, because they didn't cure you, they conditioned you. I'd spend the rest of my life here – till my money ran out – quarrelling with Mary Smith and the Welsh Twit, being told what I *really* meant by Dr Weiss, being visited by people I couldn't talk to.

A little bit of this seemed to get through to Sid in the end, because he stopped and looked at me, quite anxious: 'Not tiring you, am I, Johnny?'

'Course not,' I said, but I think he got the message, because he dried up after that, and we just sat there till he said, 'Know how you feel, Johnny. Know what it must be like.' You've no idea what it's fucking like, I thought, but I didn't speak. He was certainly a trier, though, Sid. 'I can see you up there in the Palladium,' he said. 'On stage. Them all falling about, like they always did.'

I could see it, too, but I didn't know whether I liked it. For one thing, what were they laughing at? Something really funny, something original and true, or one of those easy gags you can always slip in for a quick giggle, the kind Maurice used to be so good at writing, the kind some comics never get beyond. Easiest of all in the Palladium, where they've paid so much for their seats they reckon they've been done if they don't laugh. When you come on you're a star, and it's harder to stop them laughing than to start them. I didn't say anything; I just found myself shaking my head.

'You'll feel different once you're there, on stage,' Sid said. 'Once you hear the laughter. The best tonic for a comedian, that is, laughter.'

'Maybe I ought to play myself some tapes of it,' I said, which wasn't fair to Sid, when it was me I was pissed off with, not him, thinking that he might be right, maybe that's all it did need. Conditioned reflex. Laugh at me and I'm yours.

'Thanks, Sid,' I said, 'thanks for coming.' I took his hand, but I couldn't look at him. I could hear him breathing, sharp and heavy, waiting; but I'd got nothing more to say.

'Okay, John,' he said at last, 'take care,' and he got up. I still didn't look, but I could hear him crunching through the leaves.

You believe in your mission, you believe in your message, but we must ask ourselves to whom are they directed?

Everyone and no one, Doc. Everyone in general, no on in particular.

But it seems to me that you are quite ambivalent.

How's that, then?

You are hating your audiences as much as you love them.

Every comic does. If they laugh, he loves them, if they don't he hates them.

This is quite understandable. It may even be quite Messianic. Christ, after all, rebuked the Jews and the Greeks for their indifference.

I'm in the clear then, am I?

But is your message for the world a message of hate or a message of love?

Neither. It's a message of laughter.

What's wrong with love and hate, anyway? You find it everywhere, Doc Weiss says so himself. Love-hate your mother, love-hate your father, so why not love-hate your audience? Who in any case love-hate you.

But you love them only when they are laughing and to hate them when they are not laughing is to deny them a separate identity. *They* laugh, therefore *you* exist.

You sound like my wife again, Doctor.

'You, you, you, you!'

That was when she knew I was leaving her. Stood there in the middle of the lounge in Hampstead Garden Suburb, in that house that had cost me thirty-five grand, stood there under the chandelier, in front of the brick fireplace that was never used, and screamed at me, 'You, you, you!'

Bob was in his room upstairs, mucking about with his model racing cars; I hoped to God he couldn't hear her. 'Bob!' I said, pointing upwards.

'You think *he* doesn't know? You think *he* hasn't noticed? He's not a little child any more! Daddy's tired! Daddy fell asleep! Daddy's gone away for a rest! He's seen you, he's heard you!'

That room we were in; it overpowered me, now. The whole house did, the whole house was her, flock wallpaper, fitted carpets, heavy curtains. Her. Provincial. Weighing me down, hemming me in, where June's flat was all light and colour, white woodwork, wicker chairs, bright woollen rugs, low tables, abstract paintings on the walls. Ethel was house-proud, but she didn't run a house, she ran a prison. It was forever, her house – I always thought of it as hers – somewhere where you stayed until you died, somewhere where you couldn't grow, and I needed to grow. How could I tell her all that? Whereas June's flat was a place that didn't oppress you, it allowed you to breathe, you could be what you liked. If you stayed you stayed, if you went you went. It was just like her. She lived in the place, she liked the place, she made it as nice as she could, but she didn't make a religion of it. It was like her car – she nipped about everywhere in a little, souped-up, psychedelic Mini with black windows and cassettes – it was something she thought of when she used it. It didn't use her, and she didn't use people. She was free, she was happy, she was doing her own thing, she didn't need to possess anybody.

'Oh, June's like you,' said Ethel, 'two of a kind, you are. Go your own way, and to hell with the rest of the world. But don't you try crying on *her* shoulder like you have on mine!'

I knew I never would, I'd never have to, any more than she'd cry on mine. We didn't want sympathy, we wanted inspiration, and that's what we knew we could give each other, what I admit I got in the beginning from Ethel.

June would never have talked all that crap about audiences, identities and that, she's been up there on that stage and she knows. She knows that if a performer doesn't look after himself, doesn't think about himself, he's finished. '*Fucking* audiences!' she'd say. She always came out and sung like she didn't give a screw and they loved her for it. 'Look at them!' she'd say. 'They're like sharks. The slightest smell of blood and they're in there tearing your flesh. Look what they did to Judy Garland. They could always smell the vulnerability. They could smell that she wanted to be loved, poor bitch. *I* don't want their sodding love!'

Nor did I. What I wanted was their laughter. I knew that cruelty, just like she did, that viciousness you find in audiences; it was the cruelty of the world. I've heard comedians called sadists, too, to their audiences, to the people that work with them, but I don't think comedians start out like that. If they get to be, then it's through experience, to protect themselves, for self-defence, because the first impulse, the thing that starts them going, is wanting to make people laugh, and what's cruel in that?

'Egomaniac,' that was something else Ethel used to call me. 'You're an egomaniac! You're too bloody sick to think of anybody else!' Whereas June understood. 'Of course you're an egomaniac. We're all egomaniacs. We need to be to defend ourselves.'

If a performer doesn't think he's interesting, who else is going to? I've been in railway carriages with two or three other comedians, at cocktail parties and at dinners, and I admit it's like a duel, you're all jockeying and manoeuvring, you've got this fixed smile on your face, but you're not really listening to the other fellow's gags, the other fellow's stories, you're waiting for the moment that he stops, when *you* can jump in, and you get very skilful at that, you can tell within seconds when a bloke's almost done, then bang, you're in, unless he goes you one better with the old false finish and picks up again just when you're opening your mouth.

**But we have still to reconcile your ambivalence towards**

your audiences with your belief that you also have a mission.

If you can't see it, Doc, I can't explain. Every performer has this. He starts with a belief he's got something to give the world, but then he finds he's got to fight like buggery to get it across.

There is an obvious analogy here between the performer and the tiny child, who also believes in his own significance and who becomes resentful when he is frustrated. For the baby, too, the world exists only in relation to itself, and his relation to it is solipsistic. What your wife might have called egomaniac.

There you are again, cutting everything down to size. You should have been a fucking demolition expert.

I am not demolishing, only analysing. The comparison between the child and the artist is not a new one. The artist has also the innocence of a child.

Look, Doc, don't let's mess about. You're calling me a phoney, aren't you? You're saying I do everything for *me*, that all this mission stuff's just ego-message. Right?

Again you are imputing to me ethical judgements. I am not interested in blaming you, only in helping you.

You could have fooled *me*, Doctor.

I am not denying that unconsciously it is possible to hold two quite conflicting ideas in one's mind at the same time. It is our task to bring them into relation with each other and in time to form a synthesis.

It ain't as easy as that, Doc. I *can* hate audiences. I *do* want to help people, and I think I can help them by making them laugh.

I think, but I'm not sure of anything any more. That's the effect this place has had on me, it and him, his digging and probing. How is it helping me to pull me apart? It's like walking. If you thought of every single movement as you made it, you'd be paralysed. When you're doing things you take them for granted, you understand them without being aware of them, but the trouble now is I'm not doing anything, I'm hanging around like a big useless ponce, having myself shrunk by Dr Weiss and squabbling with everybody in the group therapy. Sid could even be right; that the real therapy's going back on stage and making people laugh, that this would pull it all together, work the synthesis, or whatever fancy name Weiss wants to call it. Has a lot of fun with me, he does.

And yet, if I'm honest, I have to say I'm frightened to death; that they *won't* laugh, and then what happens to the synthesis? Everything would break up into smaller pieces than ever so that even Doc Weiss wouldn't be able to help.

> All the psychiatrists and all the Doc's men
> Couldn't put Johnny together again.

The trouble is, the longer I wait the harder and harder it's going to get, the further away I'll be from my last laugh. Even now I've got to the stage of reconstructing laughs, which is part of the phobia, thinking of what you said, how you said it, and how they reacted. I don't think I'd be able to go on stage without taking something, not one of those tranquillizer bombs they keep feeding me here, because all they do is make me more placid. It would have to be more like a purple heart, Bob's the one to ask, except that whatever he's taking seems to turn him off, not on. They're all on the contemplation kick, so far as I can see, though God knows what they bloody contemplate.

We're back again here to the old business of kill and cure. Take away a comedian's megalomania, or whatever name you give it, and you're stripping away his shell, you could leave him helpless. That's good, Dr Weiss would say, at least he's got rid of his megalomania, a step towards reality, he'd say. Labelling things again. Call it megalomania and it's bad. But call it self-protection and it's surely good. Who's right? *He's* right as a psychoanalyst; I reckon I'm right as a performer.

> I've just come out of a mental hospital.
> You've just come out of a mental hospital?
> That's right, I've just come out a mental hospital.
> And did they cure you?
> Yes.
> How do you know you're cured?
> Because I can't work.

No, but seriously. Lying awake at night on that horrible hospital bed with its bars across the bed head – very appropriate those bars – or ambling around that big, boring garden in the rain, these thoughts come closing in on me. The Doc says that when people laugh, it's because you lift their inhibitions. Which is what I want to do, my aim; keep lifting them, lift them for good. But if I succeed, if I ever do lift them for good, then that's the end of laughter. No, but seriously. Which must mean laughter's a disease, or anyway a symptom of one.

'You know what you're doing, Doc?' I've said to him. 'You're turning me into a fucking intellectual, like you are. I'll tell you one thing, though; I'll never turn you into a comedian, like I am.'

Or was.

'Is, was, will be,' June would always say. Great for me she was, at times like this. 'Luckier than singers, comedians are. Singers' voices go in the end. Comedians are okay if they can *whisper*.'

That was in the worst days, the really, really black days, much blacker than now, or they seemed to be, maybe because I hadn't been conditioned then, no one had got hold of me yet and turned me into a patient. And *as* a patient, what I notice more and more is that there's a lot of envy in psychologists. It's plainer in the Welsh Twit than what it is in Dr Weiss, but I can feel it there, as well. They're not envious in the way all those twots in the group therapy are envious, because I've been famous and rich and that; they're envious because they've never done anything and never will. It's all second hand. After all, what's a psychologist's life? He never goes anywhere, he never does anything, he never takes a chance. If he's somebody like Dr Weiss, he spends nearly his whole life in one poxy consulting-room, with just an occasional treat now and again when he can give some poor bastard the old electric shock treatment or jab him with an insulin needle. If he's doing group analysis at least he gets a bigger audience, but it's the same old thing, he's still living at second hand. God knows what makes a bloke a comedian, I've heard a million fucking explanations by now, but if you ask me what makes a bloke a psychoanalyst it's not having the bottle to go out and do things for himself, he'd rather do it all through other people, I know the jargon, we're acting out his fantasies, and at the same time he resents our being able to do it so he gets his own back by taking us to bits. That's his way of getting power. That's how he reassures himself.

A great idea, that is, Dr Weiss and me changing places, me telling all his bloody patients what's wrong with them, putting everything back to front, like a boxer's really afraid of finding out he's yellow and a sex maniac's afraid of being impotent, while Doc Weiss goes on the halls. The Laughing Psychiatrist. A Smile, A Song and A Syndrome. 'A funny thing happened to me on my way to the nut-house. Expensive? I'll say our treatment's expensive. We're the only sanatorium in England where you even pay for your free association.'

Or maybe we'd team up as a double act. That'd be good, that, me lying on the couch, him sitting there behind me in a white jacket.

'Doctor, Doctor, what am I going to do about my Oedipus Complex?'

'Oedipus, Schmoedipus, just put your mother on the Pill.'

One thing that shows me things are bad: I don't keep wanting to ask him how much longer, when'll I get out of here? Before, it was the one question that was always in my mind and if I didn't ask, it was because I was frightened. Come back and ask me in six months, he might say, or; maybe a year, maybe two, who knows? Besides, I'd got a funny feeling that he wanted to hang on to me. He'd have a label for that, and all, he'd call it persecution mania, but I'm still suspicious. He wants to get to the bottom of me, the Doc does, and there's one big question that he hasn't solved, he more or less admits it: why I get depressed. I don't know either. I wish I bleeding did. Guilt, he's been saying. Guilt about what? Ah, that's it; he can't tell you. Just guilt. Round we go in circles. If it was guilt about *something*, it wouldn't be no bother, but it ain't. It's the worst kind of guilt; the kind you can't get at.

'Look, Doc, I get depressed about not being able to make people laugh, that's all. It's logical enough.'

'But what is *causing* such an anxiety?'

Very deep, the Doc. Deep enough to drown.

Sometimes he asks me about other comedians. Are they all like me? Do they all worry?

'Most of them.'

All of them? How do *I* know? That's a ridiculous question. The first time I was ever at the Palladium, Jack Benny was top of the bill, the suavest thing I've ever seen. So confident, it made you nervous to be near him, in fact I *was* nervous to be near him, he was such a hero of mine, such a legend; those wartime broadcasts on the American Forces Network coming over our prehistoric radio upstairs above the pub, big as a bloody coffin, with a great round drum of brown cloth across the middle. What poise he had, what authority! I'd stand in the wings watching him and wonder could I ever be like him, strolling on in a sharp grey suit, carrying that old violin he could hardly play, so cool he could have been walking into his own front parlour. He could get effects with just an expression or a gesture that you'd beat your brains out to get. I'd watch him and I'd think, there's a bloke really believes in himself. There's a bloke *knows* it's going to go right, every time he walks on a stage, and that it'll go on and on being right.

There were so many things I wanted to ask him, how's it done, what's your secret, have you always been like this, were you always so sure? Because part of it, obviously, was the prestige. He was Jack Benny, he was a great, great star; whatever he did, people were ready to laugh, and because he knew this it made him all the more confident, one thing reinforced the other.

Of course I didn't ask him any of these things, I was far too shy, and the biggest question of all, the sixty-four dollar question, I didn't dare ask him: 'What do you think of *my* act, Mr Benny? Will I ever be in your league?'

Very polite he was but remote, living, you might say, in his own legend, a thing I came to notice about a lot of the biggest stars, though whether because they thought it was all real or because they used it to keep people at a distance, you could never really know. Personally I was never able to be like that, not even when I'd made it, but that was just me, maybe my uncertainty, and in some ways life might have been easier if I could have done.

'Evening, Mr Benny,' I'd say, when I saw him, very deferential, like saluting a superior officer, and he'd always nod and say, 'Good evening, young man.' Offstage, from all that I could tell – he moved around with quite an entourage – he seemed very calm, solemn almost, more like a businessman than a comedian.

Just once, at the very end of that week, when I realized it was now or never, I got up the courage to talk to him, caught him outside his dressing-room when I'd just been on, it had gone well and I was feeling good. Poured it all out, I did; I must have sounded like a right berk, oh Mr Benny I'm such a fan of yours, listened to you in the war when I was a kid, never thought I'd be appearing on the same bill as you.

He listened to me very patiently – that was the word – as if he'd developed a technique for when people rabbited on at him like this. In the end I took a deep breath and said, 'Mr Benny, if you'd just forgive me asking this, is there any advice you could maybe give me, anything you think I ought to do?'

He didn't answer for a few moments, like he was considering it very deeply, then at last he said, 'Yes, I'll give you one little piece of advice. Never try too hard.'

It took the wind out of me, that, I don't know what I'd been expecting though I suppose what I wanted, what I was really angling for, was praise, something I could take away and treasure. Jack Benny told me that I'd really got it. Jack Benny told me I could be as big as he is.

'Thanks, Mr Benny,' I said, 'thanks very much,' then he gave me what you'd call a gracious smile and nod, a bit like royalty, put his fingers on my arm and said, like he'd just thought of it, 'And good luck!' End of conversation.

Really crestfallen, I was. He went into his dressing-room, the door shut, and I was left there feeling I'd been hit in the stomach. Good luck. How many people had got that smile, how many people had had that nod, how many people had heard those words? Yet he was right; even then I realized that. I *did* try too hard, it was something that I'd have to watch, but then hadn't *he* ever been anxious, hadn't *he* ever been over-eager, or had he just stepped straight out on to a stage with everything in its proper place?

Never mind; I was *at* the Palladium, however low down the bill, and one day please God I'd be where he was.

*What a thrill it was to make my first appearance at the Palladium on the same bill as the man who had been my boyhood hero, Jack Benny, surely one of the all-time comedy greats. And I never forget the advice the old maestro gave me. 'Don't try too hard,' he told me. 'If you're really funny, then the laughs will come.' How right he was.*

Out of Ethel's scrapbook, that; don't ask me what hack churned it out. From my four-part, exclusive life story, as published in the *Sunday Dispatch* or something like it. 'Well, we can *say* he said that, Johnny, after all it does make it sound better.'

It came just before I got my radio show, the Palladium appearance. I was playing up in Glasgow, and Lou wired me. I was so excited that I sent out for a half a dozen bottles of champagne and gave a party in my dressing-room. By the time I went on stage I was a bit pissed, the first time it ever happened and I wish I could say it was the last time, though up there it was really more of a giggle, reaching out for the microphone, missing it nearly falling over, turning it into part of the act, a bit of the old Jimmy James. 'It's all right!' I told them. 'Just to show you I belong to Glasgow!'

The Palladium! All those times I'd walked around it like a bloody shrine, when I was playing the Windmill. If I did try too hard you could understand it, because a supporting comedian, on a bill like that, either he grabs them as soon as he comes on or he never gets them at all. It's hard enough at any time, making an impact in ten minutes, but when the top of the bill's another comedian and that comedian's one of the biggest in the world, then you're really up against it. It's him they've come to see, not you. Who's this, they're asking themselves, especially the fancy people in the stalls, never heard of him. It might have been a bit easier if it had been like the old Sid Field shows, he'd come on early, go off, reappear, give someone else a chance, like Terry Thomas in that scene as the disc jockey who loses all his records and has to sing them himself. But the Palladium show would always build, now; acrobats, jugglers, singers, another comic, till at last on came the star, and stayed on for the best part of an hour.

'You've got to have a writer,' Lou Gold said, and he found me one called Ron Gresham, very smooth, very slick, smiled a lot, knew all the old American comedy routines inside out, even spoke with a bit of an American accent himself, though I think he came from somewhere like Barnet. He was another of those easy-way-out blokes, he could have been a lot funnier if only he hadn't gone for the obvious laugh. He wore a lot of Brilliantine on his hair and a big, toothpaste smile that he switched on and off like a lamp. 'Great, Johnny, terrific to meet you, good to be working with you.' It worried me; he couldn't be that fucking nice, but I never found out; he'd built up this showbiz barrier and he stayed behind it.

He was very big on the 'in' gags. 'They say Jack Benny's mean. *I* don't think he's mean. All this stuff about moths flying out of his pockets. His suits don't *have* any pockets.'

No, no, I said, not me.

The other thing was he had this stereotype in his mind of what I was: a Cockney comedian.

*This gangling funster is as London as a fog, as East End as jellied eels, as Cockney as the Old Kent Road.*

Ethel's scrapbook; week of the show, I remember when I read it; I was pleased but annoyed, pleased they'd noticed me, annoyed they'd type-cast me. I wasn't interested in being a regional comic, a local comic. Regional comics date, even the good ones are like rockets, go up in a blaze of sparks and come down with only the stick. Al Read with his Manchester act, the monologues and that, Arthur English with his Cockney spiv. Great when they're new, but they don't develop, they're tied to their own time and place, they can't hope for more than a limited run. All right, I'd think, I *am* a Londoner, I admit I'm a Londoner, I'm not ashamed of being a Londoner, but I'm *more* than a Londoner. That's where I start, it isn't where I finish. Who could tell you where W. C. Fields came from, where Tony Hancock came from, or Sid Field, come to that? It was a trap, this Cockney thing.

I'd even toned the clothes down, none of the Palais de Danse stuff now, more like one of those second-hand-car salesmen, everything smart but just a bit too smart, just this side of flash; still the snap-brim trilby, a pale blue tie with a mermaid painted on it, but brothel-creepers instead of brogues and a bright green check tweed suit.

What I did was I came running on, singing, to the orchestra: 'When you're smiling, when you're smiling, the whole world smiles with *you*.' A few more bars of that then the music stopped and I said to them, 'Ladies and gentlemen, I have pleasure in introducing you to the bravest comedian in the world. Me.'

A good laugh for that, and I'd pretend to be offended. 'Straight up. I'm serious. You are looking at a hero. The only comedian with the courage to *start* his act with a song instead of saving it till last, when he knows he'll be safe. That's the difference between us; I come running on, they go running off. I'm not kidding, I've known one or two, they sing their song, they run off stage, out of the stage door, straight into an armoured car, and they're away. It's a funny thing though, isn't it, when you come to think of it? Why should a comedian *want* to go off with a song? I mean, I can understand why most of them want to go off after they've *sung*. But did you ever hear of an opera singer going off with a gag? If he did, it might sound something like this.'

Then they'd play a recording of the Figaro aria from *The Barber of Seville* that I'd mime to like The Bernard Brothers used to do then, when it was a new gimmick. After the last, 'La-*la*, la, *l-a-a-a*,' the music stopped and I'd say in a cod Italian accent, 'Thank you very much. An' now I wanna tell you a story. There was-a these-a two barbers . . .'

Great it went, I'd got them, and from then on they'd always stay with me.

The first laugh I got on the first night; I can't describe how it felt, what it did to me, how it lifted me up, how it filled me to the brim with this great, great feeling everything was going to be all right. My first laugh on my very first appearance at the Palladium; it was something you couldn't buy and you could never repeat; and something you could never feel sure of till you'd heard it.

Thinking about all that's made me think a lot about laughter, it's made me start working out my own theory, which I suppose I can thank Doc Weiss for, because he does get you thinking, though whether it's good or whether it's bad, Christ knows. He takes it all for granted, his theory, Freud's theory, all this lifting the inhibitions stuff. To me, it doesn't go far enough. From what he tells me, it must have been worked out sixty years ago and if Freud was anything like him, then he never laughed in his life.

This laughter, Doc. To me it's more like an orgasm.

An orgasm for whom?

For *both*, don't you see. The comedian *and* the audience!

But the comedian is not laughing.

I know he's not, but it's like masculine and feminine, see? They both come at the same time! Like you say: the active and the passive. The comedian's the man, he makes her laugh. When she comes, so does he.

The comparison is not exact.

I know it's not. I'm not a psychologist, am I? But there's other things that fit. A comedian *builds up* to a laugh, he prepares it, just like screwing.

You mean that there may be a symbolic form of love play.

That's it! But if you don't get the laugh, you haven't made her come, and if you can't get laughs, then maybe you're impotent or she's frigid.

It interests me that you should regard your audience as a woman.

For Christ's sake, Doc, aren't I allowed to have a theory? Has it always got to be down to me? Why don't we just say I think audiences are cunts?

This may in effect be what you mean, but we must also remember that not all laughter is caused by comedians.

Jesus, Doc, I wonder what you'd do if you had Freud on the couch.

We are concerned not with hypothesis but with analysis.

Give me strength.

# *Chapter 4*

Johnny come lately, Johnny come quick,
Johnny's done greatly, Johnny's so slick.
Some people think he's too clever by half,
But Johnny's come lately to make you laugh.

Believe it or not, a close-harmony group used to sing that at the start of my show, The Radio Rovers, two men and a couple of birds, the men in blazers, the girls in bright pink dresses, all grinning like lunatics. It seems prehistoric, now, but that was radio then, except for *The Goon Show* which was far out and miles ahead of its time, Sellers and Milligan and Secombe, and even they had a bloke playing the mouth-organ. Dead as the dodo, those days, television's buried them, though in another fifteen years I reckon we'll look back on *these* shows and think the same; diabolical liberty, how did they ever get away with it? In fact I often think that about them now.

Still, it was that show that made me, *Johnny Come Lately*, so I can't really knock it, even though I wince a bit whenever I remember it. It followed the usual formula of that type of programme; they'd sing, I'd come on and do some patter, the quick-fire, stand-up sort of stuff, which was the only part of the programme I really enjoyed, we'd go into a sketch, The Radio Rovers would sing a song, we'd do another sketch, and then they'd sing us out. It wasn't bad, Maurice could be quite clever, but that formula was like a straitjacket, I was fighting all the time to burst out of it. I'd listen to the Goons, all that surrealist stuff they were doing then, and I'd envy them.

At the same time the lolly was rolling in, I could pick and choose whatever stage shows I wanted anywhere in England, and I'd proved my point, I'd arrived, I was happy. We had a fair old cast in that show, a lot of good radio pros like Molly Rivers; a great, huge woman with a colossal bust, forearms like pillows and a plummy accent who was meant to be my fiancée. Most comics in those shows had a radio 'wife', but I was allowed to have a fiancée, which I suppose was progress. 'Johnny, you *can't*,' she'd keep on saying, which became the catch phrase of the show, people were saying it everywhere, 'Johnny, you *can't*,' you'd hear them say in shops, on tube trains, in the street. In fact that was the name they gave my next radio show. Fame at last.

If only I could have left it there, been satisfied with that, maybe I would have been better off. To be honest, I suppose I had the arrogance but not the self-satisfaction. Some comics I've known have had both, they get their break and that's it, they settle for what they've got, or what they've got away with, going on with the same crappy routines year after year. I don't say you have to change, though personally it would have driven me nuts always to stay where I was, never to grow. I don't say some comics won't reach a sort of perfection after a time; and nobody can keep on developing forever, you've got to stop somewhere. It just amazed me that people whose acts were so bad could go on with those acts and still seem so pleased with themselves; when I met them, this was what I wanted to ask them about. Maybe it was just fear again; that inside themselves they knew they couldn't be any better, so they settled for that and grew a skin over it. Other times I'd think there was maybe something wrong with me, who was I to be so special? Why couldn't I just join in those sessions when comedians got together and rambled on and on boasting about what they'd done in Wigan, how they'd paralysed them in Bradford? 'I'm not saying there wasn't a dry seat in the house, folks, I'm only saying that the audience went out the theatre by canoe.' Cabaret, I used that in. You could never have used a gag like that on radio.

They sensed this in me, the old hands, this holding back. One of them said to me once, after a session like that, a real old-timer, very funny in his way, vaudeville-style with loads of double meanings, 'Johnny,' he said, 'you're *not* different. You'll find that out. You're just younger.' I wondered whether he was right. I wondered whether at his age I might be like him – though he *was* a good comedian – content with just the custard-pie stuff and the straightforward blue gags, living on my reputation. Maybe I would. After all, he was still working, wasn't he? And maybe that was why. Many, many times, in years to come, I'd wonder about that, whether you needed this to survive, this self-satisfaction. When a comedian has to put up with so much from outside, he can do without the strife from inside.

Every week, on *Johnny Come Lately,* I was meant to have some smart idea for getting rich, and every week it went wrong; selling refrigerators to the Eskimos, starting a gold rush on Clapham Common, selling Buckingham Palace to an American tourist. I was a kind of failed con-man, a lovable operator; it would do for the moment, but it wasn't me. I liked what I got out of radio, the fame, the loot, the freedom in a way, but I got more of a kick out of cabaret or stage shows.

I woke up laughing this morning, the morning after that session with Dr Weiss, because I had this phrase running through my head: All Audiences Are Cunts. Only, of course, there were good cunts and bad cunts. Next thing, if I wasn't careful, we'd be back on the old line about audiences really being my mother; or my father, God forbid. What an audience that would be! The one thing that spoiled my first night at the Palladium: my father sitting in my dressing-room like a fucking monument, wearing a blue serge suit that should have gone out with the Ark, and an invisible sign above his head: We Are Not Impressed: 'It's better than work.'

It shouldn't have hurt me but it did. Doc Weiss would have all the reasons, of course; trying for my father's approval and not getting it, while there was old Ted, tramping the streets in his bloody great boots, sorting out suspects in the cells and probably taking a few backhanders like any copper, the apple of the old man's eye.

But I think it was simpler than that, which it often is with Doc Weiss, who could give you fifteen different reasons why you blow your nose. I think it was just that when you've had a success like that, you want everybody to be happy with you, and if someone isn't, then it blights things.

When eventually I topped the bill at the Palladium, just a couple of years later, I couldn't bring myself to ask my father for the first night, which upset me, because it meant I couldn't ask Mother either. 'You *can't* not,' Ethel said, 'you *can't* not,' but I just couldn't face it, knowing he was there out front, the great big bulk of him, maybe even being able to see him, see that sardonic look on his face, like *he* saw through me if nobody else did; the thought of him in the dressing-room afterwards, giving off bad vibrations; hostility, envy, or whatever it was. It choked Mother, I knew, but how could I help it? It was sheer self-preservation. He grudged me my success, he grudged me the money, and when he was down on his luck and dying, in a little flat with Mother over Clapton, it was murder to do anything for him, he'd take nothing from me, I had to go all round the houses, which made me hate him instead of feeling sorry for him, because he was depriving her, as well.

It was only when he died that I was really able to help her, buy her a little seaside house near Southend, where we'd once gone on those day trips, that she shared with her sister who's a widow, too. Him and his fucking pride, that other people had to suffer for.

There was a lot of needle between me and Ted in the old man's last weeks, he'd had a stroke and a heart attack, not the first of either, and he lay there in a ward in Guy's Hospital like a whale on a beach, poor bastard, huffing and panting, just about able to recognize you, hardly able to speak. Ted was there every day, like Mother, I came when I could; when I was free and when I could force myself. Ted would stand the other side of the bed and glower at me, sometimes in his copper's blue uniform with sergeant's stripes (he was moving up now) sometimes in plain clothes. There was a lot of the old man in him. If he loved him that was okay with me, but why should I pretend? Because a man's dying doesn't change how you feel; that's just hypocrisy, superstition. You were entitled to be sorry for him, and I was, but we'd lost each other long ago.

He hated being helpless, you could tell, a man who all his

life had been proud of being strong, and he hated me *seeing* him helpless. For him, I was someone who'd cheated. I couldn't make it like he had or, according to him, like Ted had, like a man, through strength and through aggressiveness, so I'd gone round the back alleys and come out ahead of both of them; but it didn't count.

Those big hands, that thick, creased neck, those great, white, hairy arms; they were useless to him now. If he had to turn over the nurses had to do it, and it took three of them. My mother would sit there by the bed, very quiet and weepy, in that same old hospital stench of bedpans and disinfectant and methylated spirits, and I felt sorry for *her*. Whatever he was, he was all she'd got left.

Two or three times I went, but that was all I could take. I was only once alone with him and that couldn't have been for more than about ten minutes, though to me it seemed like ten days. There was one moment he looked at me with an expression I'd never seen on his face before, pathetic really, a sort of appeal, like he wanted me to reassure him; that I *didn't* hate him, that he *hadn't* been that bad. His lips opened, there were thick strings of saliva between them like tiny ropes, he gave a funny little moaning noise, but that was all he could manage, then it had gone, his eyes closed and he was asleep. By the time he woke up Ted and his wife were there, she'd been in the police force too and she looked it, big square-built blonde woman with calves like bannisters, eyeing me like she wanted to arrest me.

No, I never made the old man laugh, not *with* me, anyway, and when it came to his funeral, I didn't cry. Fucking funerals, I hate them, the misery and the lies. Don't speak ill of the dead, okay, but don't speak cobblers either, especially somebody that's barely known them, like the old fart in the graveyard in Hackney, bleating away about the old man's kindness, his principles. Ted glared at me across the grave like he was challenging me to deny any of it, my mother was crying with Ted's wife's arm around her shoulders as if she was running her in. A few of his old pals – there'd never been many of them – stood around in their best suits looking like they were embarrassed, too. Ashes to ashes, dust to dust. And sods to sods, I thought.

It's terrible at times to be a comic, conditioned reflexes twitching even at a funeral.

We were meant to go back to Clapton afterwards, but I couldn't face it, I kissed my mother, hurried Ethel into the Bentley and drove west across London, drove like the clappers, through at least a couple of red traffic lights, away from all that poverty and grime and misery that I wanted to put behind me forever.

The fact that you should drive away like this shows that your conflict still was unresolved.

How resolved can you get, Doc? I'd just seen him buried, hadn't I?

A physical death is not always a psychological one.

You mean I'm trying to make his ghost laugh?

Metaphysically, perhaps you are.

That's great, that is. An audience that's *really* dead. That's all I'm short of. Mind you, he wouldn't be any tougher dead than alive.

When Ethel and I got home from the funeral we had the most stupendous fuck; I suppose the Doc would make something out of that, as well, a celebration, maybe. Anyway, the best fuck we'd had for years, almost as soon as we got inside the door, rolling about all over the living-room, never waited to go upstairs to the bedroom, in the house we had then up in Highgate. I suppose what I might have been saying was he was dead but we were still alive. She seemed to understand it, Ethel, she went at it as hard as I did, like something had gone, something that had stood between us, and it's true that for a time things were very good, almost like the days before Bob.

As for my mother, it may sound a terrible thing to admit it, but I didn't want to see her now any more than I had him. I knew she needed me and that, I knew I should have been with her, should have had her over, but to see her weeping and wailing about him, missing the old bastard, was more than I knew I could stand. So I sent her things, the cowardly way; flowers and fruit and cakes and cooked meat and that from Harrods and Fortnums, places I hardly knew existed a few years before; even a diamond brooch from Asprey's, wondering what Ted's face would look like when he saw her wearing it.

Ethel understood, she was always good about that, though at first it threw her a little coming from a family where people liked each other, then running across one like ours. She'd got on all right with both of them; the old man fancied her a bit, I could tell from the looks he gave her, the remarks he made, which were as near to jokes as he could ever get. *She* drove over to my mother a few times, took her out for a run in the Bentley, took her for meals. She was great, never got on at me about it, I was really and truly grateful. I don't think I was callous, any more than I meant to be when I broke up with Ethel. It was just that the past was past. I resented being dragged back.

Back, back, back. That's what I hate about this place; the dragging back. No future, you could understand that, but not even any present, because the present is nothing, you're hanging in the air, the present's just a trapdoor to the past, which robs you of the one great thing about the past, it's over, you've lived through it, however bad it was, you've left it behind. I don't want to hear that I turned Ethel from my wife into my mother, even if it may be true, because what good can it do me? It's like some archaeologist who spends all his time digging up poxy little bits of pottery. One day, maybe, he'll have enough to put them together and make a prehistoric soup bowl; so what?

We were at it in group therapy, as well, Ivan was my son, the Colonel was my father – I wish he had been – Mary Smith and Mrs Casey were Ethel and my mother and Christ knows what old Tight-Arse was; maybe he was Ted, he wouldn't have made a bad copper. We were all playing things out and working things through and generally disappearing up our own arseholes. Even the old Colonel blew his top one day with Mary Smith who told him he had a lot of anal characteristics. 'My dear young woman,' he said, 'a little reticence on your part would be a great blessing, whatever caused it,' which the Welsh Twit said was good; he was showing his aggression.

'What was he doing in the war, then?' I asked.

'That's different,' the Welsh Twit said.

'I see,' I said, 'that's not aggression, that's just killing people.'

Nothing was real in group therapy, nothing was what it seemed to be, at least according to the Welsh Twit; it was like a hall of mirrors, and they were distorting mirrors, if you asked me. 'Maybe we all ought to dress up,' I told the Welsh Twit one day, after some remark about my treating Mary like she was Ethel who was really my mother. 'Put the Colonel in a grey beard. Put Ivan in a cap and blazer. Put Mary in a grey wig, Mrs Casey in a red one, and when they feel like it, they can swap.'

'This is group therapy,' he said, 'not psycho-drama.'

Maybe it was, but it seemed to me that the only thing that got acted out all the time was hostility. Maybe they reckoned it was like squeezing poison out of a snake; by the time they put you back in the world again you'd got no aggression left, so good for the Colonel when he snarled at Mary.

You couldn't be sure of anything any more, what was good and what was bad. Like I'd started jerking myself off, something I'd never done since the Army. Was it good or bad? Normally: bad. The old mallarkey they told you as a child, play with yourself and it'll drop off. But now, maybe good, because it meant at least I was getting interested again. If June came down another time, would I want her? There was nothing here I wanted, least of all Mary Smith, who'd taken to smiling at me now in the sessions and trying to chat me up outside them, which was worse than all the bitchiness. Maybe a fuck would put me back in the world. Not fucking was part of what was wrong with this place, part of its not being real.

Permission to fuck, please, Doc.

Yes, but once only, and for no more than thirty times.

Discouraged, screwing was. Mustn't upset ourselves.

'Of course we do not exercise supervision, but our patients are put on their honour.'

Trusties.

Who did I think about when I was wanking? June, mostly. Now and again about old fucks – we were living in the past, weren't we? – though never about Ethel. Mostly June. Or who I thought was June. Maybe she wasn't June, so when June came I wouldn't want her, I'd want whoever else it might be.

However good it was, though, it could never be as good as our first fuck, just as Ethel and I never had anything so great as that first time in her digs at Fairleigh, not even after the funeral.

Going back to her flat, off Baker Street, after the Talk of the Town, trying to follow her Austin Healey that she had then and drove like a lunatic, where was the hurry? Jumping lights, cutting people up, but no tension, just excitement, expectation, knowing it was going to happen, that something new was starting, something important. That marvellous feeling inside me that I'd been good that night, good for *her*, playing for her, to her, like a matador dedicating a bull.

And the first thing she said when we got inside the flat, 'You could be *so* much better.' That really deflated me. I'd got no confidence at all then, I was just about able to work, but that was it.

'What do you mean,' I asked, '*better*?'

'Oh, you were *good*,' she said, she was bustling about, she always seemed to be on the move, switching on lights, throwing her coat on a chair, ripping open letters then crumpling them, picking up bottles. 'You probably always *are* good. You could *do* much more with your invention, your intelligence.'

'Do me a favour,' I said, 'it's as much as I can manage to get on a stage.'

'Oh, yes,' she said, 'the whisky. Do you want one now?'

'All right,' I said, and I sat down, which I needed. I'd come in feeling right randy, but if what she'd meant to do was to turn me off, then she'd done it. I still couldn't take my eyes off her as she moved about, though; she was looking fabulous. She'd changed into silver tights with a black, sleeveless top, and the boots. Her skin was tanned, like she went bathing all year round, and there were these little golden flecks of hair over her back and down her arms. She was slimmer than Ethel but not thin; firm, no fat on her.

'That might be *why*,' she said. She had this way of throwing things out, a style I wasn't used to, leaving gaps for you to fill in. With Ethel, everything was rounded off and down to earth, nothing left to the imagination.

'Why what?' I said.

'This drinking,' and she poured me out a whisky. 'Repressing talent's like repressing aggression; it can turn cancerous.'

'So I'm getting cancer,' I said.

'Not physically; maybe morally.'

'Moral cancer,' I said. 'That's nice, that.'

'It *can* be cured,' she said, then bent forward and kissed me, and suddenly we were away. It had been bad for so long, not just with Ethel but with whoever I tried it, that I'd almost forgotten how great it could be. She was wild, June, marvellous with her hands, marvellous with her tongue, she seemed to be everywhere at once. At the same time, she behaved like it was a sort of conspiracy between you; while she was going down on you or you were screwing her, she'd suddenly dart you these mischievous looks, these smiles, that somehow added to it all.

We fucked in her bedroom, on her big, broad, low bed, where there was plenty of room to roll about. It had a red and black woven cover on it, and I remember her ripping it off, looking at me with that smile. What she could only do with those gestures!

That bed; me and that bed. The part it would play in my life. The best and the worst. The best screwing, the worst boozing. How many times did I come on it, how many times did I puke on it, how many times did I lie there so depressed I thought I'd die? Christ knows how she put up with it, or who else would have done, who else would have helped me like she did. Not Ethel. I was beyond anything Ethel could do; the big reason why I'll never accept her version of it all, that I was guilty, she was innocent; that I used her, then I dropped her. Of course she helped me; while she could, when she could. The early times. Later on, it needed more than she could give me, like if you're really ill you go to a specialist, not a local G P. I don't blame her for that, but why should she hold it against *me*? Ethel's version is I left her for someone younger, someone prettier, someone I fancied more, someone I could boost my ego with, and all that's true, up to a point. What she could never stomach, and is just as true, is that June helped me when she couldn't. The sex bit hurt but she could take that because it made *me* look bad, just another middle-aged lecher, but the other was too much for her.

All those interviews she gave the papers.

*'If Johnny wants to play the fool off stage, that's his business. I feel sorry for him, but I feel sorrier for any woman who gets mixed up with him. She doesn't know what she's let herself in for. I've had fifteen years of Johnny and his insecurity, fifteen years of trying to be his Mummy, and now I'm going to enjoy myself.'*

Came down on me like vultures, they did, the bloody reporters; what had I got to say, what did I think of what she'd said?

'Nothing,' I told them. 'I'm happy, I'm glad *she's* happy.'

June also has been a mother figure, I think.

Fucking hell, Doc, she helped me, women are maternal, that needn't make them mother figures.

Certainly she helped you. You became dependent on her, also. But she seems to me more masculine than Ethel.

Maybe she was a father figure, then?

It is not impossible to be both.

Always got an answer, eh, Doc?

Maybe she wasn't that feminine, June, in some ways, but she was female; that was what I loved about her, that she'd got all the positive things and none of the faults. Sensual as hell, great body, lovely face, yet none of what usually goes with it; the moods, the tears, the reproaches, the demands.

'*We* don't make demands, it's men who won't accept responsibility.' Mary Smith.

'She's quite right. They're like greedy children, men are.' Mrs Casey.

'Rather a generalization, that,' the Colonel says.

'You'd be as bad if you weren't so repressed,' says Mrs Casey.

You can't win, not in group therapy. These were Ethel's

arguments, anyway. I'd heard them again and again when I was married to her; you stood here, she stood there, stuck forever in the same position like molten lava had rolled over you, where June had gone beyond them, so that you could, too. Doc Weiss' idea is that she was calling the tune, that she liked it because she had the power. 'Your drunkenness, your depressions and your helplessness were therefore acceptable. It is this that may even have made your relationship possible.'

When she came down again, we did fuck. In my room, quickly, much too quickly, because they don't leave a lot to chance when you've got visitors, nurses would just 'happen' to drop in to see if there was anything you wanted.

It was a bitter day, a sky like a shroud, tiny little snowflakes swirling about, fingers freezing if they weren't in gloves or in your pockets. She came driving down in the same crazy way, spraying gravel, cornering the drive like a race track, wearing a round fur hat, a short fur coat, a mini dress, and no stockings. That turned me on more than anything when I had her in my room, those bare legs, my hand on the flesh of her thigh, very white and so cold, roughened by the little hairs.

'*Care*ful!' she said. 'They're probably listening.'

Under the hat, above her jutting cheekbones, her eyes were glittering, full of sex.

'You look Russian,' I said, 'like a Russian cat.'

'A very cold cat,' she said.

I moved my hand between her thighs and started to play with her and she wriggled, giving herself up to it like a cat, again, exciting me more and more. 'Not *now*,' she said, 'not *here*!'

'*Here*!' I said, and stood up and kissed her, still keeping my hand there.

'Hadn't you better lock the door?'

I was so randy, it had been so long, that I didn't even wait to undress, I rolled her on to the bed, that lousy, creaking hospital bed that hadn't been built for such things, pulled down her pants and fucked her. Lovely round white thighs, still cold, lovely thick pubic hair, dark blonde, darker than the hair on her head. The fur hat coming off her head, her lovely face moving and moving on the pillow.

I came much too fast, and when I had she got off the bed very quickly where we'd always used to lie there afterwards beside each other saying how great it had been. '*Well!*' she said, pulling down her skirt, going to the mirror above the basin. 'You do take people unawares!'

'I'm sorry,' I said, though I'm not sure what I meant. Sorry I'd jumped on her, sorry I hadn't made her come, sorry for myself because I was afraid I might have lost her.

'*Sorry*,' she said, 'there's no need to be *sorry*,' and she turned round and smiled at me, which made me feel a little bit better. Because I was terrified of losing her. She was my last chance, my way back; if she didn't want me any more, if she didn't believe in me, where could I go? I suddenly wanted to ask her, 'Do you love me?' but I couldn't, partly because I was frightened of the answer, partly because you never asked June questions like that. Any sort of slop, any sort of sentiment, was out. Everything had to be brisk, clean, taken for granted. At the same time, I remembered how *I'd* felt when people asked me did I love them, Ethel especially, in bed beside me, moving close against me, 'Do you love me, Johnny?'

'Yes, yes,' I'd say. I couldn't look at her. Fuck off was what I really wanted to tell her. 'Of course I love you.' And I got a hint of what Dr Weiss was getting at; me asking her, when normally it should be her asking me, the woman the man. I felt ashamed of myself, I felt terribly weak, weaker than I'd felt when I got pissed and flopped about her bed, because then you were beyond it, you were too far gone to care. It was terrible to feel so ill, so helpless, and that was how I did feel with her being there in the room, so beautiful, so strong and successful, so well. How could she want me while I felt like this, whatever Doc Weiss said? She'd looked after me before because she believed in me; what was there to believe in now; I felt like crying. I'd cried a lot when we lived together, boozy tears, but this was different. It was worse. She'd despise me if I cried.

Being here, in the sanatorium, classified you; you were sick. Before, while you were out, you could always kid yourself, even in the nursing homes, the drying-out places. You weren't sick, you were just depressed, you had a drinking problem, you were going through a phase. But here, among the nuts, you were a nutter, and when someone came in from outside, it really hit you.

She started talking to me, very bright, about Ronnie Scott's club where she was singing now, with an American jazz group. I listened a bit, I took some of it in. There was a lot of stuff about who was on hash, who'd been busted by the police, how she'd been round to see some actress, and her boy-friend had been there in bed with her; 'She said, "What do you think of him? Isn't he gorgeous?" and there he was with these drooping bosoms and this terrible pot belly, just like a great, white slug.'

She didn't gossip like most girls did in show business; all the stories she told were very hard, very tough, almost cruel, and it came over particularly strong to me now; how would *I* stand up, I wondered, what would she say to *me*?

There was a knock at the door; one of the nurses, Eddie, and I let him in. 'Hallo!' he said to June, giving her a look. 'Anything you need?' he said to me.

'Nothing I can get here,' I said.

'Now, now!' he said. 'That's not nice, is it?'

When he'd gone, June sat down in the armchair and lit a cigarette. She always smoked Gauloises so I associated their smell with her like you do perfume with some women, and whenever I smelt it, it would always give a pang. 'Ethel came to see me,' she said.

'Ethel?' I said. I couldn't believe it. They'd been like cat and dog, although they'd never actually met. June had phoned up Ethel once and given her a right slagging off after one of her newspaper interviews where she'd said again that she was glad to be shot of me, that June had done her a favour, but that she needn't think when things began to go wrong she could unload me on *her* again. June asked her why she didn't just belt up; if she really believed all that, she wouldn't have to keep on saying it. I wasn't there to hear any of it, thank God, but Ethel said to her then, 'I'll tell them what you really are, which is a bloody whore,' to which June said whatever she was at least she didn't take any money off me, and so on.

'Stupid bitch,' June said, when she told me about it. ' "You're enjoying it," I told her. "All this publicity; you've never felt so important in your life."'

Now here was Ethel coming round to see her, and at once I got very agitated. What did she want, Ethel? What was going on? I felt so powerless here, so cut off from everybody, like a ghost making signs that nobody notices. 'What?' I said. 'What is it?' and my hands were shaking. 'Nobody's hurt? Nobody's dead?'

'No,' she said, 'everyone's *well.* How can I tell you anything while you're in *this* state?'

'Tell me *what*?' I shouted, I was in a right frenzy by now. I got up from the bed and stood over her. '*What?* You're fucking tormenting me!'

'Bob was picked up by the police,' she said, 'for being in possession of cannabis. Ethel bailed him out, but he's due to appear in court next Thursday.'

'The stupid young sod,' I said, and sat down on the bed again with my fingers over my face. She came across and put her hand on my shoulder. 'I wouldn't have told you,' she said, 'except she wants to come and see you. That's what she asked me to say.'

There were so many emotions going through me I was spinning like a windmill; anger and fear and love and guilt. At the same time I felt so bloody impotent; shut up here like this, what could I do? It was like being tied in a sack.

I started striding about the room because it was such murder to sit still. 'Where is he?' I said. 'I must speak to him. I must phone him.'

'He's still in Cornwall,' she said. 'You can't phone him. They don't have phones in hippy communes.'

'Fucking hippies,' I said. 'They did it to him. I must be there in court. I've got to speak for him. I'll talk to Dr Weiss.'

'*He* won't let you go,' she said. 'Besides, what could you say, even if they allowed you to speak?' and I knew she was right on both scores. Bob could be jumping out of the window of a burning house and it still wouldn't be real for Doc Weiss, not as real as what went on in his consulting-room. 'Why should you want to go?' he'd say. 'Let us discuss that.' And if I did go, if I did get a word in for Bob, what would I look like but the absentee father, the bloke that saw him once every five years? We've got a right one here, they'd say. Neglects the boy rotten, walks out on the mother, never gives him a stable home background, then comes down here doing the loving father bit.

'It's a first offence,' June said, 'he'll probably just be fined, and you could always pay *that*,' which brought Ethel back to me. ('Money! You think you can buy your way out of anything! Pay for this, pay for that, but never give anything that matters, anything that might hurt you.')

'Is *she* going down?' I asked.

'Oh, yes,' June said, 'she's going.'

'Have they got a good lawyer?'

'I think so.'

'I'll have to see her,' I said, 'I'll have to talk to her,' knowing that I dreaded seeing her, talking to her, after all these years, even assuming I'd be allowed to.

I remembered how he'd looked when he'd come to see me; how it had been like trying to walk to someone through a fog. 'You know he was here?' I said. 'I wish to God I'd talked to him about it then,' though I knew how useless it would have been. He'd gone where I couldn't reach him, influence him. We might make contact now and then, there might still be some love left on both sides, but he was out there on his own, like a boat in a storm, you could only watch from a distance as the waves rolled over it and pray each time that it would still be there.

'What'll happen to him?' I said. I hadn't meant to speak it aloud.

'It's only cannabis,' June said. 'They all use it, it's part of their scene.' Just as it was part of her scene, the jazz world, where everybody was on something or other, which had always put a barrier between them and me. For them, I was square, I never turned on, I only drank. As for June, she could take it or leave it, she never made a fetish of drugs like they did. Now and again she'd smoke pot in her flat, on her own or when some of the musicians came round, but she was always in control, which was more than you could say for me at that time.

Was it only cannabis that made Bob like he was that day, or was it something much worse? And if it wasn't yet, then would it be later?

'Cheer up!' June said. 'It's not a *real* crime, he hasn't killed anybody. They might just as well arrest people for being in possession of a bottle of whisky.'

I shook my head. You could still go inside for it, real or not. The terrible thing was I couldn't see him coming out of all this; so far as I could tell there was nothing he wanted to be, nothing he wanted to do, other than what he was; which was nothing. Maybe that was why he'd come to me the way he did, that was what he was trying to ask me, like a sort of appeal, in desperation, feeling himself being sucked under, hoping I could be the one who'd pull him out.

Pull him out! Who was going to pull *me* out? A great comedian with a message for the world who couldn't even get through to his own son. And yet I *had* made him laugh that day, just once or twice, and I felt that if I could only be with him for a while, get him laughing again, then that could be the way back for him, the way out of the drug scene, the hippy scene, back into life. We'd laugh together, and maybe I could get back, too.

'Tell her to come,' I said. 'Ethel.' So she did.

It wasn't easy to swing it.

At this stage of your analysis I certainly would not advise it. As for your friend June, she should first have talked to me.

And you'd have stopped her.

I would have found perhaps a less disturbing way to tell you.

She did it for the best, Doctor.

But hardly in the best way.

If I'd found out later on it had been kept from me, I'd have done my nut.

The meeting must be very short, and must be in my presence.

Have a heart, Doc.

So we compromised. He talked to Ethel first.

All these bloody phantoms. Popping up in my analysis, popping up in the flesh. There was lots of flesh on Ethel, now; double chin, plump legs, round body. Middle-aged, she was; she'd surrendered. My age, almost exactly; how did I look to *her*? She'd touched up her hair to a brighter blonde and it was obvious, pathetic. Very tired she looked; no life in her eyes. A lot of little lines around them, lines on her forehead. Did I feel middle-aged? Had I surrendered? God knows what age I felt; I'd been buffeted about so much in time, pulled back into the past, ten years, twenty years, thirty. I'd lost touch with time. And Christ knows I'd lost touch with her. She was a stranger. All this till death us do part crap. Who needed death?

She was wearing a navy blue coat and skirt, the kind of thing I'd never seen her in before, a white frilly blouse and a cameo brooch; she'd always gone for those. When she sat down, her knees looked the size of melons. Why deny it? I thought. When sex has gone between you, everything's gone.

'I'm sorry about all this,' she said, like she'd learned it off by heart.

'Can't be helped,' I said.

One thing she still carried round with her was this atmosphere of what you could only call reproach; she gave it off in waves, like a scent. It's *your* fault, she seemed to be saying, while she sat there. You paid him no heed, now look what's happened to him, and I felt myself getting angry, just like it always made me; one, because it was unfair, two, because it was so bloody useless.

Although she'd changed so much, although it had been so long, I found I could still pick up messages from her, and the one that was coming through was resentment: it's all right for you, when things go wrong and you can't take it any more, you run away and hide in a place like this. I can't hide, I have to stay out here in the open and try to cope. Which again was unfair, because what pressures had she had to put up with, compared to all mine? She could say what she liked; things hadn't been too bad for her once I'd started making it; houses and cars and clothes and servants. It was easy to despise them once you'd got them. I remembered what Bob said; that she'd been worried. Worried about where the next bloody bob was coming from, most likely. And now she'd seen me, now I wasn't actually in a padded cell or foaming at the mouth, where was all the sympathy?

So it went on, this silent conversation, while outwardly we hardly talked at all. I hoped she wouldn't cry because I'd only be disgusted, then I'd feel ashamed of myself.

'You know he could get three years,' she said, and that really frightened me.

'Three years?' I said. 'How could he get three years? A first offence! Who told you that?'

Now all her misery and her anxiousness came swelling up, so that she forgot about resenting me. 'The solicitor said he could,' she said. 'The police say he had two pounds of cannabis.'

'Probably planted it on him if I know them, the bastards, which I do,' I said. 'Who've you got defending him? Have you got a Q C? It's only a little noddy court down there. If they sentence him, he's got to appeal.'

'He's not a Q C,' she said, 'but the solicitor says he's very good. I met him. He's very young and sympathetic.'

'Young!' I said. 'They need someone experienced! That's why I want a Q C!' and again I had that feeling of being in a cage, of things happening all around me that I couldn't control. I was going nearly crazy with frustration. How could I leave everything to *her*? I wanted to get to a telephone and talk to people. 'Look,' I told her, 'money's no bloody object.'

'It never has been, has it?' she said, the silly, sour bitch, but I made myself be calm, it was Bob I was concerned with, not her and her little jabs; the present, not the past. The walking, breathing past, she was.

'It's not too late to change,' I said, 'not even now. Who are the solicitors? I must get on to them.'

She told me who they were, as if it made no difference. 'Bob just doesn't care,' she said, 'he's completely fatalistic,' and I was afraid she was going to cry again. 'He says if he goes to prison, then he goes to prison. "If I can't get pot," he said, "I'll meditate,"' and then we were both quiet, both left with nothing to say and too much to think. She couldn't reach him, that was obvious, I couldn't reach him, and if we neither of us could reach him, how could we save him; especially when he didn't want to be.

At one time she *would* have cried, it was the logical next step, she'd have put her head on my shoulder and I'd have tried to comfort her, but all that had gone. We'd no more comfort for each other. The only thing left between her and me was this kid who'd turned his back on both of us. She could blame me for it as much as she liked; she was still no closer to him than what I was.

'We can't let that happen to him,' I said, 'he doesn't know what he's bloody talking about. He doesn't know what prison *is*. If he'd grown up where I did, he'd have heard enough about it not to be so airy-fairy.'

'But he didn't, did he?' she cried. 'He grew up with all the things *we* never had.'

'Like drugs,' I said, 'we never had drugs.'

'Do you think if it hadn't been that,' she said, 'it wouldn't have been something else?'

It was the old game with a new twist. She was still blaming me, but she wasn't so sure of her ground any more, because she knew she couldn't get to him either. Not only that, but he'd come to see me, hadn't he, come of his own free will whatever he'd said about coming for both of them; even if when he did come I couldn't do anything for him. It must have killed her, that, his having any love left for me.

'Look,' I said, 'for Christ's sake let's have a truce, shall we? We're trying to help him, that's the only thing that matters.'

'Of course,' she said. Then she did start to cry, this middle-aged fat woman, the tears oozing out of her eyes and running slowly down her fat cheeks. When I'd first seen her cry, when I'd known her first, it used to tear me to pieces, I'd do anything to make her stop, she looked so pitiful, like a little child, like a beautiful child. This, now, was like some terrible caricature. All I could do was watch her and hope to God she'd stop, when suddenly she put out her hand, not looking at me, just held it out, like she might be sticking it out of the window of a car, and the last thing I wanted to do was take that hand, it made me angry with her. It had gone, all that, what was she up to? But she wouldn't put it down and I couldn't just ignore it, so in the end I did take it, and as soon as she felt my hand on hers, she grabbed it like the jaws of a trap. My one reaction was to tug myself free, what the hell did she want from me, but I fought it down, I tried to imagine that the hand wasn't mine, it just happened to be there at the end of my arm, and hoped that she'd soon get tired of it.

Which she did, suddenly she dropped my hand as if it was something she'd picked up by mistake; she sniffed, turned away from me, took a little handkerchief out of her handbag, and blew her nose. 'I'm sorry about that,' she said. 'After all, I did promise your doctor. I know how important it is that you shouldn't be disturbed.'

What did she want, for the love of God, a reconciliation? The bitch. She'd never been fair to me.

Not wanting to disturb me; that was a good one! When she left I felt like I was on the rack; pulled here, pulled there, pulled everywhere. I lay on the bed wanting to scream, though if I did scream, I knew just what would happen; patter of heavy feet along the corridor, male nurses, tranquillizer, sedatives, good-night.

The only thing to do was walk out; put on a coat and go. I'd got a few quid, enough to get me to June's. There was no use telling Dr Weiss, who'd only turn it into the same old game. Why should I feel responsible? What was I going to achieve? Round and round we'd go, never making sense to one another, him talking his language, me talking mine. I could hear him now: 'To do such a thing would have the most serious effect on your recovery.' And then I heard Ethel: 'It's *very* important that you shouldn't be disturbed.' She was a cow, but I knew what she meant, I could put myself in her position; in a way, I was even in it now. Someone's drowning, but I mustn't pull him out; it might affect my treatment. Someone's been run over, but I mustn't go to help; what about my recovery? How big a price must you pay for a recovery, and when did it get too high to be worth paying?

I'd decided, then; I'd go. I'd tell them I was going for a walk, slip out after tea, when no one would be looking for me, and away up the drive. Once I was off the grounds, they couldn't touch me, could they? Tomorrow I'd see the lawyers, by Thursday I'd be down in Cornwall.

Thinking of it, I began to shake, my stomach started throbbing, just like it would before a big first night; sweat broke out in my armpits and started running down my sides.

We had tea in the lounge downstairs, a big room with french windows that looked out over the lawn, chintz-covered chairs and sofas, very, very restful, nice pictures of cows and landscapes that wouldn't give you any ideas, and a piano in the corner where a little brown wizened old woman with dyed black hair in a bun would sit and play *The Merry Peasant* like they'd put her on piecework, her therapy, thank God she wasn't there now.

I sat in another corner with the Colonel, who seemed even quieter than usual, though I didn't take a lot of notice, wanting to be quiet myself, being so keyed up. When I picked up my cup of tea, silly little shallow cups they gave you, it rattled in the saucer like a pea in a whistle. When I picked it up again, I took it in both hands. There were these soppy little sandwiches they used to give you, brown bread and cucumber, that day. I tried to eat one and I nearly choked, the last thing I wanted, drawing attention to myself like that, the whole room frozen, teacups turned to stone, conversations killed, everyone just watching me.

'Are you all right?' the Colonel asked, like I'd been wounded. I tried to tell him yes and started choking again. When I'd recovered, I had to sit around for twice the time I'd meant to knowing they'd been watching me, and that added to the strain, I was sweating all over, I was dreading one of the doctors would come past or maybe one of the nurses and ask me what was wrong. But they didn't, and when enough people had started to get up and leave, I left, too, though the Colonel went on sitting there, still as a waxwork. I couldn't give him more than a nod the way I felt, the way things were, which rather choked me because I might never see him again, but he didn't respond, he didn't notice.

I'd left my overcoat, the sheepskin, on the stand in the hallway. No case; that would have been a giveaway. Mary Smith had to be out there: 'Going for another of your constitutionals?'

'Yes,' I said, and just brushed by her, closing my ears to whatever bloody stupid thing she said as I went through the door, I didn't want to be upset.

I stood at the bottom of the stone stairs, shaking, though it wasn't that cold. It was twilight, a bad time, I always thought, when things like trees could go grotesque and bushes threatened you. I'd meant to walk out into the grounds, across the lawn, away from the drive, then gradually go back, but I changed my mind, I wasn't calm enough. I went straight up the drive towards the entrance, the stone gate posts, freedom, real life, or whatever the hell lay out there. I hadn't got halfway up the drive, though, when I stopped. My strength just seemed to have gone, and yet I had plenty of strength, I went for long walks every day, didn't I? But my heart was booming away, I was sweating worse than ever, my legs were like paper, and in the end I had to sit down. I felt terrible about it, I felt disgusted with myself. I got to my feet after a few minutes and I tried again, but it was still no dice. I'd had it.

Again I sat down, and this time I cried, what use was I to anybody, what use was I to my own son? I sat there long after I'd stopped crying, I sat there feeling chilled right through, not caring if I got pneumonia, not caring if I fucking died. A car went past once, down the drive, somebody arriving, no one I bloody knew; I hoped they wouldn't see me and stop, but they didn't, they went crunching on over the gravel.

Eventually I managed to get up and I walked back, despising myself with every step I took; every step was a sell-out, it was a step away from Bob.

When I was upstairs and lying on my bed I thought, what bloody good would I have been if I had gone? I'd have made things worse. I'd have screwed things up even more. It was my one excuse, and it was a lousy excuse. I couldn't help him because I was crap, because I'd lost my nerve. For the first time ever, through all the depression, all the drinking, all the disappointments, I really thought of doing away with myself. What use was I to anyone if I wasn't any bloody use to my own son? If I hadn't got bottle enough for that, the way I was, then where would I find it to get up in front of an audience again? If I'd had a tube of sleeping-pills beside me, then, that would have been it; I'd have shaken out a handful of them and swallowed them, no problem, the easy way to go. I thought of slashing my wrists with a razor blade, but I couldn't find the guts for that, either; it sickened me, the idea of that. Bob would come up in court and I wouldn't be there. They'd maybe send him down, and he probably wouldn't appeal. I started thinking of him in a cell, cooped up with a couple of right hard cases, the place smelling of shit; it was too much to take.

I rang the bell. I wanted a sleeping pill, I wanted a tranquillizer. Anything to fucking well obliterate me.

But it wasn't me that tried to kill himself; it was the Colonel. Of all people. The last one you'd ever think of; I'd have reckoned he'd call it cowardice in the face of the enemy. Very brave man, the Colonel, won medals and that, M C, D S O, saw it once on a list here in Doc Weiss' office; though he never talks about it, another thing I admire, when you come from a profession where they spend their whole lives talking about themselves, shouting to make themselves heard, to keep their spirits up; I did this, I did that.

In group therapy, he wasn't there. Next day, that was, next morning. 'Where's the old Colonel?' I asked. 'Not like him. Absent on parade.' I *felt* something wrong. I looked at the Welsh Twit's face, even more bloody miserable than usual, I remembered how the Colonel had seemed the day before, at tea, and I had to ask, I had to hear. 'What's wrong with him?' I said. 'Where is he?'

'He's all right, he's all right,' the Welsh Twit said, which meant he wasn't, though it meant he was alive, and suddenly we were all hammering at him, me, Mary, Ivan, even the old bank manager, come on, tell us, what's happened to him, while he went on saying, 'He's all right,' like some bloody talking doll. You could tell how much the Colonel had meant to everybody, how much they'd respected him, even when he'd said so little, even people like Tight-Arse, who you'd never think would care about anybody but themselves. In the end the Welsh Twit couldn't keep it up, he had to tell us. 'The Colonel is quite comfortable now,' he said, 'but I'm afraid that last night he tried to end his life.'

It just fell on us, that. It stunned everybody, and perhaps me more than anyone. Then Mary Smith began to cry, very loud, great noisy sobs, and Mrs Casey started to cry too, not so loud, and I admit I felt tears coming up into my own eyes, I had to take hold of myself, it was terrible, and it was terrible for two reasons. First, because of the Colonel himself, such a fabulous old fellow, second because if the Colonel tried it, him so decent and disciplined, what chance had all the rest of us? Plus my own situation of having wanted to do it myself, while all the time the poor old sod was actually going ahead.

So that's what it had done for him, group therapy; all the shit about breaking down his inhibitions, showing him his complexes, helping him to free himself, whatever that meant. I suddenly found myself getting very angry. The Welsh Twit: what had *he* ever faced? Bullets, like the Colonel? A stiff neck if he slept in a draught was about it. It was the old jealousy at work again, for someone who'd gone out in the world and done something, who'd been a bloody hero, not just a ponce in a white coat who spent his time indoors on his arse, living other people's lives.

And suddenly it was too much for me and I turned on the Welsh Twit. 'Why didn't you leave him alone?' I said. 'Why didn't you *all* fucking well leave him alone? Pushing and prodding at him. He's twice as good as any of you. He's a bloody gentleman for a start.'

'Like you, I suppose,' said Tight-Arse.

'No,' I said, 'not at all like me. Dead common, I am. But I know a gentleman when I see one. A real one; not just some twot who's got money or a title. And don't you start,' I said to Mary Smith, who was opening her big mouth. 'You were one of the worst. You loved having a go at him,' which set her off crying even louder than before. The Welsh Twit tried to soothe it down like he always did, but this time he couldn't, because he was in it up to the neck himself, he was the worst bloody offender of the lot. We were all shouting and crying and yelling at each other, till in the end Mary Smith got up, went out and banged the door. That stopped people for a moment.

'I don't think there's much point going on while you're in this condition,' the Welsh Twit said, in his most pompous bloody way, trying all he knew to get back in the driver's seat. Then Ivan asked in a very quiet voice, 'How did he do it, Doctor?' and it made me realize again what a shower we were; instead of finding out how he was, exactly what he'd done to himself, all we'd been doing was having a go at one another.

'I don't think that really matters,' said the Welsh Twit.

'Yes, it does fucking matter,' I said. 'What's all this secrecy about? We're not kids. We care about him. We want to know.'

'I'm afraid he slashed his wrists,' the Welsh Twit said. 'He was found in time. He's quite comfortable.'

'Can we see him?' I asked.

'Not yet, not yet.'

Though I realized, as soon as I thought about it, that he wouldn't want to be seen. He'd felt ashamed, the poor old bastard. One thing was dead certain; we'd never see him in group therapy again, which as far as I was concerned meant fuck group therapy, because I could imagine what would happen. We'd sit around discussing *why* we'd reacted like we did, how we really felt about him, what he really signified to us, which to me would mean taking away his dignity worse than ever we'd done when people got on to him about his problems, anal this and inhibited bloody that.

When we left the room, the others all stayed together talking, but I wanted to be on my own and I walked off out of the house, not bothering about a coat, although it was cold with a rain that blew into your face like needles.

I suddenly remembered what he'd said to me once, the old boy, when we were out here, strolling around. 'It must take quite a lot of courage to stand up there in front of an audience time after time, and try to make them laugh.'

What an irony! I hadn't thought about it at the time. Him, who'd been bombed and shelled and shot at, faced the lot, talking about the courage just to face an audience, where the worst that can happen to you is you don't get laughs, because they don't even throw things, not nowadays. We talk about dying, but we still get off stage alive. Bullets; they can really kill you.

At the same time, in a funny way, recalling this cheered me up; it made me feel that maybe I wasn't as chicken as I'd thought last night; or at least that once upon a time I hadn't been. If *he* thought I had courage, a bloke that had won medals, then maybe I did; and maybe, please God, I could find it again.

I started walking very quickly, I suppose I was muttering to myself; a couple of patients I went past, both dressed up like explorers, looked at me like I was mad; but so were they. I can do it again, I was telling myself, I can do it again.

There was something else I would never have admitted to myself then, but I realize it now. The Colonel's trying to kill himself had somehow got me off the hook. It was the other side of what we'd all been thinking in group therapy. If he'd tried to kill himself, a hero, then I was entitled to think about it, too. It was this place that did it to you, the treatment, the loneliness, the being cut off from everything. He'd felt like I had; hopeless. It could happen to anybody, and whatever the reasons may have been, he'd tried it, I hadn't. It didn't make me braver than him, that was ridiculous, but at the same time it didn't make me any worse.

I got ever so excited; again, I wanted to go in and see him, talk to him, tell him I understood and try to thank him, though I knew they'd never let me and, like I've said before, I knew it would only sicken him. But I wanted to tell him, 'Look, Colonel, at least you had the guts to try, while I was just lying there and thinking about it, never had the bottle.'

Remembering what he'd said to me that time led me on to thinking about things I *had* had the courage to do, cheering myself up; the moral courage, anyway, because there'd never been a worse soldier than what I was, never learned to slope arms properly, let alone hit the target. But like him, I'd had courage once, so why not again?

It wasn't just standing on a stage that had taken courage, either; it was the challenges, the changes, never knowing what was waiting for you, because there'd never been a time like ours for comedians, our whole world changing in a few years, everything you'd taken for granted suddenly turned upside down. No wonder so many cracked up, no wonder so many couldn't take it, seeing the ground cut away from under them like that, stars one day, finished the next, and even those that did come through, people that were lucky like myself, knowing things would never be as easy again, that we'd never have the same freedom, the same ... not peace, you could never call it that, but let's say elbow-room.

We all know about the old comedians, the music-hall comics, got away with the same handful of routines for years, putting in a week here, a week there. What a wonderful life! Didn't have to beat their brains out, always chasing something new, didn't have to keep relying on writers, or if they did, it would only be now and then, just for the few acts they did. Harry Lauder, Dan Leno, George Robey, Harry Tate, Harry Champion, all those. And of course they loved them for it, audiences. People *wanted* what they knew. Maybe it reassured them or something. Even as late as Sid Field, everyone wanted the golfing scene. Radio made a bit of difference, you were playing to a huge audience instead of just as many as could fill a hall, but even there you could still get away with the same basic themes; Will Hay and his schoolmaster act, Al Read and his Manchester sketches.

Then wallop, television! Like a great, big open mouth that gulped down everything, the biggest mouth in the world, swallowing your gags, swallowing your routines, taking everything and giving you back nothing; except money. We didn't know we were born till television came. I'm not saying comics hadn't always been morose bastards, hadn't always been worriers, but this was like getting off a bicycle and taking a jet plane. The whole business had gone crazy, it was moving so fast you could hardly keep up with it, no matter how good you were, and you would never, never get ahead of it.

Because it wasn't like radio, the television; it was no good thinking you could just turn your back on it and shelter in your backwater; at least not until the working men's clubs got going, in the North, and that wasn't for a while. As television grew, variety died, Bang, bang, bang, they started going out, the halls; first it was the little ones that didn't matter so much, at least to people like me, houses in the outer suburbs or the smaller provincial theatres, but all of a sudden it was happening in places you'd taken for granted, houses in London you'd reckoned you'd be playing till you packed it in; Collins' Music Hall in Islington, Shepherd's Bush Empire, Finsbury Park Empire, even, in the sixties, the Golder's Green Hippodrome; if you appeared in these places at all now, it was because the B B C had taken them over as television theatres.

It was like a man climbing a mountain, with a bear up his arse. Suddenly he comes to a chasm, a bloody great abyss. He can't go back, he's got to jump it, and if he doesn't get across, that's it. Thank God I did get across and once I was across, it was like jumping into Paradise; at first. What was I worried about, you wondered. You were bigger than you'd ever been, richer than you'd ever been, much better known. But you weren't to know it would turn out like that; not everyone had got over. You could call it a leap in the dark, you couldn't be sure what was on the other side, all you knew was you just had to make it across. But then, after you'd succeeded and it all looked so good, it began to dawn on you that there were drawbacks, too, that maybe what you'd got into was more like an open prison than a Garden of Eden, very comfortable, very lush, but still with high walls, barbed wire and warders. What's more, the walls were closing in, very, very slow, maybe just a little every year, but it was happening. Do what the people wanted and it was all great; you could even do what *you* wanted if it was what they wanted. But if it wasn't, then watch out. And if you'd been fighting all through your career to do what *you* wanted, then it was harder still.

That's how all the little nobodies came up, all the little pimps and ponces who'd never have lasted five minutes in the old days, on the halls. People would say, 'How do they get on, little no-talent bums like that' and I'd say 'What do you mean? It's *because* they've no talent, it's because they're nonentities. They're disposable, like plastic cups; the system created them and the system throws them away.'

Now and again, in places round the West End, fish bars and that, I'd find myself surrounded by them, and I'd feel like one of those old sharks with all the little pilot fish around. Like I've said, I've never been too happy sitting about with a lot of other comedians, all trying to upstage the others. I even did a radio sketch once about a home for old comedians; still going on in their wheel chairs about the things they'd done, and all dying off in them, one by one, laughing themselves to death at their own jokes.

But at least the old lot had a bit of substance to them, at least they'd been through the mill, they were proper pros, even if they might be egomaniacs as well. This new lot were anonymous, they even looked like one another, all young, all trendy, nearly all dressed by the same tailor in whatever way was 'in'. Suits with narrow trousers when they were fashionable, cravats when they came in, safari jackets when they came in, long hair when *it* came in. They wore their clothes like uniforms, terrified to be a minute out of date, where the old lot didn't give a shit. They dressed like they wanted to, and you could take them or leave them.

These others, though, you felt they were a sort of Mafia, they kept together in a way the old comedians never had, armed truces it used to be with their lot, but you felt this was an unhealthy way, it grew out of fear and ambition, always in one another's pockets, always in and out of one another's flats and houses, playing for these silly Showbiz football teams because that was part of it, that might help them, too, and rabbiting on and on about it, like it was real. So I was out of place among them, as well. I hadn't joined in with the old gang, I didn't join in with this lot, but I'd rather not have joined in with the old lot, if you see what I mean.

The new ones came from the same sort of backgrounds as comedians always had, from the working class from Scotland and the North, a lot of them, but they came too quickly, before they'd developed a real personality, and once they'd arrived, which was usually overnight with the slow ones, they set about knocking off the rough edges, rounding off the corners, till they all seemed the same. I know I've said you can overdo the local thing, that real comedians should be universal, but that's not the same as deliberately tearing up your roots.

Again, perhaps you couldn't really blame them: it was what television wanted. Style their hair, dress them up in a hundred-guinea suit and a frilled shirt, spend twenty thousand pounds on the production, give them a hand mike and a big hand, and they were away. Anyone would be away. They'd got a captive audience that paid nothing. Turn the switch, change channels, and all you got was the same kind of crap on the other side. Talk about fucking evolution. For years there'd been people around like myself, people like Frankie Howerd, people like Tony Hancock and Ken Dodd, all done well on television I admit, trying to develop our comedy, push it forward, do something original, and along come these little nig-nogs pushing it back thirty years, with routines I'd have been ashamed of in the Fairleigh Follies.

It seemed to me that the bigger the technical advance, the worse the bloody product, which was *their* word, the going word: product. Something you put into the machine, because it had to show something. I remember getting pissed one night in a West End night club with another comedian, a bloke a few years older than myself, from up in the North. '*They* don't want us, Johnny,' he said. 'They don't fucking *need* us. I'll tell you; in twenty years' time, they'll be doing it with bloody robots.'

Which was why I had to get out of the sanatorium; to fight all this. It was my nightmare, the form my crack-up had taken, that I was a computer, a robot myself, which was what they wanted me to be.

It didn't start like that, not at first. Oh, no, you were doing them a favour then. Please, Mr Lucas, thank you, Mr Lucas. Terribly kind of you to appear on television, Mr Lucas. Talk about selling your soul to the fucking devil. Later on, any little ponce of a comedy director in charge of an arsehole series gave himself airs like he was Cecil B. De Mille. Why not? If he didn't get you, he could get someone else. It would still go out on the box, and if it went on the box people would watch it, because they were too bloody stupid and idle to switch off and do something else.

My first television show. *The Johnny Lucas Show.* Very original that. Always original, television. 1956, that must have been; B B C. The other lot had just started. I'd done the odd appearance, mostly in phoney cabaret things where you wouldn't really know the difference if it wasn't for the lights blinding you and making your make-up run, the cameras spying on you here and there, the cables lying across the stage like boa-constrictors.

I had to have a writer for *The Johnny Lucas Show*; no arguing with that, it was part of it. Television shows: writers. Even more than with radio shows. They gave me a glum little Northern bloke from Blackburn or somewhere whose suits smelt of sweat and who'd say, 'I've done this sketch with you coming on as a Pearly King, it's very visual,' and I'd say, 'Do me a favour, son. You're sure you don't want me to come on as the fucking Tower of London?'

In the end we compromised. I let him write the sketches, which I could ad lib a bit anyway, and I did my own patter.

'Television?' I said on the show. '*Television?* Well, yes, I've *heard* about it,' I said. 'That's wide-screen cinema for poor pygmies.'

But soon the cinemas would start closing, too.

I wouldn't say I enjoyed it, that show. I wouldn't say I've ever really enjoyed television. To that extent, it's been like radio; I've enjoyed what I've got out of it, though seeing yourself on the box is even worse than hearing yourself on the wireless. In the very early days, that didn't happen, the shows went out live, but as time went on, everything was 'taped'. It was part of the whole process; *they* were in charge, not you, and if you stepped out of line, did anything they didn't like, out came the scissors and snip!

Watching yourself. You got used to it in time, you grew immune. At first it's a funny mixture of feelings; you're embarrassed and you're chuffed and you're worried. It's flattering, it's a giggle; at the same time, you feel very naked and helpless.

They're watching you round their sets, all over the country, and it's too late to change anything. How do I get away with it, you wonder, a big ugly bastard like me, great hooter, pulling faces that would turn milk sour, arms waving like windmills. Still, they were laughing – very innocent days, those, no canned laughter – so I couldn't be as bad as I looked.

Later, when you were used to it, you just watched everything with a dead professional eye, your delivery, your accents, your timing.

*But above all it is timing that makes Johnny Lucas the comedian he is; the timing that allows Jack Benny to say more with a shrug than a lesser man could say with a soliloquy, which enables Bob Hope to turn the dross of a machine made script into the gold of pure humour, which let W.C. Fields work wonders with a monosyllable.*

They're always on about timing, critics, it's a word they've got hold of and they won't let it go, like knowing about car engines and hanging on to 'carburettor'. In fact that's a fair comparison, because if you haven't got a carburettor you're liable not to have much of an engine, and if you haven't got timing, you're not going to be much of a comedian. I mean, if you're going to run, you might as well have legs.

Interviewers kept asking me about timing too, were you born with it or did you develop it, and the answer, naturally, was, both. Without it you'd never be funny in the first place. After all, if it was only their material that made comedians, they could pull anyone in off the street to deliver it; which I must say was beginning to happen. On the other hand, as you went on, your timing obviously got better, it was like anything else. A cricketer got better, a chef got better, a juggler got better. Either they'd got it or they hadn't, but after that, it was experience, the feel of things. The trouble with the new lot of comics was not only hadn't they got it, but they didn't have the experience, either.

The other thing about television, the worst thing, was you lost your privacy. It was like one of those fables, Midas and the Golden Touch; what you'd wished for all your life you get, then you wished you'd never got it. Fame; that was what you were after. People looking at you in the streets nudging one another and saying, 'That's him,' asking you for your autograph. I'd had a little taste of it early, when I was up in Fairleigh, but there it was a touch double edged, you knew you were only a big fish in a small pond, it might never happen again. Still I admit that when I got to London I missed it a bit, walking around and being nobody again.

When I'd made it in radio, made it at the Palladium, that was just about right. You *would* get recognized, but not that often, especially outside London. Name in gold on the back of a chair in Isow's; even old Lou didn't have that. Headwaiters looking after you at The Caprice, the White Tower, and that. Good table in any night club you went to. Your life was still your own, though. Then television, and it wasn't; you might as well be living in an aquarium. Not only did everybody recognize you, all the millions that were watching your show, but worse than that, something you never got before, they reckoned they knew you.

'*Hallo*, Johnny!' they'd say, and they'd get quite narked when you looked blank at them. *They* knew who *you* were; how come you didn't know them? It was another way in which you lost your identity. On one side of you the system, the machines, the blokes with even bigger cigars than Lou Gold, the big-headed directors, all trying to manipulate you; on the other side the public, that reckoned it owned you.

One or two comics I knew, blokes of the old school, would treat them like shit. 'Look,' they'd say, 'I'm very sorry, I don't know you, I've never set eyes on you, now do you mind, I'm having my lunch,' but I couldn't do that, though I knew one of them was quite right when he said to me, 'In the old days maybe you had to put up with it, but not now, not when there's millions of them. If you tell one to fuck off, how long's it going to take him to get round all the others?'

It got so you couldn't use buses or tubes any more, even if you wanted to; you'd need a disguise. It wasn't even as if there was anything flattering about it, because it happened to everyone that went on the box if they appeared often enough, even to the little nig-nogs, just as much as to me or Ken Dodd or Frankie Howerd. It was indiscriminate, and so it was an insult. Why did I despise them, the audiences, Doc Weiss would ask. Well, *that* was why I despised them, because they'd got no fucking standards, because they were pig-ignorant, because they'd lap up anything they saw on that screen, good, bad, or indifferent.

You could tell it from the studio audiences, which was *them* again, the other side of the set for a change, mostly just viewers who wrote in and got a free ticket. They laughed at anything. They were *there* to laugh. To me, they weren't audiences, they were a lot of bloody whores, and that's how the studio managers treated them, telling them when to laugh, telling them when to applaud, holding up cards in front of them. Who needed canned laughter? You could have come on and showed them your arse, and they'd still have laughed. I know I've complained a lot about audiences, audiences that would give you nothing, audiences that sat on their hands, but in a way that was part of it all, you looked forward to the duel, and every time you won it, every time you had them laughing, you felt you'd achieved something. Going back to what I've said, it was the difference between a seduction and paying for it, though of course nobody had paid them, not directly. They were paid by being there, by feeling part of it, it was *their* laughter all those millions of people were hearing! To go back to this, especially now I'd had time to think about it so much, time to bring out what I'd been feeling all the while, that was a really terrible prospect.

But you have despised your audiences long before the television.

Not despised them. Sometimes hated them.

Because they did not laugh.

That's right.

But while you hated them for their hostility, you also despised them for their stupidity.

If they laughed at me I loved them, though, didn't I? I still despised the telly lot, whether they laughed or whether they didn't.

What you are saying seems to me that you were prepared to tolerate your audiences only when you could control them.

We're back again to calling me a phoney, are we?

I cannot see the distinction between the television audiences and the others, except that television is much greater.

A theatre audience pays. A night-club audience pays. A telly audience sits at home and turns the switch.

Yet it may still contain the paying people.

It contains the whole damn world.

And is your message not for the world?

Yes, but collectively.

Hierarchically?

Collectively.

When I look back at the first time I topped the bill at the Palladium, it's almost like looking back at the Garden of Eden. Whatever may have been wrong with it, it was nothing compared to what was coming.

Great I was, that time, at the Palladium, even though I say it myself. I don't think I've honestly ever been any better; something I can admit now I'm floating up here in outer space, though when you're working you don't like to think that; that your best performance is behind you. What I prefer to think is that this was when it all came together; not only was *I* good but the opportunity was there, I could come on and do what I wanted.

Well, nearly what I wanted. In some ways you can get away with a lot more now than you could then, the kind of jokes, the language, but in another way it's an illusion, because the scope's narrower than it used to be, the control's much tighter. Within the limits, you can say things you never could have said in the fifties; sex jokes, queer jokes, but it's like being shut in between two walls; you can jump as high as you like, but you can only move a few feet either way.

Fifty minutes I was on at the Palladium, including the quick changes, which is a long time when you've got no one with you. Even Bob Hope had Jerry Desmonde, like Sid Field did, but I was on my own, bar a bit of rabbiting with the conductor of the orchestra. At first it worried me a little, but once I got into it I loved it, there was room to spread yourself, this great feeling that the whole stage was yours, the whole theatre was yours, the plush seats, the spotlights, the gilding, the fancy boxes, the lot. I did plenty of patter, which I loved, told jokes, ad-libbed a fair bit, sang a song or two, if you could call it singing, and did some sketches, characters I'd invented, like the old sergeant-major, except he was dead and gone now, he belonged to the past.

Maurice Franks was the scriptwriter, but again we worked on it together. I was using him more and more to play off of; he'd put up an idea, he'd suggest a gag, and I'd work on it and make it better. Or *I'd* suggest something, he'd say it couldn't be done, and I'd show him that it could.

'Suez,' I'd say, 'we ought to do something about Suez.' It was just after they'd invaded Suez, the Canal and all.

'Can't do that,' he said. 'People are very, very touchy.'

'Then you do it indirectly,' I said. 'How about a song? "I've Been On A Cruise To Suez". Old boy who gets on a liner that's going up the Canal, then can't understand why everybody's shooting at him.'

We worked the lyrics out together, got the music put to it, and it went tremendous. People were so choked about all that had happened, whether they were for it or against it, and they jumped at the chance of a laugh. I kind of talked it rather than sang it, putting on an old buffer voice. The end of it was the boat got stuck there, it was the longest holiday the poor old sod had ever had; the French pilots had packed up and the wogs didn't know how to get it through, which was just what had happened.

> 'They can't find the way, so I'm going to stay.
> 'I'm hoping to be here for years.'

Nowadays I suppose they'd call that racialistic, but it fitted in with how people felt then, and as far as I was concerned, I was sending them both up; not just the wogs but the old boy as well. You had to, you had to be impartial, making both sides out ridiculous. It was the same with politics. Most comedians make the odd gag about politicians, some of them imitate them, but apart from a few of the Yanks, Lenny Bruce and those, they don't really *care* about politicians, it's not their business to care, that's for the satirists. To me, comedians should be above politics but beneath them, at the same time. Humour's more permanent than politics, and anyway, politics themselves have always been the same, politicians are always cunts. If you work with that in mind, you can't go far wrong.

I used a few props for the acts, put on a floppy straw hat and a moustache as the old boy in the Suez sketch, came on once in drag with a red wig and sang a song called 'All Change For Stockholm' about having been there to have the sex operation, but what I originally came on in was a single-breasted, midnight blue suit I'd had made for me by my tailor, cream-coloured shirt, dark blue tie. I was taking a leaf out of Bob Hope and Jack Benny's book; what you came on in was yourself, never mind what you did later in the act. If you were Max Miller, okay, you wore the multi-coloured suits this girl used to make for him in Brighton, if you were Bud Flanagan you wore the moth-eaten straw hat and the fur coat, but I was finished with the London bit. If I wanted to do a Cockney act, all I had to do was play up the accent.

I didn't run on to the stage this time, just walked on quick, though the music they played for me was 'When You're Smiling' again, which was a bit of a superstition. Blimey, what confidence I had then! I could do with it now, and all. The confidence that came from getting laughs, laugh after laugh, night after night, every little thing coming off, so that you'd take risks, you'd do more and more off the cuff. 'Is that a cigar,' I'd ask a bloke in the front row, 'or are you trying to torpedo me?' First off they booked me for two weeks, then they extended it to four, then to six, and finally to eight. I was walking on air. I bought myself a new Jag, bought Ethel a Mini, flogged the house in Highgate, bought the one in Hampstead Garden Suburb.

They were all coming to see me, the critics, the people in the business, asking me to do things, writing about me, even the posh blokes that I couldn't make head nor tail of.

*To understand Johnny Lucas it is necessary to understand London; not the hybrid, heterogeneous city of today but the London of Marie Lloyd and Charlie Chaplin, of Vesta Tilly and Bud Flanagan, even Noël Coward; there is a lot of Coward in Lucas' Suez song. This is a comedian who routs respectability with a diphthong, destroys decorum with a glottal stop. His effects are as calculated as a Pavlova pirouette, his vulgarity as natural as the North wind. With one sardonic lift of the eyebrow, he puts hypocrisy to flight and beckons you into his own world of Bacchanalian irreverence, where ripeness is all, and a beer in the hand is worth any number of slices of pie in the sky.*

I reckoned I could conquer the world, then; I was going to do it all, like Bob Hope; films, America, the lot. It was always just about to happen, the States, I always seemed to be going out to lunch then at the Savoy and places with these blokes in bow ties and horn-rimmed glasses and crew cuts with cigars, who told me how God damn great I was and how they knew I'd make it big over there. It was just a matter of the timing; it had to be right, the timing. I'd agree with them, though I'd no idea what they bloody meant; to me, the time was right away. I was ready for Broadway, I was ready for Las Vegas; I was ready for wherever they put me.

'Beautiful,' they'd say, leaning over the table and looking into your eyes, 'beautiful. The way you handled that audience. The way you put that song across. The way you conceived that character. You're a real comedian, Johnny, and you know why? Because you're funny on your own. You stand up there, pal, and you're funny. I mean that. Our comedians? Sure they're funny, they damn well should be funny, they have a hundred people working for them. What you see up there isn't just one guy, it's an end product. Like the war; how many men did it take to put one soldier in the field? We don't have comedians like you any more. We make ours by committee.'

After a couple of hours of that, a bottle of wine, a brandy or two, you wouldn't walk out of the restaurant, you'd float out, which was what they were good at, making you feel fantastic, that it was all going to happen. Then nothing.

As for films, I made British films; and what films. I was going to be Danny Kaye doing Walter Mitty, I was going to be Bob Hope in *The Road to Morocco*, but that didn't happen, either. How could it, in England? What we made were small-budget pictures full of jokes about tits and lavatories, with a lot of stage comedians like me in them, playing silly little parts for peanuts.

Looking at it now, I realize there's only one way to make it in America; to be born American. If I'd popped out of a hole in Michigan instead of Mile End, there'd have been no stopping me.

Everything was opening out, though, I was meeting people I'd never have dreamed of meeting; people in the theatre, people in films, producers, directors, writers, politicians, sports people, always going out to restaurants, always being asked to parties. I was the big novelty, everyone wanted to take a look at me. 'And to *use* you,' Ethel would say. 'Watch this one, keep an eye on that one.' Very shrewd, she was. It was good to have her about, to keep my feet on the ground, or anyway never more than a few feet off. She enjoyed it, too; not the parties so much, the invitations, but my having really made it after all this time, it had proved her right, she'd really believed in me, she'd gone out to work for me, and now I'd done it. It was good between us then, good in bed, she was still very pretty though she'd put on a bit of weight. I don't say I didn't have a bit on the side now and then, I wouldn't have been human, but nothing you could ever call serious. The Windmill days, when she was everything I wanted, those would never come back, I think she knew it, too, but now she'd got Bob I think she'd accepted it; in fact that's where it had started, with Bob.

Everyone liked her, especially Betty, Lou Gold's wife, who was also from the North, who'd also been a dancer, nice and fat and friendly. It helped her, that, because she didn't find it easy settling down; Highgate, and now this Hampstead Garden

Suburb. The sort of area *I* wasn't used to, let alone her. A lot of Jews, who all kept themselves to themselves, and the others round us people who probably weren't making near as much as I was but had the schools behind them, the accents; people that wore bowler hats to work and belonged to the golf club. On one side of us, in the new house, we had a solicitor and on the other side a stockbroker. They'd say, 'Good morning' and 'Good afternoon' if they were mowing their lawns or cleaning their cars, but that was it. They didn't have to put it into words, their whole attitude told you; you'd got no right to *be* there. As for the Yiddishers, they weren't as toffee-nosed, they hadn't the confidence, but that was a club you joined at birth.

It hadn't been so bad for me, I was out and away such a lot, but it was bad for Ethel. For her sake I even joined the golf club, though I was about as good as Sid Field in his sketch and about as interested. The Christian golf club, I joined; they wouldn't have Jews so the Jews had one of their own. But I couldn't face it after the first few times; a lot of twots with caps and purple faces, knocking back double whiskies in the bar, haw-hawing about keeping the Unions down, and why didn't we bomb Cairo?

'You're a comedian, are you?' one of them came up and brayed at me, bloke with a bright pink face and a R A F moustache. 'You make people laugh.'

'That's right,' I said, 'and there's some people make *me* laugh.' End of conversation. They were quick enough to come round if they wanted something, flogging raffle tickets, asking for donations to the church bazaar, but that was it. We weren't them, they weren't us, not even if I could have holed in one. When Bob went to the local kindergarten, Ethel said the mothers would smile at her like they were trying to freeze her to death, while the Jewish ones priced everything she wore.

Maybe it was a good thing in a way. It showed you that you'd always be an outsider, which a comedian should be. You've grown out of your own class, the working class, and the middle class don't want you. I'd envied them, growing up in the East End, their houses, their clothes, the way they walked around as though they owned things, but now I'd got to know them I didn't envy them, I detested them. At least the people in the East End were what they were, take them or leave them, but this lot were forever putting on an act. I may have done it on stage, but they did it twenty-four hours a day, and they were frightened. Frightened about the mortgage, frightened they couldn't afford to send their kids to a posh school or buy a new car, frightened they couldn't go somewhere flash on holiday. No wonder they hated us; we'd come up from nothing and paid cash for everything, while for them it was all on hire purchase. We'd won the rat race without even being entered for it.

I did a sketch once on my telly show about a family like that; that shuts up the house for the summer and tans itself with sun ray lamps, because it can't afford to go abroad.

Sometimes I'd come home and I'd find Ethel in tears and it would choke me, I'd want to go round and smash their windows, but it worked out all right in the end, we had our own friends, showbiz people mostly, jumped-up people like ourselves. We'd give big barbecue parties on the back lawn in the summer and I'd enjoy those; I'd imagine them smelling the smoke, looking out of their windows, and spitting blood.

Five great years you could say I had. Earning and spending like a lunatic – if it hadn't been for Ethel, I'd have probably gone through the lot – all the birds I wanted, pick of the bookings all over Britain. That's when I look at it now, when I know what came after. Then, you don't think of it as good or bad, you aren't comparing it with anything, you just know you're happy, things are going well, people are laughing, though you're not satisfied, which I wasn't; who's ever satisfied? I wanted America, I wanted the world, I still want them, though now I realize it's a thousand to one I'll ever get them, likely enough I'll never even work again. That night I tried to walk up the drive was enough; I hadn't got it in me to walk *out* of the place yet, let alone do anything when I got out.

And they'd know; that's the other thing that worries me. It must have got around. 'He's in a mental home.' A tiny little world like that. They must have been guessing, anyway, me being away so long, and so many people knowing; Ethel, June, Lou, Sid. It wouldn't take much to let it out, just a hint. 'He's been in a mental home, he's been in the bin.' I could imagine the looks, the whispering, people suddenly shutting up when you came into a room. Because there was still this fear about. You could go into hospital to have a leg off, you could be cured of cancer and come out again and they'd accept that, but mental illness, that frightened them, as though they were afraid they might catch it from you. I didn't know if I could face that, not on top of all the rest.

As for America, I did make one appearance there, which was almost worse than none at all, because it gave me the taste, it showed me the excitement, it built up my hopes, and then it came to nothing.

On one of those televised shows it was, where there's a host who introduces different acts and rabbits with people. I flew with Ethel to New York. She hated it, but as soon as I got there I knew this was for me; or should have been. I'd seen it hundreds of times on the films, I'd dreamed about it since I was a kid, but it still surprised me; the vitality of the place, the electricity, the charge you got from looking up at those skyscrapers, even the aggressiveness somehow seemed part of it, like it went with the place, there was no time to be polite, and anyway a lot of them behaved like they were playing character parts, the waiters and cab-drivers and cops and newspaper-sellers.

The taxi-driver we had from the airport said, 'You British? What're ya doin' over here?'

'I'm a comedian,' I said, 'I'm going on television.'

'Okay,' he said, he was a tough looking, swarthy bloke who hadn't shaved for a few days, and he wore one of those peaked leather caps, 'so make me laugh.'

'You drive me for nothing,' I said, 'I'll make you laugh for nothing,' and he did laugh.

'Hey, that's good,' he said, 'I like that. I never thought you British could be funny.'

On the show they didn't think I was funny, not the studio audience. They wanted to laugh all right, they'd laugh at anything they understood, a lot of fat middle-aged women in hats they must have borrowed from the Confederate Army, falling about at any silly little thing the host said, the most sycophantic bloody lot I'd ever seen. As for him, he was a pain in the neck; a big, fat fellow in glasses who delivered about five words a minute and was shitting himself in case he offended anyone in Nebraska or Milwaukee. 'I don't think we really ought to say that, Johnny. It's a real good gag, *I* like it, but maybe our audience just wouldn't quite get it.'

So they cleaned me up and filleted me and took out everything they thought was 'too British' and even then the studio audience sat and looked at me as if I was talking Japanese. I wanted to say something that would really shake them, some double meaning that even *they'd* get, like, 'Very forgetful, housewives can be; come into town, a lot of them, stay too long, and when they get home they find they've got one in the oven,' but what was the point? It wasn't even as if it was going out live and you could offend them in Milwaukee.

So after I'd been flogging a dead horse, or a lot of dead mares, for ten minutes, the host came waddling on to the stage, put his hand on my shoulder and said, 'Thanks, Johnny, that was really great. Wasn't he great, ladies and gentlemen? You know, I asked him, folks, how come you London guys are so tall? And you know what he said? He said, that's easy. We have to see over the fog.' Believe it or not, he got a hand for that, a really big one, like it was such a relief to them that at last here was something they could really understand.

Afterwards we had dinner in Sardi's, amongst all the red plush. He was a big man there, everybody saying, 'Hi!' and hoping to be on the show, though God knows why. I looked around the walls at all the pictures, all the playbills, taking in the atmosphere, remembering how people had been applauded when they came in after a really great opening, and had this terrible feeling of so near but yet so far, knowing that I'd flopped, that I'd maybe never be in here again, and Ethel knew how I felt, I could tell from the way she looked at me, so sympathetic, how she once put her hand on mine. She didn't say much; I didn't say much, either. They never did ask me again. 'Too British.'

It depressed me, but not for long; there was too much happening in England. In England, I couldn't go wrong. Every eighteen months or so, I had a new television series, patter and sketches again, filling in with dancers, a singer, maybe a 'guest personality' who'd join in one or two of the sketches. It either had to be that or situation comedy and I didn't fancy situation comedy because you got locked up in a show, you were at the mercy of the writers; more than ever at their mercy. It was bad enough in the sketches, but situation comedy was one long sketch. Even Tony Hancock, who had the best situation comedy of the lot, who could hold you just on his own for half an hour, had to escape from it in the end and do something else. People said he was mad, especially when the new show wasn't in the same class, but I knew how he felt. He wanted his freedom. He could feel the walls closing in.

To me, a stand-up comic is a stand-up comic, whether he's Frankie Howerd or Ken Dodd or me, and if you put him in sketches and that, you're wasting him, he feels very uneasy, he's used to being on his own. It's like caging a bird. Whatever song you get out of him won't be his best. That's why we don't come off in films; Bob Hope's the only exception. That's why, doing all this television, I felt the *need* to get out and play to audiences, to play night clubs and theatres, like a soldier who's been put in a desk job.

You wanted to be back on your own, away from the writers, away from the directors – or producers, as they called themselves – who sat up in the control room like God, among all the little winking lights, looking at half a dozen screens at once, giving out orders, hissing, 'Camera one! Camera two!' all tense, like they were firing six-inch guns. It wasn't surprising that it all went to their heads. After all, what were we, the performers? Not even flesh and blood. Just little figures flickering on a screen. Press a button and we'd disappear. 'They're *all* monsters,' June used to say. 'They all wish they were working in films where the director really *is* the boss, and anything he doesn't like just gets snipped in the cutting-room.'

What it usually turned into was the same old battle, patter against sketches, I'd want the patter, they and the writer would want the sketches. We'd sit around in these terrible drill halls and church halls and dumps where we used to rehearse, in places like Shepherd's Bush and Fulham and Battersea, miserable, dark, dusty places in miserable suburbs in the dead afternoons, and argue.

'It's very *nice*, Jack,' that was Geoff Perril, the camp one, who'd been at Oxford, curly red hair, cavalry twill trousers and corduroy jackets, 'but it *does* throw the sketch out of balance.' Or there was Tom McIlhatton, a little bloke from Belfast, like a ferret, suede jacket, he wore, 'Great, great!' everything was great, until he got his hands on it and cut it. 'Great, great!' The little bastard.

I'd sit in front of the television set when the series ran and I'd want to smash things. Ethel would try and calm me down. 'No one will notice,' she'd say. 'Nobody will know.'

'*I* notice,' I'd tell her '*I* bloody know! He's castrated it! He's cut out everything that's good and left in all the crap! *That's* not me! Those sketches aren't me!'

She'd say they were good and I was good in them and all the stand-up stuff they'd left was good, but it wouldn't console me. 'I'll phone him!' I'd say. '*I'll* tell the bastard!'

'Not now,' she'd say. 'Wait until you've cooled down, Johnny!'

'*No!*' I'd say. '*Before* I've cooled down! Now, when I'm really in the mood to tell him!' So I'd brush her aside and pick up the phone and dial his number and he'd come on the other end, 'Great, Johnny, great, you were really great!' which was what he lived by, he was an evil little bastard, he thought I couldn't read him.

'What do you mean, great?' I'd say, but he'd already taken some of the wind out of my sails. We're all a soft touch for flattery, comedians, because we don't recognize it as flattery, we always think it's true. Tell us we're great and we'll let you rape our wives and kidnap our children.

'Look what you fucking did to my solo at the start!' I'd say. 'Murdered it! Castrated it!'

'It wasn't me!' he'd say, and how could you prove it was? 'We had two minutes to cut, we over-ran. I couldn't cut the sketches, I couldn't cut the song, I took all I could out of the dances, I'd have taken more, but they wouldn't let me!'

They! What a marvellous get-out that was: They. You never knew who They were; the Head of Comedy, the Chief Controller, the Director-General, and if you did find out, you could be sure there'd be another They above them. I've run sketches in my mind in which you go up and up and up the ladder until at last you reach the ultimate, God, and God tells you, 'Look, it isn't Me. It's They.'

'It *is* Them,' June used to say. 'There's no God, there's *only* Them. That's what makes the world how it is: the Them-ness of things. The Universe is hostile to human beings.'

'There's a few human beings I'm hostile to and all,' I'd say.

Geoff Perril was one of them, the big ponce. I never knew what he was doing in comedy at all. Intimate Revue was about his mark, the sort of thing that thank God went out about the late fifties, full of queens, camp as a row of tents, incomprehensible to anyone who'd spent his life more than a couple of hundred yards south of Shaftesbury Avenue. At the same time, with all the camp stuff, the Oxford stuff, he was dead ambitious, he was a power maniac. This was only a stepping-stone, this job, and I was a stepping-pebble. Ethel saw it, though he was always so polite to her that it made you sick; 'How *are* you, Mrs Lucas? How *very* nice to see you, Mrs Lucas,' and she never asked him to call her Ethel.

'I don't know why,' she said, 'but he gives me the creeps. He's too good to be true.'

Dead right he was too good to be true. Or rather, he wasn't good *enough*. In his own way, his taste was just as bad as Tom McIlhatton's, who thought a pratfall was the funniest thing there'd been since Buster Keaton, 'Great, great!' If Perril couldn't have in-jokes about Binkie Beaumont and Hermione Gingold, he wanted basic lavatory stuff that wouldn't have worked at the end of the pier. I used to say his ideal punch line was a flushing toilet.

'I don't think it really *works*, Johnny,' he'd say, when I came up with an idea for a sketch. 'I think it's one of those wouldn't-it-be-funny-*if* things,' which would make me want to hit him. What we'd do instead would be crap. He'd say, 'Jack and Billy have this sketch about a man who's looking for an aphrodisiac,' the most unoriginal thing you've ever heard of, vintage Salford Working Man's Club, 1942; they were both from the North, Jack and Billy, come up the hard way and for my part couldn't go back quick enough, but they were professional. They could run you up any sketch you liked in half an hour. It would be terrible, but it was professional. I never thought I'd be praying bring back Maurice Franks, but I was. I don't know about osmosis and all that, but compared with these two, him and I were Siamese twins.

Nothing they wrote was really me. They couldn't find me a character, like Galton and Simpson found for Tony Hancock; how could you expect them to? Their whole lives had been different from mine. They were quick all right, but it wasn't a Londoner's quickness. To me, they were neither one thing nor the other, they were a new type that didn't belong to the South *or* the North, that came from the North and couldn't get South quick enough. It wasn't the old swede-bashing touch of coming to London and pretending you hated it, keeping your accent and shouting your mouth off how much better things were in Bradford. If anything, it was the North they hated, that they were always sending up, its phoney attitudes, its meanness. You could never imagine them writing for the Northern comics, Robb Wilton, George Formby and those.

I thought myself they had their eyes on America, London just happened to be on the way, *I* just happened to be on the way. One was a little chap, prematurely bald, who wore his hair like a monk, the other was bigger with a lot of black wavy hair. They both dressed sharp, drove flash cars, got around the West End a lot. What they wrote was probably quite funny, but it was written for nobody or anybody, not for me.

Still, like I said, you couldn't go wrong. The show got tremendous ratings, it got well reviewed, no one seemed to notice I was pulling one way while the scripts were pulling the other.

The next series it was just the same. I moved over to commercial television for this one. The writer was a tall bloke with a lisp, even taller than I am, who'd been very successful in radio and should have stayed there. They were radio gags, his, radio gags from the late 1940s, they embarrassed me. At least Jack and Billy had this veneer of being up to date, even if some of their ideas were so corny. With this bloke Teddy Kempton it was all corn, it needed a combine harvester, not a comic. There's nothing worse than comedy which dates, which belongs to its time but isn't funny any more. These stupid plays on words.

'The Duke of Wellington? How do you know he was the Duke of Wellington?'

'Because he gave me the boot.'

So I started getting a reputation. I was difficult to work with. Lou Gold told me that, between a couple of forkfuls of chopped liver. 'They're saying that you're difficult to work with.'

'*You'd* be difficult to work with and all,' I said, 'if they gave you the kind of scripts they're giving me.'

'What do you want?' he said. 'You've had wonderful ratings, marvellous notices. I can book you anywhere.'

What did I want? Why even try to explain to him? By his standards I'd got the lot; money, celebrity, recognition.

'The day I find a comic who gets on with his writer,' he said, 'that's the day I'll have seen everything.'

He understood one thing, Lou, he worked for one thing, Lou, and that was success, which was something concrete, something you couldn't analyse or categorize. There it was, success, and you were glad to have it, whatever shape or form it came in. Don't make waves, don't rock the boat, you're successful. When you weren't successful, didn't you use to come crying to me? And listen, if word gets round you're difficult to work with, maybe you won't be successful.

I looked round Isow's; everybody here was successful, or pretending to be. You could see it in their suits, you could see it in their big, padded shoulders, you could smell it in their cigar smoke and hear it in the way they talked. If you were Jewish, that seemed to be the one crime; not to be successful. Only a *goy* could start worrying about *how* he succeeded. He reassured me, Lou, and he depressed me. He was totally right but absolutely wrong. June had him summed up. 'He's an agent, darling. Who wants to earn ten per cent of nothing?' I'd got a big car, a big house, a lovely wife, what did I want, blood? People were paying, weren't they, people were laughing?

So when the crack-up came, the first one, Lou was the last one who understood it. How *could* he understand it, when I couldn't understand it myself? In his book, I should have been walking on air; fail, *then* you can crack up! And cracking up at the Savoy, of all places! The finest room you could play in London, the finest audience, people with titles, film stars, millionaires. If it had been the Goat and Compasses over Wapping or somewhere, he might have understood it.

Standing there at that microphone like I was paralysed, clinging to it like I was afraid I'd fall if I let go. Loud, posh voice from the audience, 'I say, is the fellow drunk, or something?'

Not drunk, God bless you, Your Lordship, just incapable. Not pissed, but petrified. Frightened of you and them and it; of everything. Not able to open my mouth. Hardly able to get out of my lousy dressing-room. If you knew how long it took me, Your Lordship, just to get up out of my chair, just to come away from the mirror, just to walk as far as this room we're in, you'd never credit it. Sid saying, 'Anything wrong, Johnny, anything I can get you, Johnny?' rushing around the place, poor bastard, like an old hen. What could *anybody* do? He was a dresser, that's all, and he'd never seen anything like it. Neither had I. Never. What was the matter with me, why couldn't I go out there, what was I afraid of? The last three nights I'd done it, the show, and it had gone fantastic, 'Haw, haw, haw!' They'd laughed their heads off. What was different about tonight? 'Have a drink, Johnny, pour you a whisky?' No, not even a whisky. That would all come afterwards, far too bloody much of it, bottles of it, rivers of it, but it wasn't what *caused* it. No, no, the fellow wasn't drunk, not then, though he would be often enough.

We see that the fear was an irrational fear, otherwise you would have experienced it not on the third night but the first.

Too bloody true.

In this case it was not that you were afraid that people would not laugh, after all they had already laughed. You were afraid even of appearing.

Terrified.

And on the stage you were also terrified.

I told you; paralysed.

So we must try to discover by what.

Them. Just going out in front of them.

But you had *been* twice in front of them, therefore it is clear that they no more than symbolized the cause of fear.

That's a great help, isn't it?

By eliminating what things are not, it becomes easier to find out what they are. Also we must relate it to your endemic fear, that people will not laugh.

It wasn't that. It didn't get as far as that.

Also it was more than that. Not only that they would not laugh, but that they would be actually aggressive.

It was just *fear*, Doc. Not fear of them, not even when I got out there. Just *fear*.

It seems to me perhaps an extension of the *same* fear. If an audience refuses to laugh, then the next step may be that from passive hostility it will pass to being actively hostile.

I never thought that. I never thought anything.

We were talking of course of unconscious processes. That they will not laugh at you, that they may attack you; all this, again, implies a motivation of guilt, a feeling that you *deserve* to be attacked.

I've known a few that do; comedians.

So we must decide for what you are afraid of being punished, and who it is that would be punishing you.

Who did I need? I punished myself.

I'll say I bloody punished myself; liquid punishment. Bottles in the dressing-room, bottle in the car, bloody distillery at home. They were terrified I'd be done for drunken driving, Ethel, Sid and Lou. Once, on the way home from a show at the Astor, I fell asleep at the wheel, just felt it coming on in time, pulled into the side and went out like a light. I woke up feeling like the Tin Man in *The Wizard of Oz*, stiff and creaking everywhere, cold as a witch's tit, and when I got home, Ethel was going spare. She'd sat up all night, she was sure I'd been in a smash, she'd started ringing police stations and hospitals, though thank God nobody had picked me up. After that, she made me hire a chauffeur, a nice little old boy somewhere in his sixties who didn't mind how late he worked or how pissed I was. Not that I worked a lot. For months, I never worked at all.

I packed up the Savoy that same night; I said I felt ill, then that I *was* ill. I felt worse than ill, I felt bloody suicidal, more miserable and depressed than I'd ever been in my life. It wasn't even a question of being afraid people wouldn't laugh at me, and not daring to face them. I wasn't even interested in facing them. I wasn't interested in anything. There was nothing I wanted to do, nowhere I wanted to go, no one I could stand seeing. I locked myself up in my room and I drank. Sometimes Haig, sometimes Vat 69, preferably Ballantine's. I wasn't fussy. Now I come to think of it, maybe the youngsters *have* got something, with this pot, if what they say is true, that it doesn't have after-effects. Maybe this is why Bob turns on, through seeing me and what it did to me, drinking, staggering about in a dressing-gown, three or four days' beard, eyes as pink as a ferret's. A bloody commercial for Alcoholics Anonymous I was, long before I ever thought of going to them. Terrible, the hangovers, the pain throbbing in your head, the filth in your mouth, the geysers rising in your guts.

But there was something much worse than that, which was what Ethel and the rest couldn't understand, and that was *not* drinking. I'd take physical discomfort any time. I'd take bursting heads and aching guts and bloodshot eyes any day of the week rather than it: the misery.

I moved out of Ethel's room and into the spare bedroom. I didn't want to be with anyone, anyone who watched me, anyone who reasoned with me. If reason had anything to do with it, I couldn't feel the way I did.

I cancelled a two-week booking Lou had made for me in Manchester, I cancelled a cabaret date at the Milroy. Even when the taste began to come back again, when the misery started lifting and the fear returned, then the fear started lifting, too, I knew I couldn't do it sober; that I'd have to be high. I reckoned I could handle it, though; after all, I'd been getting very skilful, like a doctor prescribing my own doses. What I needed first thing in the mornings, just so I could face the day; maybe half a bottle. What I needed to keep the wolf from the door at least till lunchtime; another half bottle or so. Lunchtime; though of course I wouldn't eat any lunch, I'd hardly eat at all. If I was lucky I'd fall asleep then, which might mean I wouldn't need another dose until the evening; best part of a bottle, then, to help me back to sleep. But I've known days when I could finish three; and later it would get worse.

It did start easing off after the first two or three weeks, like whatever it was had been pacified by my not working. The end of it was I took this date at the Astor, as a test, really, as an incentive. I'd sleep through most of the day, leave home near midnight after half a bottle or so to keep me going; more if I felt really shaky. Bottle in the car, to help me along the way. Then in the dressing-room, what amounted to three quick doubles, and I was on, floating through the air like a bird, quite ready to face a firing squad, let alone an audience. The only problem: would I be able to stand up?

Very funny I used to be then, too. You can't beat professionalism. Until I started miscalculating, or not so much miscalculating as starting to need more and not being able to take that more; feeling worse, and not being able to beat it without going over the top. It was a very, very fine balance, I'll tell you. Poor old Sid, it was terrible for him; flapping round me in the dressing-room, watching every time I poured the whisky, watching every sip I took, every swallow, 'That's enough, Johnny, that ought to do it, Johnny, watch yourself now, Johnny,' trying to hide the bottle when he thought I'd had too much. '*I* haven't touched it, Johnny, honest. Last time I saw it, it was here, right on the dressing-table,' and then when I'd find it in a drawer or in a cupboard, 'Wasn't me, John. No idea how it got there.'

'Lying cunt,' I'd say.

That night at the Astor, I didn't feel no different when I walked on. I'd had two doubles – well, maybe a double and a treble. Neat; always neat in the dressing-room, you don't want a bloody great soda syphon standing around there, though at home, I'd often take soda, sometimes ginger ale, I'd never been mad about the taste, but who gives a fuck about the taste? It was what it did to you that mattered.

Maybe I'd had too much in the car on the way that night, maybe I'd eaten even less than usual that day; a stone and a half down I was, by then, I must have looked like the walking dead. The orchestra played 'That's Entertainment,' I went out to the little stage, took hold of the microphone and adjusted it, looked up and around at the audience, and there *wasn't* an audience, no faces at all, no definition, just these blobs and shapes, blobs for the faces, shapes for the bodies, pulsing backwards and forwards, backwards and forwards, like heartbeats. What could I say to these shapes, these blurs? I said what I felt. 'Funny looking mob *you* are tonight,' I said. 'Like a lot of bleeding frog spawn. Still, that's better than most night-club audiences, all as pissed as newts.'

The frog spawn started laughing then, 'Ha, ha, ha!' it was throbbing all the more. And I kept on ad-libbing; I'd forgotten my act. Now and then snatches of it would come back to me and I'd put them over like a dummy, then I'd lose the thread and have to ad-lib again. I knew I was swearing quite a lot, fuck this, cunt that, which wasn't accepted then, it was before the permissive society and all that. I could tell the old frog spawn wasn't that pleased, I was getting a few bad vibrations, seemed to hear a shout or two, but couldn't make out what they meant. Then there was a bloke beside me saying, 'Mr Lucas, Mr Lucas!'

'Who are you?' I said. 'Another fucking tadpole?'

'Mr Lucas, are you quite all right? Would you like to come off?'

'Come off?' I said, 'I've hardly got on. What's the matter with you?'

Then Sid was there too, on my other side, he was taking my arm. I said, 'For fuck's sake, Sid,' then the frog spawn seemed to come rushing towards me, to engulf me, and it blacked me out, I was just frog spawn too, the whole world was frog spawn.

When I came round I was in bed at home; the doctor was with me. Nice fellow, big yiddisher chap, curly dark hair, no bull-shit. 'Too much strain,' he said, 'too much tension. Just as well you *did* fold up; it was going to be that or your liver. I could send you to a clinic, but I don't think you're that far gone: yet. Go away somewhere hot for a month with Ethel. Can you drink? Yes. Stick to wine if you can. If you must have spirits, no more than the equivalent of one double whisky a day. Ethel's going to watch you. If you've got any sense, you'll watch yourself; while you still can. Try and take some exercise. Can you swim?'

'No,' I said.

'Well, learn to swim. It'll be something to do. Try to develop some interests. When did you last read a book that wasn't a gag book?'

'Can't remember,' I said.

'That's the trouble with you show-business people,' he said, 'no interests; except in themselves. All right. Enjoy yourself and behave yourself. You're on your honour; and if you play silly buggers, you'll be on your back.'

We went to the sun; we went to the Canary Islands. It was hot all right, there was sand, there was sea, and I nearly went mad. Going away was meant to stop me drinking, but why I'd been drinking was to stop me worrying, and if I couldn't drink, what else could I do but worry? Maybe if I'd come away with some nice young piece of crumpet out of the chorus, some little raver with a pretty face and big tits who loved to fuck and hadn't a brain in her head, it might have worked, just temporarily, swopping one distraction for another. But I didn't want to fuck Ethel, that was the lousy thing, which added yet another problem, as if I hadn't got enough already.

It hung there between us all the time. I hadn't seen so much of her, so often, for years; in her bikini, which wasn't really right for her, which might have been when I knew her in Fairleigh, but bikinis hadn't been invented. She wasn't fat yet, but she was getting plump. It was years since she'd been dancing and though her legs were still good, dancer's legs, solid but not fat, she'd begun to put it on around the middle and the upper arms, chubby, here and there a bit puffy, and she was one of those people that don't turn brown, not for quite a while, anyway, but go red.

Lying beside her on the beach, I'd notice other things about her, I'd nothing else to do; a mole beneath her arm, among the stubble there, hanging like a little brown growth. The lines around the corners of her mouth when she wasn't talking or smiling; it was a sad mouth now, it drooped, which maybe should have made me feel bad but didn't, it only turned me off. We had single beds, thank God, but just the same I didn't like to share a room with her, I couldn't stand the lack of privacy. That's one of the things about drinking, you get very secretive, very resentful of anyone who's likely to interfere.

June handled it a lot better than Ethel did, she'd make less fuss, she'd never nag me, just do the things that had to be done, treat it as a fact of life, the collapsing, the vomiting, the setting fire to the bedclothes, like a baby messing its nappy. Mind you, she knew she was taking *on* a drunk, whereas with Ethel, to be fair, it was seeing me turn *into* a drunk, being frightened it was happening, still hoping she could stop it. June could take it for granted, Ethel just couldn't face that it was going on.

When she found a bottle of whisky in our room that I'd hidden under some shirts in a drawer, she nearly went berserk, she tried to pour the whole lot down the bog. If I ever slipped away into the bar, she'd follow me there and stand beside me, hissing in my ear like a snake, 'You *know* you shouldn't, you *know* what Dr Lewin told you,' till one night I just turned on her and told her to fuck off and she ran out of the room in tears. I shouldn't have done that, for a day we didn't speak to each other, lying five yards apart on the beach like we were strangers, sitting opposite each other at meals in dead silence. I was ashamed but I resented it, the way she kept after me, even if I knew she meant it for the best.

The best. What *was* the best? For me, the best had gone, it had disappeared that night at the Savoy. After that, things could never be the same again. 'What *is* it?' she'd sometimes ask me, Ethel. 'What *is* it, Johnny?' She was desperate. In some funny way, like women have, she seemed to blame it on herself, and this would irritate me, too.

'I don't *know*,' I'd tell her. 'If I knew I could do something about it, couldn't I?' which was shrewder than what I thought. Now, after all this time with Doc Weiss, I've learned that's exactly what *would* cure me, to know, but I still don't know, nor does Doc Weiss, so I'm still not cured.

Lying on that beach, hot as a furnace, under the big coloured umbrella, looking at the bronzed young crumpet strolling past, looking at the speedboats and the water-skiers out at sea, a sea without a wave that I still wouldn't swim in, I thought a lot about Sid Field. I was beginning to understand what might have happened to him, which I never really had before, to see that maybe it was nothing to do with success or failure, or rather that success didn't save you from it, from the misery and the boozing, from the misery that causes the boozing; even then I realized that perhaps the success had something to *do* with the misery. If Sid had started drinking because he was frustrated, because he had to hide that marvellous talent in the provinces, then maybe success had been just as hard to deal with. It hadn't cured things, it might even have made them worse.

I couldn't talk to Ethel about this, the way I later could with June. It wasn't that she was stupid, she'd certainly never pull the Jewish mother act on me like Lou Gold, but it was too deep for her, and at the same time she was too much part of it, too involved with me.

What I was frightened of was fear, of the fear coming back, so I was frightened of performing in case *that* made the fear come back, because that was what had begun it. I'd think of all the comics who'd been drunks; it was easier to think of ones that hadn't. Tommy Trinder hadn't. He was a teetotaller. Maybe that was the only way, the only alternative you'd got; once you'd started drinking at all you were lost, a time would always come when you'd drink too much, almost like it was a comedian's destiny. Tony Hancock, on top of the world, a marvellous comic, out on his own in television, and everyone knew he was drinking himself silly. It seemed like there was no escape;

once you became a comic, that was what you were locked into.

I'd think of the Vaudeville Club Lunches when I had to speak, getting up in front of the mike and looking round table after table of flushed faces, pair after pair of bloodshot eyes. My profession. 'Blimey,' I told them once, 'what with the orange blossoms and the gin blossoms, I thought I was in a fucking flower shop.'

'Buy yourself a wreath while there's time!' one of them shouted.

I had a television series coming up, and I knew I couldn't do it, I was dreading going back to London; I hardly said a word on the plane, and I must have had half a dozen whiskies, I ignored Ethel. It was Geoff Perril again, nearly two months of the bastard, two months of those terrible scripts, two months of those poxy studio audiences. Yet if I pulled out, what would happen? Even if they didn't sue me I'd be missing for a year, no Johnny Lucas on the box, that was like death nowadays, it could easily be the end of you. There were a hundred little no-talent ponces ready to jump up and take your place, do whatever they were asked, speak any line they were given. It would soon get around, if it hadn't done already: 'He's a drunk, don't use him.'

Till the very day I was supposed to do it, the day of the first reading, over Hammersmith, I kept changing my mind; I'll do it, I won't do it. Geoff Perril asked me to lunch at the Mirabelle. I ducked that, I got the little secretary I had to ring and say I had 'flu. Then on the day itself, I was so pissed there was nothing to be done, paralytic, slept right through the morning; apparently he phoned and phoned, Ethel telling him I wasn't well, and that was that.

Lou came round, but I wouldn't see him. He phoned me: 'Listen, do you know what you're doing?'

'I know what I *can't* do,' I said.

'You know how easy it is these days to be forgotten.'

I knew that all right, and I knew why he was shitting himself, too. He didn't want to cross the Bluestones, who ran the television company and half a dozen theatres and Christ knows what else besides.

'I'll tell them you're ill,' he said, 'maybe they can postpone the recording.'

'They can postpone it for a year,' I said, 'and it'll still make no difference. You might as well stop kidding yourself, Lou.' Then I went back to my room and I got into bed with a bottle of Ballantine's beside me. I was a patient and that was my medicine. Very comfortable I was there, in my red silk pyjamas and the purple sheets.

Ethel came in with a face like a wardress and said, 'You're not going.'

'No,' I said, 'I'm not fucking going. So what?'

'I see,' she said, in the same flat voice. That was just what I needed, reproach.

'If that's all you've got to say,' I told her, 'fuck off. I've had enough from Lou. Terrified he'll lose his ten per cent. Shit scared of the bloody Bluestones. Don't worry, there's plenty in the bank, you'll never starve.'

She didn't answer; just shut the door and went out. It wasn't fair, I shouldn't have said it, I can see now she was choked, but what I wanted then was understanding, sympathy. Sympathy with the way I felt, understanding that it wasn't my fault, that I wanted to work, that I didn't want to drink, that I'd got no choice. As for understanding what was wrong, *I* didn't know, so how could she?

Three weeks later I was drying out in a nursing home; in Kent, this one, in a nice little village, not far away from Dover, Tudor houses, oak and elm trees. The place stood just across from the graveyard, which may have been appropriate, behind a big brick wall. The house was brick as well, Queen Anne they told me, though I wouldn't have known, and God knows what she would have thought of the people who lived in it now and turned it into a sort of rich man's Skid Row. They must have made a packet, the people who ran that place, and they ran it like an assembly line; sedation, injections, out you went; until you came back again, which I did, twice.

'It may work, it may not,' Dr Lewin said. 'It's a crash course; you might be lucky. You're not addicted, yet. I said, *yet*.'

The sedation part was all right – at least you didn't know anything; you had all the advantages of death without being dead. The Vitamin B shots I could have done without; a little ginger-haired Irish nurse would use my arse as a dartboard, always taking two or three shots to get the needle in, but I *did* feel better, I admit that. Not eating's part of drinking; you can waste away.

The fellow who ran the place was a small, dark, brisk, bald bloke who drove around in a Rolls-Royce, as well he might, looked as if he didn't mind a drink himself, and had a good line in patter, though it didn't sound so good the third time round. 'We don't regard alcoholism as a disease here, we look upon it as a symptom. The disease is not in the patient, the disease is in the society which exerts stress on the patient. Remove the tension, and the symptoms will disappear. We don't believe in Alcoholics Anonymous. To us, all alcoholics are individuals; individuals first and alcoholics second.'

I never did make any sense of that, I don't think anybody did, but he'd got a captive audience. The state we were in, we'd swallow anything; after all, it was swallowing that got us there in the first place.

The pattern was, I'd do a few weeks there, feel better and better, go for country walks – though walking through the village wasn't that great, they looked at you like you were Dracula – go home, accept a booking; and drink myself silly the day I should have opened. Not just in London, either; I did it in Oxford, I did it in Liverpool, I did it in Brighton. Thank God I had Sid with me, to look after me. The fear was back again; the fear of fear. Doc Lewin put me on tranquillizers, but it wasn't enough; you might as well have taken aspirins for cancer.

What would happen was the same every time. I'd turn up wherever it was, I'd breeze through the rehearsals, half a bottle a day, no more, then the day we were due to open, I'd freeze. I'd be paralysed before I was paralytic. Sid would try everything; pleading with me, encouraging me, hiding the bottles, but it never worked. I knocked him down once, up in Liverpool, I was choked about that, I bought him a pair of gold cuff-links. Poor little bastard, he didn't know what time it was, any more than I did.

'If you could just get over it *once*,' he'd say, 'just do it once. Get out there on that stage and put it across, that's all it needs, Johnny. It's an invisible barrier.'

I did it once; at Newcastle. Three parts pissed, got through the whole thing beautifully, couldn't believe it was happening, gag after gag that brought the house down – they're always a good audience, Geordies, if you take it a bit slower – even did well with the ad libs. 'Why don't you come down the pit and do an honest job?' a bloke shouted from the gallery. 'Me?' I said. 'I've been down more bloody shafts than *you* have.'

The next night I never even got on stage, flaked out in the dressing-room. Back to the nursing home, another five weeks, and try again. Only for three weeks, this time. It may not have been a disease, but the symptom was bigger than the sodding individual.

'You're getting addicted, I'm afraid,' Dr Lewin said, and who was arguing? From needing it to get off the hook, I just needed it. There was no subtle little distinctions any more, just this need that blotted out everything else. No more drinking so as not to feel frightened, drinking not to feel depressed, drinking not to worry about the audience laughing. Just drinking.

And then the nightmares, the hallucinations, blending with each other so that you were never quite awake and never quite asleep. Nothing as nice as pink elephants. The audience that suddenly all turned into crocodiles and came snapping at you, hundreds of them, swarming out of their seats and slithering towards the stage. The cat that burst out of the wall with its claws bared, snarling at you. The tarantulas that dropped from the ceiling, one after the other, very softly, plop, plop, on to the bed with their bent hairy legs, plop, plop, beside you on the pillow, plop, the next one would drop on your face.

Cats and crocodiles and spiders, they were all real, more real to me than any people, than Ethel, very pale now, even I noticed that, hovering round me like a lost ghost, driving me nuts. 'You'll have to go and dance, then, won't you?' I yelled at her one day. 'You'll have to go back to bloody dancing!' More real than Bob, poor little bastard, who was sent away somewhere. More real than Doc Lewin and that big, curly head of his, mouthing things like, 'It's all a question of will-power, in the end.' Will-power! Had he ever tried stopping a tank with a catapult?

It frightened me to death, experiencing all that; maybe it was the best therapy I could have had, shock therapy, to be shit scared of it ever happening again. It took the nursing home to pull me clear of it, it wasn't the last time I'd have to dry out, but it would never be that bad again. Fear was bad, cats and crocodiles were worse.

When I got out this time, after God knows how long, nobody talked about working, not even Lou, who'd taken as much as he could stand. Working; that was something so remote I couldn't even think about it, far more remote than ever now. I was convalescent. For nearly two years, that's what I was; convalescent. Work was like the top of a mountain. You could just about see it through the swirling cloud, thousands of feet above your head, but first you had to climb this rock face, get up on to a plateau, and this plateau was just being able to exist. No more than that. To stay clear of the crocodiles. It wasn't much to ask, yet it was everything.

I'd manage a week or two without a drink, not a drop of it in the house, promising Ethel, who'd been worn to a wraith by now, never mind a ghost. Then it would be too much for me and I'd get cunning. Solitary drinking, I'd tell myself, that's the thing you've got to avoid. When you're on your own, and you pour it down your throat like water. Communal drinking; now that was different. So I'd drive into the West End, and meet someone in a pub; but that wasn't so good, people recognized you, or weren't sure they recognized you, which was even worse. '*Aren't* you Johnny Lucas?' like they couldn't believe it, and once, even, '*Weren't* you Johnny Lucas?' Did I look that bad, that old? So I gave up the pubs for the drinking clubs, where people looked as bad as I did. Poxy little places. Round Soho, Smithfield, all over the place, but always seemed the same. Bar in a tatty room, one flight up, boarding-house wallpaper, seedy smell, always in the middle of the afternoon, the feeling time had been kicked to death there. Same with the people, too; they went with the places like furniture, all pale as paper when they weren't pink and mottled, all bloody miserable, all zombies. I was one of them; I avoided the ones with a mirror behind the bar.

Most of them broke. Taking drinks off you, borrowing money off you. 'I don't know if you *could* help me, old boy; just a fiver, just till next Thursday.' Betting men, a lot of them, on and on about dogs and horses, boring shit out of me, I never gambled. At least they had that, though, the one thing that seemed to keep them alive apart from booze, waiting for the result of the 2.30, passing one another dud tips.

They'd give you little lectures if they found out who you were: 'Now the trouble with you, Johnny, if you don't mind my saying so, if you'll forgive me for saying this, and I mean, I admire you, I thought you were great; where *you* went wrong, Johnny ...' One piss-artist to another, the democracy of drunks.

I'd never seen so many handlebar moustaches since the war, so many R A F ties, heard so many phoney accents, so many pathetic war stories. 'Baled out over the drink, and I tell you no lie, I was in that bloody water for thirteen hours before the Air-Sea people picked me up, bobbing about on a Mae West, very useful lady.' It was like a museum, but that's where I belonged; a museum. Where Are They Now? Try Rupert Street.

*The tall, pale, dark-haired Londoner sat down beside me in a fashionable Mayfair restaurant last week and asked for a jug of water. 'That's what it's going to be from now on,' he told me. 'This is the new Johnny Lucas.'*

*The Cockney comic who made millions laugh, whose television shows topped the ratings, who could command a king's ransom in cabaret, has not worked for a year.*

*'I have been through hell,' he said simply, 'but I have learned my lesson. I've found out who my real friends are and who was just climbing on the bandwaggon. I think success may have come too quickly for me, as it so often does these days. It caught me unprepared; the wealth, the national fame, the adulation of*

*thousands of fans. I admit I got a big kick out of walking into a luxury restaurant and always getting the best table, of being chauffeured round London in my Bentley. But now I believe there are more permanent things in life, that a comedian's fame can be as fleeting as the laughter of his audience. Johnny Lucas will be back, Johnny Lucas will make people laugh again. But it will not be the same Johnny Lucas.'*

After which I went straight up the road to a drinking club in Soho and knocked back four or five doubles. Puke-making, those interviews; God knows why we allowed ourselves to be conned into them. '*Them*,' June would say, '*those* shitty little men,' the licensed sycophants, the stars' friends, arse-crawling their way from London to Hollywood and back again, knowing that flattery would get them everywhere and anywhere, parasites' parasites, living off our insecurities. My insecurities. My fear I'd be forgotten, that even a crappy article by him in his crappy newspaper, an article I could predict word for word before I even saw him, was better than nothing, dead silence, total disappearance.

There were two articles he did for people like me. Number one, I have learned my lesson. Number two, it's great to be working again.

*Yes, Johnny Lucas is back, and London is laughing again.*

Until the next time.

Lou was good; I'll say that. Always kept in touch, had me and Ethel round for meals, tried not to look when I poured my own drinks. Never a drinker, Lou. Kept trying to find me things that might interest me.

Now and then I'd do a one-night stand, not too far from London, the most I could cope with, and sometimes I couldn't cope with *them*. No television; too much of a risk. Once or twice some radio, nothing too taxing, just the odd quiz game and that, where if you didn't want to speak you could get away with it.

Where are they now? Still in Hampstead Garden Suburb, and if you can't find us there, try Soho again.

When I set the bed on fire and Ethel thank God smelled the burning, threw a jug of water over it, I had to be dried out again. I'd had the Kent place, this time I went somewhere different, in Surrey. Very picturesque again, nice old house, lots of big trees. Twilight sleep, salt-free diet, very understanding doctor. How about aversion therapy? Every time you take a drink, you get a shock.

No thanks, Doctor.

Okay. Just an idea. It works with some people.

Maybe I'd get hooked on the electric shocks.

Yes. Very funny.

Still, each time I came out, I seemed to stay out a little longer. I worked a little more, I drank a little less. I started taking dates outside London, very cautiously, not too far away at first, then a little farther; Watford, Derby, Coventry. Had to be careful, like Lou said; I couldn't afford to take rubbish. Take rubbish, and rubbish is all you'll get offered, you'll finish in the South-East London desert. I had to do The Great Comedian Who's Been Resting bit. Slowly, gradually, making his way back.

Working-men's clubs; I eventually took a few of those, as well. It wasn't Lou's scene, it wasn't my scene. He didn't understand booking them, I didn't understand playing them. Everything I'd always detested about the North and nothing that I'd ever liked, all concentrated under the one roof, in one repugnant bloody hall; like an Odeon cinema gone mad. Even for me, the most vulgar rooms I'd ever seen, they all looked like they'd been built by Pools winners. All gilt and crystal, all chandeliers and thick-pile carpets. Three-quarters of the audience pissed, arrogant and noisy and provincial. Everyone as good as you were; what were you doing up there, getting paid? Glorified beer halls, was what they were, only they weren't content with being beer halls, they were trying to be something bigger. When I first played one I thought it would destroy me, the hostility, the boozing, but instead I got angry, like I had that night once in Wolverhampton. I thought, you bloody swede bashers, and when they heckled me I gave it to them back.

*Yes, it's great to be working again, and I honestly think I owe it to the Northern clubs. Playing them was a whole new experience. They really put you on your mettle. To hold those audiences, you have to be good.*

It was as if the old barrier had broken down, the invisible barrier between the audience and the stage. There was a stage there all right, but the magic had gone, the mystery. You weren't the boss. It was their club, they'd paid for everything, they'd asked you along, they were as good as you were; and probably pissed as well. Beer going down their throats in rivers.

'Why don't you speak English, you Cockney bastard?' one of them shouted at me in a club in Manchester.

'Because I'm like you,' I said, 'I'm shit-ignorant.'

Another time, in Bradford, someone asked, 'When are you going to say something funny?'

'I did,' I told him, 'you were too pissed to hear.'

So that's how it was when I met June; still hanging by a thread. What you might call Between Clinics. Even the Talk of the Town were doing me a favour. Some Yank had let them down at the last moment, rang up Lou Gold, got anybody for us? Johnny Lucas, he said. What, him? they said. You must be joking. The stand-up comic who can't stand up. The only comedian who dies before he gets out of the dressing-room. No, no, straight up, he says, he's a new man. Drinking? You're crazy. Never touches it. Heard how he wowed then in the Stockport Working Men's Club? And what he did in Macclesfield? How they kept him on for an extra week in Carlisle? So they shopped around a bit, couldn't find anybody else, came back to Lou and said, All right, but God help you if he hits the bottle.

So naturally there was a lot of, 'Look, Johnny, for *my* sake, I'm asking you to do this for *me*.'

'What are you on, then,' I asked, 'ten per cent of the laughter? By the time I go on that stage, I'm liable to feel like Sinbad the Sailor.' He didn't smile, I don't think he saw it. Like I said, he was never very quick on gags, Lou. If he could book you, you must be funny, if he couldn't book you, what was funny about that?

At home, Ethel was going around like a Salvation Army woman, Keeping An Eye on me, obviously under orders from Lou, the worst thing she could have done, building up the tension instead of relaxing it, making it all seem now or never, make or break.

'Stop fucking following me!' I'd tell her. 'You're making things worse, not better!'

She didn't shout back at me, which made it worse still; she was restraining herself, I had to be treated like I wasn't responsible for what I did.

It nearly didn't happen. I felt like getting drunk to spite them, fuck them. I'd string them along, I'd do all the rehearsals, then when the first night came, forget it. Maybe that helped me, taking off the pressure. I was working towards something that would never happen, so why worry?

The rehearsals went okay, the director was okay, one of the old camp-spectacular kind, then the opening came, and there was June. What I'd needed, what I'd wanted, what I'd prayed for, someone to bring me back to life. Someone to understand me, not forgive me. I was sick of being fucking forgiven.

When I left the house and moved in with June, I felt like I'd been let out of prison. Jesus, I was actually happy: how long had it been since I was happy? It wasn't a question any more of could I work at all, of every show I did being an achievement, look, I've done it, I've come through, I wasn't pissed. It was a question of actually growing again, of reaching for the things I wanted to do.

'You've never *stretched* yourself,' June said. 'You've never taken risks. That may have been the trouble.'

At first I resented that. What did she mean, I'd never taken risks? I never took the easy way out, did I, not even when I played in clubs? I never fell back on race jokes or the old-fashioned smut. A lot of my act was dead original, look at what the posh papers had written about me.

'It could be *more* original,' she said, 'it could be *more* personal. Like Lenny Bruce, or Mort Sahl. You could go around with jazz groups, like they do. No one does that here. It's all telly and Palladium and clubs; you need a new kind of audience.'

She played me records of these two, and I saw what she meant. They were both funny all right, both very quick, but they weren't me, I could never be like them, and deep down, I didn't want to be. For me, they weren't comedians, they were satirists. I couldn't really put it into words, it was something I felt; what I had to do, which might not be as clever as them, but was more basic, more universal. They were a lot cleverer than I'd ever be, they knew more, and yet I knew more than *they* knew. I was more the real thing, what comedians *should* be.

'I don't mean you should *imitate* them,' June would say. 'Just be yourself, like they are. Let yourself go. Say what you want to say, not what you're expected to, or what someone's written for you.'

That part was something I'd always felt, through all the years I'd had to compromise; with poxy producers, with deadbeat writers.

'You *are* funny,' she'd say. 'Why should you let yourself be turned into a ventriloquist's dummy?'

And she was an example to me; the way she worked, the way she lived, everything on *her* terms; she was free. She'd turn down an offer from Las Vegas for two thousand pounds a week – '*I'm* not going to sing a lot of shitty songs for shitty gamblers' – and go on at some jazz club in Soho for fifty, because she liked it there. 'Do your own thing,' she'd say, 'do your own thing.'

I'd try new routines on her, a thing I hadn't done with Ethel for years, and I realized I hadn't cared what Ethel thought, I'd lost respect for her, whereas June encouraged me. If she liked something, it would really give me a charge.

Another thing: she was against the clinics. '*They're* no bloody use,' she'd say, 'just clip joints. They don't dry you out, they soak you. If you're going to be cured, you'll have to cure yourself.'

'Help me,' I said. I'd never said that to anyone.

For the first few weeks I lived with her, things were so great I hardly drank at all, but when I was away or when *she* was away, things were different, the fear could return, always lurking around, waiting its chance, pouncing. Not always the same fear. Sometimes the misery, which was what you were afraid of, which was worse than the fear, that you could only escape by losing yourself, and that meant drink. Or it was the other fear, that they wouldn't laugh at you, coming back now; now that I was safer from the misery. I could get that when she was there, too. You needed to drink for that, as well, though not as much, not to lose yourself, just enough to take the edge off things, to blur them, so you could go on stage not caring. The trouble was, it was still difficult to draw the line.

June was away a lot, sometimes in Britain, sometimes on the Continent, sometimes in the States, and they were all bad times. 'Come with me,' she said, and I tried it once or twice, once to Liverpool and once to Rome, but it was no good. I felt like a ponce, I wasn't part of it, and I knew I never could be what she wanted me to be, an English Lenny Bruce, with all the hip talk. They weren't me, I wasn't them.

'You're like a baby,' she'd say, when she'd come home from a trip and find me pissed out of my mind. 'Mummy goes away and baby wets the bed.' But that would be it. No sulking, no silences. She'd clear up any mess I'd made and it was over; till the next time. And she hadn't got Ethel's hang-up about *things*; *my* carpets, *my* armchair, *my* bedclothes. I don't mean June wasn't bothered how she lived. Like I've said, everything was very bright, very smart, very neat, it was just that they were only *things* to her. If you burnt the sheets, okay, so you could buy some more. They were sheets, that's all. If you smashed a glass or a vase, you could always replace them.

I never did knock it off with anyone else while I was with her, but I always had the feeling if I did, and she found out, she'd laugh about it. I admit I wasn't the same. When she was away, I'd worry. There was one bloke in the group that often used to back her, a pianist called Tony Schneider, Jewish fellow, slim and curly haired, about thirty, who I wasn't too happy about. I didn't like the way they joked together, the understanding that they seemed to have, the secrets, though I never dared to mention it. I knew what would happen; she'd go off like a bomb. Anything that for her cut in on her freedom.

Like you could never tell her she was late; which she always was. Always. You arranged to have lunch with her at one o'clock, you could depend on sitting in the restaurant there till quarter to two. She said she'd see you in some club at midnight, you'd be drinking on your own till one in the morning. Always apologized. Always had some excuse; the rehearsal had gone on too long, the show had finished late, somebody had phoned her from New York, she couldn't find a place to park, until you realized this was *her*. And if you protested: *wham!* 'I'm not some bloody little housewife with nothing to do who can plan her day to the last minute! You're lucky I got here at all!'

'All right!' I'd say. 'Okay! All right!' There was no doing anything with her in that mood, even if I'd felt stronger than I did. In the end I realized she was late for one reason, because she wanted to be late.

To be late was obviously an act of defiance, and perhaps of independence.

Even I got that one, Doc.

It is clear that the hostile impulse was satisfied by the action itself, but that when challenged, the sublimation would break down.

Yeah, I'll say it broke down.

It seems to me that she was not late as women usually are late, that the motivation was not one of self-aggrandizement, but of resentment.

Who did she resent?

I do not think she likes to be a woman.

She liked it in bed, all right.

That is not necessarily a contradiction.

She was all contradictions, June; that was part of the excitement, never quite knowing where you were, though underneath all that, trusting her, being certain she'd look after you, that she believed in you. She was tough on nearly everybody, she had them all weighed up, who was mean, who was phoney, who was always using people, yet at the same time she put up with God knows what from me. She was wild in bed, yet she could talk like a professor.

She was always reading; the flat was full of books; some of them I couldn't even understand the titles, let alone what there was inside. 'You're lazy,' she'd say, 'you're not stupid, you've just never bothered,' which was true, though what chance had I had? Doc Lewin had been right when he said I had no interests, yet at the same time I wasn't satisfied, I knew what was bad but nobody had shown me what was good. The only book we'd had in my family had been the phone book.

'Read this,' she'd say, 'look at this, listen to that.' She had friends from every sort of background, not just musicians and showbiz people, though there were plenty of those, but writers and lawyers and painters and composers, who to my amazement seemed to admire me. I couldn't understand it and I told her so. 'You see?' she said. 'You undervalue yourself. You underestimate your talent.'

What she meant was I could do more with it, which I agreed with. What she also meant was I ought to do a more sophisticated act, which I didn't agree with. To me, if something was funny it was funny for everybody, like a Chaplin comedy, or W. C. Fields getting his hat stuck on his walking stick. You didn't need to have been to university to laugh at that. At the same time, if you had been, it wouldn't stop you laughing. I suppose the thing was, a performer's two people. When I met them socially, all these intellectuals and that, they'd overawe me. If I was doing a turn, then *I'd* be in charge and I'd *expect* them to laugh.

But I did start working more, I did write more and more of my own material, I did drink less and less, I even thought about some more television.

'But on *your* terms,' June said, 'it has to be on *your* terms. Don't compromise again. Television *is* compromise. It's predigested crap for the lowest common denominator.'

Not that people were falling over themselves to offer me a

series. They were wary now, they remembered what had happened the last time, the word had got round and besides, in these last two years, the nig-nogs had been springing up like mushrooms, the little nonentities who could do anything you asked them, tell a joke badly, sing a song badly, do a dance badly. I had a name for the kind of shows they did: The Television Spectacular with a Hole in the Middle, but they never got drunk, they never held up shooting. Sometimes I'd see them on the screen with all their pathetic little mannerisms, their nervous smirks, and the rage would boil up in me, my whole body seemed to fill with rage. If June was there she'd switch the set off and tell me I was being stupid.

'They're part of television,' she'd say. 'They're just cannon fodder. Why blame *them*? Just go and do something better.'

She was right, I could see that when the rage had gone, but it wasn't an easy thing to live with.

Gradually it all came together again. I worked on a new act, a more personal act, writing most of it myself, using a young kid June had met to help me, only twenty-one, just left Cambridge but an East End boy originally like myself who hadn't had time yet to become a hack; Paul Atkins. Little plump fellow with curly hair and corduroy suits, laughed a lot, very ambitious. 'Now's the time to catch him,' June said, 'before he's a *success*.'

I cut out the clubs; there was no experimenting there. The farthest-out thing they'd understand was something about two bent Pakistanis at the Labour Exchange. I concentrated on cabaret where you were liable to get your most sophisticated audiences. I did a few guest spots on television, I did a radio show that went very well, I did a good summer season at Great Yarmouth that was healthy, too, then there I was, back at the Palladium, with nobody happier than poor old Lou; talk about the bloody prodigal coming home.

*To what he has always had, a plastic, infinitely pliable face, the timing of a Wild West marshal, the effrontery of a door-to-door salesman, he has added something more, something very pure, and something that is wholly himself. He has always been an original, albeit deriving from a long line of Cockney com-*

*ics, but now he bears on his brow the mark of the great comedian. The man and his material are in perfect equilibrium. He could not possibly be anyone but Johnny Lucas.*

We had a fantastic party after opening night, over at The Establishment in Greek Street. June got up on the stage and took off Ella Fitzgerald, I went up and did a routine about a copper pulling in Father Christmas: ' 'Allo, 'allo, 'allo! What's in this sack, then? Hit you? I never hit you! You fell off your sled!'

It felt great, but it wasn't like the first time I'd topped the bill at the Palladium, it could never, never be like that again, because what I knew now was that success didn't protect you, that success was a danger, too. You could be punished for success, like I'd seen before. The fear could jump on you like it had before. So I still kept a bottle in the dressing-room, never knowing, never being sure, afraid to be too happy.

Very happy when Bob came that night, not so happy with the way it went. Happier than I'd been here for God knows how long when I heard the news; that they'd only given him a suspended sentence. It was Ethel who told me, got through from Cornwall on the phone; the Welsh Twit came up and told me, 'Mrs Lucas to speak to you,' and my heart started banging. 'What is it?' I said. 'What does she want?' but he was smiling, 'Nothing to worry about,' he said, and I was out of that room in a flash. I should have known that if it had been bad, they'd never have let me speak to her.

'John?' She didn't sound too bright. It was always John, not Johnny, when she had the old chip on her shoulder, and it had me worried, again.

'What's *happened*?' I shouted.

'Two years,' she said, and then, as I was dying there, 'suspended sentence,' and I laughed out loud, I was so pleased.

'That's great!' I said. 'That's wonderful! Aren't you pleased?'

'I'm pleased he hasn't gone to gaol,' she said.

Pleased? I was walking on air. He was still free; what else mattered?

'They fined him fifty pounds,' she said.

'I'll pay that!' I told her. 'I'll send you a cheque for it today. Best fifty quid I'll ever spend!' I wanted her to sound happy, too, it worried me that she didn't, as if in some way there was still something wrong, that Bob wasn't really in the clear. When I'd hung up, I wanted to go round telling people, 'He's got off! My son hasn't gone to gaol!' I would have sounded mad, but so what? 'Isn't it great?' I asked the Welsh Twit; there was no one else. 'Don't you think it's terrific?'

'Yes,' he said, 'I'm happy for you.'

Who else could I tell? Doctor Weiss? 'Let us consider why you should feel so happy.'

The Colonel? I'd have loved to tell him, he'd have understood, but he'd gone. Discharged himself. A dishonourable discharge, poor old bugger. Gone without seeing any of us, like I'd been so afraid he would. Old soldiers never die; even when they try to fade away.

'How's the Colonel?'

'The Colonel has left us.'

That's how we heard; from the Welsh Twit. They wanted to protect us from *that*, too.

'Well if he's going, so am I,' I said, and got up and walked out of the room. They could stuff group analysis after that.

'We must discuss why you should so strongly wish to leave.'

I know, I know. The Colonel was my father, my *idealized* father. Now perhaps I was feeling abandoned.

No, I did *not* fucking feel abandoned. If anyone had been abandoned, it was him, he'd come here hoping to be cured of whatever it was he had to be cured of, and they'd flung him more on his tod than ever.

'To stay in group analysis will help your adaptation to the world outside,' Doc Weiss said, which I don't believe. To me, group analysis helped your adaptation to group analysis. A lot of malicious nutters picking at one another's sores wasn't the world, or if it was, then they could stuff the world. I wanted like hell to clear out of this place, or rather to be *able* to get out, because physically there was nothing stopping you. There was no barbed wire, no watch-towers, no machine-guns, no guard dogs; they were all in the mind. That time I'd tried to walk up the drive, I'd put up my own barbed wire; my own watchdogs chased me back again. I was caught in the middle, I didn't want to stay, but I hadn't the strength to go. I'd been hooked on alcohol, but now I was hooked on something worse, something I hated, on opting out. I'd dropped out just as much as Bob had. He had his cannabis, I had Doctor Weiss, going round and round the same old mulberry bush, and always meeting each other coming back. At least the Colonel had had the guts to go. He deserved another medal for that.

# Chapter 5

It was June who brought him; David Price. Looking out of the landing window, seeing the Ferrari spin down the drive, fifty minutes after she'd said she'd be arriving, I wondered who's this fellow with her, sturdy-looking bloke with glasses, curly black hair with a bald spot, a duffle coat, who I vaguely thought I'd seen before. Suspecting the worst, as always; a new boy-friend, someone she'd brought along so he could see what had happened to me. I got scared and angry then; how bloody dare she? Moving round to the next window to keep them in view, childishly thinking, well, they won't let him in, not without prior permission, the old get your card stamped bit, so they can both bugger off and drive straight back again.

I watched them get out of the car, June in that athletic way of hers, everything turned into a kind of exercise, swinging her legs on to the drive, bare legs, even in winter, black leather mini-skirt, white thighs, great thighs, all I could think of now was having her.

One of the goons came down the steps to meet them, male nurse in a white jacket. State your business. Leave your finger-prints. Expected, are you? Up the steps and into the house. Vanished. What would happen now? Two minutes, five. They didn't reappear, I had to go downstairs and see, down that great, broad, slippery wooden staircase. As I reached the bottom, they were coming out of Doc Weiss' office with Doc Weiss, who was chatting with the fellow; very friendly, smiling, both of them, June too. I *did* remember him, but not his name. He'd been over our place; *her* place.

I watched them a few moments before they noticed me, and it was him who saw me first, looking up in the middle of a laugh and seeing, surprised at first, not quite knowing what to do, whether to carry it through and say hallo, whether to pretend he hadn't seen me, whether to tell the others, but he carried it through, he did it rather well, turned the embarrassment into a great production of suddenly recognizing me, being delighted, then turning to tell the others.

*'Well,'* said June, 'what an entrance. You certainly haven't lost your sense of timing.'

'Nothing like a staircase for an entrance,' the fellow said. 'You can't upstage an actor on a staircase.'

I came down the last steps very slowly, still wondering who he was. June came across to meet me, Doc Weiss smiled at us all like Santa Claus. 'You know David Price, darling,' June said, and I remembered him then, highbrow director, the National, the Royal Court and that. June kissed me. Her cheek was very cold.

'Hallo!' David Price said, and shook hands with me, one of those grips that make you wonder where your hand's gone. 'I'm one of your admirers.'

What was left to admire?

A lot more laughing – theirs, not mine – then the doctor left us and we went out walking. Where else to go? He rabbited on a lot, this bloke, very friendly, quite funny, not what I'd expected, plenty of gossip, went on about an orgy he'd been to in Hollywood, about an actress who kept knocking it off with old critics to get good notices, the kind of scandal June always liked, but underneath it there was something more. You could sense he was putting on another act; he was enjoying himself, but it was like he was playing games with the children. What you felt there, throbbing away, was power, a tremendous energy that he put into everything he did, whether it was telling stories, directing actors or just walking, like we were now; he hurried along as if he kept wanting to break into a run. I had another impression, that all this chatter was just building up to something, something they both had to tell me.

Back and forth we went, like a three-man route march, over the lawns, between the bushes, under the dripping trees, left right, left right, laughing a lot, making a lot of noise, people looking at us – I was going to say, as if we were mad, but again, who was talking? Suddenly he asked me, did I know *King Lear*?

'Not personally,' I said. Once a stand-up comic, always a stand-up comic.

'The play,' he said.

'Ah, *that*,' I said, quick as a flash. 'Want me to play King Lear, do you? Type-casting, that is. I've had my bloody troubles, I can tell you.'

'Not Lear,' he said, 'the Fool,' which pulled me up short.

'Blimey,' I said, 'that *is* type-casting.' Then I laughed, seemed a bit ridiculous, really, me in Shakespeare, though I knew a few comedians had done it, Frankie Howerd, for instance. 'I'm too tall, anyway,' I said, and I meant it. To me, fools were little fellows, skipping about the stage, whether they were old or whether they were young. A tall fool was wrong, somehow, it gave him a status he shouldn't have, and besides, it was ridiculous. Put a cap and bells on a fellow six foot two and he looks as if he's dressing up for a giggle. He belongs in pantomime, not in a play.

'Listen to him, Johnny,' June said. 'I think it's a fantastic idea.'

'You're quite right,' David Price said to me, 'there's never *been* a tall fool, a *really* tall one, but why couldn't there be? There's nothing in the text that says there mustn't. All the more impact. All the more pathos. If the Fool's tall, it gives the part an extra dimension. It points up the ambiguity that runs all the way through the relationship. The Fool's not only wiser than Lear, he's taller; and yet he's still inferior. He's still listened to on sufferance. He can still be whipped. He's a grown man, a *well* grown man, who's treated and punished like a child.'

We were standing still now under a fir tree, raindrops dripped down from the branches; one fell on June's face, but she didn't seem to notice, it ran down her face, into the corner of her mouth, and she stuck out her tongue like a lizard, automatically, and licked it away. I thought how fabulous she looked, how natural she was in everything she did. As for David, he was the first director I'd ever met I could feel any real respect for out of all the dozens I'd known, though they'd all been comedy directors, so-called, working for laughs, anything that got a laugh was good, whether it was on radio or telly or the stage. But this fellow, as he talked, seemed to see there was more to it than that, that humour was serious – however strange that sounds – that laughter was important, that people who made you laugh were doing something with a history behind it. It amazed me how much he understood, how much he knew about *me*. He quoted jokes I'd made that I'd practically forgotten, things he'd seen me do that went back as far as the fifties. He talked about delivery, he talked about material, of how he thought I'd never really been given the right stuff to do, especially on radio and telly. 'But Shakespeare is the greatest gag writer of all time!' he said. 'Not just the Fool in *Lear*. Look at Feste! Look at the Porter in *Macbeth*! Look at the First Gravedigger! Stanley Holloway did it; he was perfect! *You* could do it!'

'I thought they all wanted to play Hamlet,' said June.

'Never,' he said, 'a pure fallacy. *East Lynne*, perhaps, not Hamlet. They tend to turn mawkish, not tragic, wind up with a song, or in the old days, some terrible monologue. I'm sure it's placatory. They want to be taken seriously. It's pathetic, but it's understandable. The result's always pure bathos, like Ken Dodd singing "Tears". Whereas the Fool was dead serious anyway; he knew he had to wrap up what he said in a jest, otherwise he'd suffer for it. "Wit, an't be thy will, put me into good fooling. Those wits that think they have thee, do very oft prove fools; and I that am sure I lack thee, may pass for a wise man."'

And I wanted to do it; it was a marvellous feeling. To think I might work again after all this time, to work with him, to do the Fool. 'You're on,' I said, 'I'll do it; if you'll take the risk, and if I can get out of here.'

'Don't worry,' David said, 'we'll get you out on parole. I'm sure we can. I'll talk to your good doctor. We'll tell him it's occupational therapy, and it could be, it could be!'

I thought so, too. Everything he said made sense to me. He understood more about comedy than fifty of those poxy television producers, full of crap about ratings and camera angles and audience reaction. He put his hand in the pocket of his duffle coat and took out a little leather book. 'Here you are,' he said, 'the script!' *King Lear.*

As soon as they'd gone I went up to my room and started reading it. I don't think I've ever read anything with such excitement, which was the gift he had, to get you going, to look at things differently, to think that whatever play he was going to direct you in was the most important thing, the most *relevant* thing, you'd ever done.

To be honest, I'd never read it before. At school we'd done it in *Tales From Shakespeare* and it had bored me to death, everything there had bored me to death. I'd seen it once on television and maybe glanced at the text a few times when Bob brought it back as homework and wanted help; from *me*! But now it was a revelation. He was quite right in what he'd said. The Fool was wiser than any of them, yet at the same time he was more vulnerable; he talked in riddles to save his skin. I was amazed how much I could feel for him; it could have been me, in fact if I'd lived in times like that, in Ancient Britain, it *would* have been me, I'd have had to be as crafty as he was, as quick on my feet, and another thing, he wrote all his own material! I reckoned that Fool, any fool in Shakespeare, was the greatest ad-libber I'd come across. He made even people like me, people well known for it like Tommy Trinder, ad-libbing maybe a few lines a show, look like amateurs. And I got to thinking all these slightly ridiculous thoughts; how much a fool would have had to ad-lib, how much he could keep up his sleeve, and I reckoned very, very little, because in a funny sort of way he was like a comic appearing on the telly, he was using up material like there was no tomorrow. The telly comic was playing to an audience of millions, the jester was playing to a tiny little one, but because it was tiny, because it was always the *same* audience, it came to the same thing. He must have had a few gags ready for certain situations, like we did, you could tell reading *Lear* that a lot of the Fool's jokes couldn't be spontaneous, they were too elaborate, but the bulk of his stuff was.

Reading the play had such an effect on me that I couldn't keep still, I had to walk about; I put on my coat, went downstairs, and made for the front door. One of the nurses came out of the shadows and he stopped me. 'Where are you going, this time of night?'

'A walk in the gardens,' I said, 'want to come with me? I've always fancied you.'

'You're daft,' he said, but he didn't try to stop me.

It was cold out, with a bitter wind that cut right through you, froze your cheeks, but I didn't care, the adrenalin was really flowing. I'd do that part come hell or high water. Whatever Doc Weiss said, whether it meant my leaving here or not, I knew in my guts that I had to do it, that it was vital to me, that in some funny sense or other, it might be a way out. If I wanted to walk up that bloody drive now, I was quite sure I could do it, but I didn't want to. I was so confident in myself that I knew I'd be able to stroll out in my own time, I was ready to talk to Doc Weiss first.

I talked to him next day, during my session, and naturally got the usual crap about let us discuss this, why is it you are so anxious you should play this part, but he wasn't dead against it, I could tell he was a bit impressed by David Price. 'Certainly now you have abandoned group analysis there is a need for something that may take its place. This might even act as a kind of existential therapy, provided you continue your individual analysis. But I do not think you are ready yet to become an out-patient!'

So he did what David Price had talked about, he let me out on parole. Word of honour; a trusty. Each day the car came down for me, mine or June's, drove me up and drove me back. I preferred mine, because she still drove like a maniac. Rehearsals in the mornings, analysis in the afternoons; the analysis sometimes milking the rehearsals. He enjoyed that, the Doc; I think it was another reason that he let me go. 'I am interested in your identification with this jester.' I could see it all going into that book of his, again.

The funny thing was, I never had any doubt I could play the part, even though the nearest I'd ever been to doing a play was pantomime, and the only time I'd ever come on in what you might call costume was as the Dame. But this was me; me taken back in time three hundred and fifty years, or more than a thousand if you bought the Ancient Britain bit. Because it was me, because I was loving it, there weren't any problems, with the language or anything else. We could come on in skins for all I cared, we could have played it up trees or under water.

David Price wasn't worried about it, either. 'It *is* you,' he said. 'It's every real comedian, past, present, or future. As soon as you're familiar with the language, you won't have any trouble at all.'

It was interesting to work with straight actors for the first time, in a straight play, to see their different approach, how they looked at things. King Lear himself was Sir Roger Cocker, a little, dark, stubby man with a very good voice who came on like an old pro, talked a lot about the Hamlet he'd done at the Old Vic, the Shylock he'd played on Broadway. To me, he seemed to have a chip on his shoulder. You expect actors to talk about themselves like comedians, but Cocker was always trying to prove something, as if he thought he hadn't had his due, that people should have taken him more seriously, like they had Gielgud and Olivier. He'd only had his title for a couple of years.

'Wonderful old ham!' David whispered to me once. 'But he's perfect for the part. Sees himself in every line.'

This became obvious whenever we discussed the play; Cocker was Lear as much as I was the Fool, it was incredible. If you criticized anything Lear did, he'd stand up for him. The way I saw the play, the way most people seemed to see it, was that this was an arrogant old man who dug his own grave; by the time he learns to behave like a human being, it's too late. When David asked each of us in turn how we saw it, this was what I said, though it embarrassed me a bit, because I felt like Leon Costa, a comic who used to come on radio describing Shakespeare's plays, getting everything wrong, and saying, 'Don't be higorant, don't be higorant.'

Cocker wouldn't have that, though; for him, Lear had been right all along. He was an old-world king, you couldn't expect him to behave like a constitutional monarch. 'He was a warrior!'

he said. 'He didn't spend his time launching ships and opening women's institutes!' The trouble was, he said, Lear was too trusting, it was part of his nobility. Goneril and Regan had taken him for a ride, and if Cordelia didn't speak up, that was *her* fault. 'I cannot heave my heart into my mouth!' he said. 'The most pussy-footed line in English Literature! The girl was obviously one of Nature's martyrs!'

At first I couldn't understand why David let him get away with all this, he struck me as a director who'd got his own very clear idea of things that nobody was going to talk him out of, but as time went on, as I listened to old Cocker ranting away, and now and again saw David smiling, I realized what he'd done. He'd chosen Cocker, like he'd said, because he *was* King Lear, King Lear as David saw him. It didn't matter whether he agreed with David's idea of the play or not; he *was* the idea. In fact after the first few readings I noticed he didn't discuss it with us much when we were all together; he'd take people aside in little groups or on their own. What he was saying was that there was nothing you could do with Lear and nothing you could do with Cocker; they were what they were, and everything else just had to go on around them, like around a rock.

'David loves playing games,' June said, when I told her about it. 'He's playing games with you, as well. He's just as much of a power maniac as Roger Cocker, but he's far, far cleverer. It's the difference between torture and brainwashing.'

I wasn't too sure about that, I'd had enough bloody brainwashing with old Doc Weiss; if I was going to get it from two sides at once, I was liable to go spare.

'Oh, *you're* all right,' June said, 'he admires you. He's always had this thing about comedians. He *wants* you basically to be yourself.'

'Meaning I can't act,' I said.

'No, darling, he thinks you take direction well. But he's chosen you *because* you're a comic.'

The Fool was cleverer than me, though. Also he was cleverer than Lear, than most of the people round him, even Goneril and Regan; they were cunning, he was clever. In fact I agreed with David when he said, 'It's really a world of brutes. It's a power-fixated world. Even Kent lives by the sword. There's only three gentle people in the whole play; Edgar, Cordelia and the Fool.' Of course, he didn't say that with Cocker there, or we'd have heard about it for the next half-hour.

I thought a great deal about it. How did the Fool *get* to be a fool? What sort of person said, When I grow up, I want to be a fool? Because there's never any background, not in any of the plays; the fool's just there, like he'd been born wearing motley. He's got no father, no mother, no family. It seemed to me that he'd have *this* in common with me as well; that we'd both had to make our own way. Like nearly every comic, we'd started with no advantages except our talent. Otherwise, a fool wouldn't be a fool. With brains like he'd got, he'd be giving orders, not taking them, he wouldn't let himself be pushed around by a lot of animals, who treated him like an animal. 'Take heed, sirrah – the whip.' That made me boil, that. He'd laughed it off, but he was obviously used to it. It was an occupational hazard. Go too far, tell them something they don't like, and they flogged him. Like he told them, 'Truth is a dog that must to kennel, he must be whipp'd out.' Who'd want a job like that, if he could get something better?

So I felt very sorry for him, not just for all the suffering that he had in *Lear* through being straight, through being loyal, but because of his whole position, and it made me realize I was lucky. In those days if you came out of the slums, and you were funny, that's all there was for you, and not many jobs like it going, either. At least if my lot made it, we were free, we had agents, we could negotiate, but there was none of that in those days, no Lou Gold, not even any Isow's, no agent going to the King and saying, 'Look, I want more for my boy.' To work under that sort of pressure, to do so much within such a narrow range, you had to be really inventive. It was amazing how much he did get into it; songs, jokes, and a hell of a lot of wisdom. No sentimental stuff, either; you couldn't imagine *him* getting up and singing 'Tears'. They were bitter little songs, the songs he sang; as often as not they had a barb to them. Yet when you considered it, fools got away with quite a lot, with jokes I could never do in public.

She that is a maid now, and laughs at my departure
Shall not be a maid long, except things be cut shorter.

Max Miller would have been proud of that.

A comic's always going to be restricted, one way or another, he's always got to find ways round the censorship, even if it isn't as direct as what the Fool had to put up with. A comedian today may *think* he's free, but there's a million things he can't say, subjects he can't touch, and not just on television; even though he may have so much more leeway now than he did when I was starting twenty years ago. Try making a joke about the Queen or sixty-nine or Auschwitz. See what happens if you break the law of libel. We're really no more free than what he was, in that way, and in one sense he's a lot freer. He knows where he stands, he knows where he is, he may not altogether like it, he may be limited, but at least he's got a certain security, till the next King comes along, anyway, and if he's lucky, that may never happen. With us, on the other hand, we've got freedom to fail, freedom to starve, freedom not to be laughed at any more. The Middle Ages, things moved slowly, what was funny today might be funny in a hundred years' time, even two hundred, while with us, an act could turn sour within five years, a comic could be finished overnight.

The main thing that worried me when we actually got into rehearsals at the Globe, in Shaftesbury Avenue, was my being so much taller than Cocker, and I knew it worried him, too. Like I've said, the idea of a tall Fool had never seemed on, to me. I'd come to accept that, but what I hadn't bargained for was there being such a short Lear. He couldn't have been more than five foot seven, Cocker, and there I was, towering above him; I could have reached down and patted him on the head. So a funny sort of battle developed between him and David Price over our positions on the stage. He was very hot on movement, David, very hot on positioning, he'd got diagrams for almost every scene, even the ones where there were only a couple of people. 'Here and here,' he'd say, making chalk marks on the stage, 'that's where I want you,' and in scenes with me, Cocker would edge farther and farther away until there'd be a big gap between us. 'No, Roger,' David would say, 'I want you closer together,' and he'd grumble and move back, then slyly move away again.

'I'm not *com*fortable like this,' he'd sometimes say, 'I don't *feel* right,' and David would give him a very patient smile and ask, 'Why not, Roger? Any special reason?' Then Cocker, who obviously couldn't give the reason without looking a twot, would mumble in a sulky voice, 'It just feels *wrong*.'

'Don't worry,' David told me. 'When it comes to the performance, every step he takes backward, you move one forward.'

I could see what June meant about his liking power and being cleverer than Roger; I could see that he enjoyed it, too. I almost felt sorry for Roger Cocker. He was a big-headed bastard all right, but it was a bit like watching a bull with a matador.

There was another thing I realized, and this was that it wasn't any coincidence, him choosing me and Roger, one short, one tall, tall Fool, short Lear, where normally it would have been the other way around. He was trying to show something; that the Fool *was* superior to Lear, at least by the time the play happened, when Lear was going senile; physically superior and mentally superior, one thing standing for the other. I hadn't quite got the gall to put it to David, I wasn't sure how he might react, but I mentioned it to June, and she smiled.

'Clever you!' she said. 'Yes, that's David!'

Whether Cocker knew it was deliberate, too, I couldn't tell, but he certainly hated it, he hated anything that took away from his being the big man. After one argument, when we were doing the scene in the hut, he shouted, 'I am *not* putting up with this petty, intellectual dictatorship!' turned his back on David and walked out. But David only smiled, like this was just what he'd expected, and said, 'All right, I'll do Lear,' and did, giving a wicked imitation of Cocker that just had us falling about. They were both word perfect, too, they neither of them bothered with a script.

I'd been a bit unhappy about movement, just like I'd been unhappy about being so large; someone as tall as I was couldn't go skipping about the stage, he'd either look like a big ponce or as if he was sending it up. I was a poor mover, anyway, dead clumsy, never any good at sports, gymnastics, dancing. June, who was very hot on all that, very graceful herself, did the modern dancing bit, went to special exercise classes with this fellow Yat, used to tell me, 'You *were* clumsy, but you've made it work for you, you've stylized it, it's funny!'

I'd usually come on with big, long strides, I'd make my gestures a little larger than life, flinging my arms about at times like windmills, very seldom using my hands the way Jack Benny did, who was much, much smaller and neater. The first entrance I made, in rehearsal, I toned down my usual walk – for one thing it wasn't my show, I wasn't going straight to a mike – and sort of compromised with how he *might* have wanted me to walk. But right away he said, David, 'I want your normal walk, your normal entrance, I want *all* your movements and your gestures to be perfectly natural. You'll be wearing the motley; that's enough.' In other words I'd look a big enough prick in that, without poncing around, but I'd been ready for that, and when I saw the costume I must say I was impressed, Max Miller's suits had nothing on it; scarlet and blue silk, almost luminous, doublet and hose, the doublet in a kind of wavy pattern, one leg blue, one leg red, a jester's cap in red and blue halves, pulled well down over my hair, with a coxcomb like the script said, a red and blue striped stick, with bells, one red shoe, one blue, curling up at the toes in the way they did then.

I had Sid to dress me, like the old days; it was pathetic to see how pleased he was, how excited. 'Together again, eh, Johnny? Together again!' He looked at me in the gear and he said to me, like he always had, 'Marvellous, perfect!'

'Don't tell me,' I said, 'on me it looks good.'

'It does,' he said, and I had to agree with him. The part felt right, and the gear went with the part. It was how I would have looked if I'd been around then, just as a soldier would have had to wear armour.

The hardest thing was the learning. I wasn't a bad study, but this was so different from anything I'd ever done, it was much more sustained, and you couldn't ad-lib your way out of trouble, plus the old-fashioned language, not to mention all those songs. David didn't give me that much direction; if anything, I got more advice from Roger Cocker. He was a great one for passing notes to other people in the cast; I reckon by the end there must have been enough to make a book out of.

'My boy,' he'd say to me, 'you mustn't mind my telling you this, but I've been acting in Shakespeare for forty years. This is my fifth Lear.'

Sometimes what he told you was useful, sometimes you could tell he was trying to protect himself, he was afraid you might steal a little of his thunder. I'd let him rabbit on. Some of it I'd pay attention to, some of it I'd ignore. He reminded me a lot of the old comedians I'd known, the same old egomania. You couldn't have conversations with him, any more than what you could with them, you either listened or you interrupted.

What he said didn't bother me much. Even with David, it was only the technical things that really interested me, diction, placing, how to sing the songs, which June helped me with, too. Because however arrogant it seemed, I knew I understood this part better than either of them.

*The face was gaunter, the body was thinner, the lines on the forehead and around the mouth a little deeper, the temples were salted with grey, but there was no mistaking the inimitable lilting voice, the humour in the dark eyes. There is only one Johnny Lucas, and now Johnny Lucas is going to play the Fool.*

*Not, I hasten to add, in his private life, but in* King Lear. *David Price, one of our most prestigious directors, has coaxed him back to the West End theatre to play opposite Sir Roger Cocker in Shakespeare's tempestuous tragedy; his first straight part.*

*'Frankly, I'm dreading the first night,' confessed the six foot two inch Londoner, who of course is better known as one of the quickest and funniest stand-up comedians in the business, star of stage, cabaret and television, 'but it was too good a chance to turn down. Do you know, there are a lot of parallels*

*between a jester in those days and a comedian today? I honestly think that in some ways I am better equipped for the part than an experienced straight actor.'*

*David Price agrees. 'I have been astonished at how quickly Johnny got hold of the role,' he told me. 'He seemed to understand it instinctively. It has been exciting to work with him, and I think you are going to see a most original interpretation.'*

It was exciting to work with him, and all, and I saw what Doc Weiss had meant, there were times when he wasn't so stupid. It *was* like group analysis, especially when we all sat down and did the readings, and especially because Cocker and I were so caught up in our parts; dig into them and you dug into us. Instead of an analyst we had a director, instead of the Welsh Twit we had David Price, which to me was a great improvement, he was twice as intelligent, he had a sense of humour, and he didn't get on your tits with his silly remarks.

But it is also not so uncomfortable. It is analysis at one remove; a kind of psychodrama.

You'd be surprised, Doc.

Because the longer we went on, the deeper we got into the play, the more the two worlds ran into one another; it was only the journey which really divided them. I was Johnny Lucas and I was the Fool; that was natural enough. But there was more to it than that, because when I lay on the couch, who was that behind me? Was it Dr Weiss? Was it Sir Roger bloody Cocker? Was it Lear? And in rehearsal, in the theatre, who was Cocker? Was he Lear? Was he Doc Weiss? When we got into costume and make-up, it was stranger still. He'd transformed himself, Cocker. The first time I saw him in his make-up, in his robes, a shock ran right through my body, like I'd been hit by lightning. He *was* Lear, he'd done it brilliantly, the white hair, the wrinkles, like a mad old man. White hair; like Dr Weiss. But Cocker wasn't real, Weiss wasn't real, only Lear was real. When Doc Weiss sat behind me, I could think of Lear. When Lear stood in front of me, Cocker in his make-up, there was only

Lear. He'd swallowed Cocker and he'd swallowed Weiss. He was a great actor, Cocker, I could see that now, watching him work; he may have been a cunt, but he was magic. Everything I'd felt for Lear, reading the play, thinking the Fool, he brought out on that stage. It wrung your heart. When you were with him in a scene, when he was wearing that make-up, you accepted him the way he saw himself.

I am a man more sinned against than sinning.

By God, you thought, too bloody true! No wonder the Fool went with him; you'd follow him anywhere. He was what he said he was, every inch a king, mad or sane.

But a king is also a father.

Dead right, Doc. You're my father, he's my father. That's what you're saying, isn't it?

There are clear analogies.

But you ain't mad, are you, Doc? You ain't a king.

I am whatever in the analysis you see me as.

Sometimes a king, sometimes a cunt.

Father-son. Lear calls me 'boy'. If he wasn't my father, why should I follow him?

I have one part in my heart
That sorrows yet for thee.

He's *entitled* to sorrow for me. Out in the rain, the bloody thunderstorm, following this lunatic. He's never been right, and now he's mad. I could have left him, nothing easier. Gone over to Goneril or Regan, they'd have been glad to have me, and when *they* went under, moved across to Cordelia. Except I couldn't have, just as *now* I never could. What Shakespeare's saying is that fools are straight, they've got a commitment to the truth. You can't interrupt them, you can't buy them. If you can, then forget them, they're not really fools; they're whores.

And my poor fool is hanged.

Me, or Cordelia? Me, of course. I never had a doubt. Wept buckets for myself. Of course I was hanged; I'd always known I would be. Whipped or hanged; my fucking fate, which I accept. If you've got a commitment to humour, you've got a commitment to the truth, and if you've got a commitment to the truth, you're liable to end up hanged. That's the chance you take. Your friends whip you, your enemies hang you, like they still do if they can. Being the Fool, feeling the Fool, it was no more than I expected. He was fatalistic, the Fool, I realized that. He didn't look for much out of life, and seeing this, I realized something else, that we, we comedians, look for too much out of life. We want it with jam on it. A fool knew his audience and he knew his limitations. Like I said, he *expected* the whip. He could even be hanged; he knew that, too. Whereas us, once we've made it, what do *we* expect – or rather, hope for? An easy passage. Laughs and birds and money. Success that goes on forever. While inside us, what we really know is that we'll be bloody lucky if we get it, lucky if we stay on top, lucky if we do keep earning, lucky if they still keep laughing. We're still whipped, but they don't call it whipping. We're still hanged, but they don't call it hanging. In those days it was kings who went round the bend, not fools. They'd set us free all right, but what we were free to do was worry ourselves mad, like I had. Which would I rather be? Daft like me, or punished like him?

I'd have been him, I think, I really mean it, though it may seem easy to say. Him, because he had what I hadn't got, more important than money or birds or celebrity, he had his sanity. However things might look, he was more his own boss than I was, and at the end, when he did have choice, he took the right choice, the choice that needed bottle. They treated him like he was an inferior being, but when it came to the crunch he was prepared to risk his life; and he lost it.

Sometimes when I thought about the Fool, when I lay on my bed in the sanatorium reading the play, over and over, I'd cry. Even in rehearsals, I'd have a job not crying. But on my own, where there was nobody to see me, I'd cry my bloody eyes out, I'd weep for the poor, brave little bastard, or maybe for myself who after all *was* the little bastard, would be until the run was ended, and even then would always have a little of him inside me.

It was funny how differently you looked at things, being him; the worm's-eye view. Like, for example, he was a randy bastard, but his humour was the sort you'd find in people who didn't expect to get much. They know a lot but they're non-combatants, they're watchers, and that's what *I* became. I watched June.

Once, when we went back to her flat together, after a rehearsal, I reached out and touched her breast. Normally that would have been enough to set her off, but this time she said, very mildly, 'Don't do that,' and moved away. It should have hurt me, but it didn't, the strange thing was I seemed to be expecting it, it didn't upset me at all, any more than it did to see her so friendly with David Price. Once, at a rehearsal, he touched her bare arm, just for a second, but the casual way he did it, the quick little smile she gave him, told me a lot. You notice things if you're a fool, yet like I say, it didn't matter. You don't *let* it matter.

'Knows his place, doesn't he, the Fool?' I said to David one day, 'knows just what he can expect.'

'He *accepts* his place,' he said. 'That was the beauty of the feudal system: no rat race.'

As for Roger Cocker, he still kept sending me the notes, he still kept trying to back away from me on stage, but it didn't worry me. I could take all that, I could take the advice, I could take this need of his always to be in the driver's seat and in the limelight, this childishness he had. It was just like Lear's. Lear was a great king, yet he was dead stupid with it. Cocker was a great actor, yet he was childish. You admired both of them, you felt sorry for both of them. Every scene he played was tremendous, better and better as rehearsals went on: the way he spoke the poetry, this tremendous voice he had, rising and thundering; in the storm scene, competing with the thunder.

Blow, winds and crack your cheeks! rage! blow!

He stood planted there, hair flying, looking up, *defying* them to move him. And the play, the part grew on him as well, changing his attitude towards me, so I wasn't such a rival any more. I was the Fool, I was loyal, I was the one who'd stuck by him.

He invited me to lunch at the Garrick Club, a peculiar old place, the kind of placc you'd expect to meet the Colonel coming down that big, stone staircase with the portraits of actors hanging above it, all gloomy and sombre yet at the same time friendly, full of good memories. *His* portrait was there too, of course, in one of the dining-rooms. The one we ate in, naturally. Painted about twenty years ago, I'd reckon, him in a black frock coat and a high collar, playing the Master Builder, staring out of the picture like he was mad; as mad as Lear.

'I was an extraordinary Master Builder, my boy. I brought insights to the part which were then quite new, but which now have been taken for granted.'

I didn't mind, I liked listening to him rabbiting on, and when he wasn't promoting himself, when he reckoned that he'd sold himself to you, he could tell a fair theatre story, like most old pros.

Just being around the West End again was great; after all this time, it was like re-discovering a country you'd emigrated from, there were recollections everywhere, good and bad. There were things and places that had changed, the Windmill ran a strip show now, Coventry Street was full of pinball arcades, got up to look like dungeons, but the Palladium was there, the Prince of Wales was there, Isow's was still there, even if they'd taken my name off the seat, the little alleys round the Salisbury hadn't changed. It was all as shabby and grubby and brassy as ever, and I loved it, it was the only place I'd ever be at home.

At the Prince of Wales, an American musical was running. At the Palladium, God help us, one of those television twits was top of the bill, a brash young loudmouth from Bootle or somewhere. I looked at him grinning out of the stills with a pink frilled shirt and long hair styled like a sheepdog's. What the hell was he doing there? I wanted to come back, just to push the cocky bastard off that stage where he'd no right to be.

As the first night got close, I felt like I'd never felt before.

It wasn't fear, fear I'd seize up and not get on at all, fear that I'd flop. I knew I'd be all right, it went beyond that, far beyond. It was like something huge was going to happen, something fantastically important, that couldn't occur until the night itself when I'd actually and finally be born, myself as the Fool, the Fool as myself. Because until we opened it hadn't really happened, however good I felt I was it wasn't real, just a dry run.

I couldn't sleep at nights, I'd lie for hours on my bed, my whole body shaking with apprehension, but of what I didn't know. My sessions with Doc Weiss were just a farce now. I didn't want to talk to him, whatever it was that might happen was something I had to keep to myself. Of course he noticed this, he talked about resistances, about who I'd got him figured for, but I couldn't have explained it if I'd wanted to. Yes, I said, no, I said, I don't know, I said. I didn't even want him at the first night, but when he brought it up, I had to invite him.

The night before we opened I took sleeping pills, the only way, I'd have been half-dead otherwise, and I woke very heavy after a wild dream. I was the Fool, I was naked out in the storm, cold as a brass monkey, with Doc Weiss there beside me, laughing like a lunatic, dressed in his white coat but with thongs on his legs and his hair flying like Lear's. 'Who's mad?' he kept saying. 'You or me?' until the misery of it was too strong for me and I had to fight my way through sleep, I had to wake up. I was wet all over with sweat, not rain.

It stretched on forever, that day. Life seemed to be going on at crawling pace, like a film shown in slow motion. I was constantly looking at my watch, thinking it must have stopped, putting it to my ear, finding it hadn't, checking with the radio, the clock in the hall, or anybody near me. I had a session with Dr Weiss which was nothing; even *he* had to give up in the end and turn it into a chat, asking me about the play, who else was in it, stuff like that.

June drove down for me in the Ferrari and if there was one thing the drive up to London did for me it was to stop me thinking about anything else. She drove like she always did, as if the Flying Squad was after her, hooting, cutting in, jumping lights, ignoring any speed limits. All I could worry about was would I ever get there alive, was I going to be sick.

We had lunch in the Trattoria Terrazza in Romilly Street, down below where there were no windows, everybody very nice about seeing me again, the proprietor coming in and wishing me luck, kissing June's hand, the whole bit, but I couldn't eat a thing and I didn't want to drink.

I was at the Globe a good two hours before curtain, before Sid arrived, though not before David Price, who shook hands with me and wished me luck and told me he knew I was going to be great, just like I had been in rehearsal. All through these last few days, right through the dress rehearsal, this thing had been building up inside me, almost being born, almost breaking through, but never quite making it, like I was in labour but not ready yet.

I went to my dressing-room, got out of my clothes, put on my dressing-gown and sat at the dressing-table, very carefully making up, a lot of pancake, heavy eyebrows, waiting for Sid, wanting to see him yet not wanting to see him, waiting to be distracted by his rabbiting on, yet knowing it would irritate me because it was serious, this, tonight, in a way that he could never appreciate.

When he did arrive, though, some of all this seemed to have rubbed off on him; he was a lot quieter than he usually was. 'Okay,' I said, 'on with the bloody motley,' and he helped me into it. I had this tenseness in me again, building up bigger than ever, almost unbearable when I knew the play had begun, and when at last I was called, which should have been the moment when my guts turned to water, I was almost relieved.

Now, friendly knave, I thank thee: there's earnest of thy service.

I was on, entering Right, my stick and bells in my left hand, taking my usual big, long strides, and I got a laugh, it was a tremendous way to enter, to this surprised, happy laughter, happy at seeing me, the double-take, me coming on the way they'd always known, even *this* audience; but as the Fool.

A lovely bit of business to start with.

Let me hire him too; here's my coxcomb

whipping off my cap with my right hand, offering it to Kent with this camped-up, supercilious stare, my eyebrows raised. I got a laugh for that, too, and I was away, as both of us, myself and the Fool. The first laugh had been for me, the second for him.

How now, my pretty knave, how dost thou?

Fantastic, great.

Sang my first song, a bloke in the orchestra giving me a few chords on a guitar.

Have more than thou showest,
Speak less than thou knowest.

That went okay, too. And all the time it was growing, this feeling in me.

Another song.

That lord that counsell'd thee
To give away thy land.

Nearer and nearer. And when it came, when I got hold of whatever it was, it was going to be mine. Not Doc Weiss' for his poxy book, riding on my back, like that lot rode on everybody's back. Not that there was a lot of time to think. Scene v, we're on again; Lear, Kent and me.

If a man's brains were in's heels, were't not in danger of kibes?

Cocker still backing away from me, but I took it for granted now. He went back, I went forward. On until the maid gag, 'except things be cut shorter,' then I was off at last, end of act, back in the dressing-room.

'You were great, Johnny,' Sid said, 'real great,' like he said at the Palladium, at Talk of the Town, at the Sunderland Empire. I thanked him, but I didn't want to talk to him.

Nearer and nearer. I sat down at the dressing-room table and I let it come through to me, clearing my mind. Guilt was it. Guilt was the word. Doc Weiss had been right, though he'd never know he's right. Guilty, m'lud. *That's* why the Fool put up with everything. That's why he let himself be punished, and that's why he's sane; because he's punished. Whereas our lot, we punish ourselves. I'd got it. We're guilty, too, but there's no one to punish us. Or we *feel* guilty. Guilty of what? I was really excited: I'd got that, too. Guilty of making people laugh? Not good enough. Then of what?

'Cup of tea, John?'

Oh, yes, there's plenty of time for tea, I don't come on again till Scene iv. And by then, I'm nearly there. In fact that's when it hits me, in Scene iv.

*Enter* LEAR, FOOL *and* GENTLEMAN.
Ha, ha! Look, he wears crewel garters.

A hard little bastard, I am.

It hits me with such force I can scarcely say my lines. I want to leap about the stage, tell everyone I've got it. In Kent's long speech, that's when it comes to me.

My lord, when at their home

It's quite clear. I was right, but I didn't go far enough. We feel guilty because we make people laugh; because of what we make them laugh *at*. Everything sacred, everything established, every old taboo. Everyone and anyone, whether it's kings or parliaments, dictators or mothers-in-law, we won't take any of them seriously and so they punish us, and if they can't punish us any more, then we punish ourselves. Let him sneer, Doc Weiss, that whole Messiah thing is true, except it isn't the sins of the world we're taking on, it's the shame, the things it hides, the things it's frightened to acknowledge, we bring them out into the light and laugh at them.

I sang my little song,

But I will tarry, the fool will stay,
And let the wise man fly

Of course I'll stay! I'm loyal all right but I'm suffering, too; I *want* to suffer. There was plenty of time to think about all this, till the end of the act, standing around with hardly a line.

'Great!' said Sid when I came into the dressing-room and I

*felt* great, like I'd solved the bloody riddle of the Sphinx. A masochist, that's what I was.

Act III, Scene ii. *Enter* LEAR *and* FOOL.

We're on the heath, the rain is pissing down, it's thundering. I'm miserable and yet I'm pleased as Punch. This great, great scene, and to me it had never seemed greater, because finally I understood it.

> Poor fool and knave, I have one part in my heart
> That sorrows yet for thee.

I was sorry for me too, but I was happy.

> Hey, ho, the wind and the rain,

I sang.

> For the rain it raineth every day.

Which I expected.

Off for Scene iii, back for Scene iv, still going great. As we came on, Cocker put his hand on my shoulder. Cocker? It was Lear. He opened his mouth, seemed about to say something, then didn't. He didn't need to. He'd felt it in me too, this joy, this triumph.

Scene vi. Now Lear was mad, right round the twist, the poor old sod. My last scene, this. From now, the poor bastard's ranting on, as daft as a brush.

> And I'll go to bed at noon,

I say. The last thing I say. A callous line, but that's the Fool, he's hard. He never gives anything away.

I came off stage. Cocker shook hands with me. 'My boy, a remarkable performance.' Into the dressing-room. Sid said, 'Marvellous, John, I mean it.' But it's bigger than me, I'm not thinking of me.

I can't sit in the dressing-room for long. I stand in the wings and watch the last two acts, Cocker's tremendous, he has me crying. When he runs off saying that they'll have to catch him, it's one of the saddest things I've ever seen. David Price comes up to me, squeezes my arm and says, 'You were quite superb, Johnny.'

So what? I couldn't miss.

And then it's over, the poor old bastard's dead, and here we are, back on stage, me coming on with Kent, terrific applause, and finally, old Cocker. An ovation; enough to bring the house down! Then we're all in line, Cocker's in tears, the great old ham, I'm crying, too, he's got my hand in his, but I'm in another scene.

I'm not on *this* stage, I'm in a huge arena, looking out again on the whole world, row after row of them, into infinity, and I'm standing in a great, long line. They're all there: Feste and the Fool, Dan Leno and George Robey, Chaplin and Buster Keaton, Groucho, Chico and Harpo. Sid Field is there, Jack Benny's there, everybody hand in hand, and all of us are shouting, 'Guilty, guilty, guilty!'

## Picture Palace

Paul Theroux

For over fifty years Maude has levelled the peepstones of her Third Eye at the beautiful, obscure and obscene and at the private places and public parts of the famous, from Gertrude Stein to Graham Greene. At her retrospective exhibition her life, measured by camera spools, is rolled out for inspection. Except for the frame that really mattered; the exposure that should have been there, but wasn't.

'Maude's voice, harsh, coarse, and yet surprisingly innocent, remains in the ear long after the book has been put down' – *The Times*

'Startlingly original, very funny' – *Daily Telegraph*

## Kiss Hollywood Goodbye

Anita Loos

Anita Loos, the pint-sized brunette, whose brilliant book *Gentlemen Prefer Blondes* laid men wide open, recalls the dizzy days as a Hollywood script-writer – when anybody knew everybody and (like Aldous Huxley) you ad-libbed your own dialogue.

Quite at her most delicious, Miss Loos *never* lets scruples get in the way of truth.

## The Dying of the Light

Brian Glanville

The story of Len Rawlings, the greatest goal-keeper of his time, who cannot cope with life away from the limelight. Among many excellent reviews, Frank Keating in the *Guardian* said: 'the best sporting novel I have read since Leonard Gardner's memorable *Fat City*'.